PRAISE FOR PHILIPP SCHOTT

Six Ostriches

"Schott's second mystery featuring gumshoe veterinarian Peter Bannerman (after 2022's *Fifty-Four Pigs*) combines the soothing sleuthing of *Murder, She Wrote* with the humble charm of *All Creatures Great and Small*."
— *Publishers Weekly*, starred review

"*Six Ostriches* is both a good introduction to the series and a satisfying follow-up to its predecessor. Whether read individually or together, these books offer lovers of cozy mysteries and animal stories a heartwarming yet stimulating read, with a puzzle that hits the sweet spot between comfortably challenging and brain-buster."
— *New York Journal of Books*

Fifty-Four Pigs

"With Dr. Peter Bannerman, Philipp Schott has created a unique brand of amateur detective, one who is as amiable as he is enigmatic . . . The reader can't help but be entranced and embraced by Schott's charming and saucily unusual first book in what should be a long-running series."
— Anthony Bidulka, author of the Russell Quant Mystery series

"Deadly and delightful, *Fifty-Four Pigs* is a delicious read with some of the most beautiful descriptions of a prairie winter anywhere."
— Iona Whishaw, author of the Lane Winslow Mystery series

The Accidental Veterinarian

"Few books . . . approach the combination of fine writing, radical honesty and endless optimism found in Winnipeg practitioner Schott's . . . Laugh until you cry — and believe, as he says, that all that really matters is that the heart of the pet (and its owner) is pure."
— *Booklist*, starred review

How to Examine a Wolverine

"An engaging study of the behaviors of pets and the people who care for them. Schott's tone is warm, friendly and folksy in his storytelling and his conversations with pet owners; even in the most stressful times, he's a compassionate and level-headed guide. *How to Examine a Wolverine* is an essay collection that celebrates the love of animals."
— *Foreword Reviews*

The Battle Cry of the Siamese Kitten

"Philipp Schott is not James Herriot. This book isn't about creatures great and small in pre-war Yorkshire — but the pets that come to this Winnipeg clinic are just as entertaining."
— *Chesil Magazine*

The Willow Wren

"Philipp Schott pulls off the considerable feat of creating empathy for his characters without ever resorting to easy excuses for their sometimes indefensible choices . . . a fine, nuanced storytelling achievement."
— Frederick Taylor, historian and bestselling author of *Exorcising Hitler: The Occupation and Denazification of Germany*

WORKS BY PHILIPP SCHOTT

DR. BANNERMAN VET MYSTERIES

Fifty-Four Pigs: A Dr. Bannerman Vet Mystery (#1)

Six Ostriches: A Dr. Bannerman Vet Mystery (#2)

Eleven Huskies: A Dr. Bannerman Vet Mystery (#3)

THE ACCIDENTAL VETERINARIAN SERIES

The Accidental Veterinarian: Tales from a Pet Practice

How to Examine a Wolverine:
More Tales from the Accidental Veterinarian

The Battle Cry of the Siamese Kitten:
Even More Tales from the Accidental Veterinarian

OTHER

The Willow Wren: A Novel

ELEVEN
Huskies

A DR. BANNERMAN VET MYSTERY

PHILIPP SCHOTT

Published by ECW Press
665 Gerrard Street East
Toronto, Ontario, Canada M4M 1Y2
416-694-3348 / info@ecwpress.com

Cover design: David A. Gee
Cover artwork: © Joey Gao

LIBRARY AND ARCHIVES CANADA CATALOGUING IN PUBLICATION

Title: Eleven huskies / Philipp Schott.

Names: Schott, Philipp, author.

Series: Schott, Philipp. Dr. Bannerman vet mysteries ; #3.

Description: Series statement: Dr. Bannerman vet mystery

Identifiers: Canadiana (print) 20230580122 | Canadiana (ebook) 20230580130

ISBN 978-1-77041-767-0 (softcover)
ISBN 978-1-77852-294-9 (ePub)
ISBN 978-1-77852-295-6 (PDF)

Subjects: LCGFT: Cozy mysteries. | LCGFT: Novels.

Classification: LCC PS8637.C5645 E44 2024 | DDC C813/.6—dc23

This book is funded in part by the Government of Canada. *Ce livre est financé en partie par le gouvernement du Canada.* We acknowledge the support of the Canada Council for the Arts. *Nous remercions le Conseil des arts du Canada de son soutien.* We acknowledge the funding support of the Ontario Arts Council (OAC), an agency of the Government of Ontario. We also acknowledge the support of the Government of Ontario through the Ontario Book Publishing Tax Credit, and through Ontario Creates.

PRINTED AND BOUND IN CANADA   PRINTING: MARQUIS   5   4   3   2   1

This book was written before 2023's horrific summer of fire.

*It is dedicated to the memory of what we are losing
in this burning world.*

PROLOGUE

A tlas and his family and friends loved their food. Their master fed
them at the same time every morning. He brought it into the
kennel room in a big pail and poured it into a half dozen stainless
steel bowls. They emptied the bowls before he even left the room.
That's how much they loved their food. There were 11 of them,
so they had to share, but they were used to that. Sometimes old
Winter still snapped at the twins when they nosed into his bowl,
but otherwise it all worked out fine. The best days were in the
weeks leading up to a race when they got extra. What dog doesn't
want extra? It was always the same, but that didn't matter. It was
food, and it was good. It was more than good — it was what Atlas
lived for. That and chasing squirrels and racing through the snow
and taking long naps with his tail curled around his nose like a
scarf. Then one night the food wasn't the same. It had a different
smell and a different taste. Also, it was at a strange time and there
was much less of it. They never got fed at night. It was delicious,
but it had changed. He wished there was more. He had to fight to
get anywhere close to a reasonable amount. Some got very little.
Too bad for them.

The next day Atlas felt tired, so very tired, and for the first time
in his life he wasn't hungry for breakfast. Then later he began to

vomit. He couldn't stop. His master was anxious. The world became grey and hazy. The last thing Atlas remembered before he fell asleep was his master stroking him and saying something soothing he couldn't understand.

CHAPTER
One

Dr. Peter Bannerman loved to fly. Ever since he was a little boy flying with his parents and his brother, Sam, to visit relatives in Nova Scotia, he was transfixed by the beauty of the Earth from above, and by the magical nature of being suspended in the air. No matter how well he understood the physics, and he understood it very well, he couldn't shake that irrational sense of magic.

There were only two other passengers on the float plane as it headed northeast from Thompson toward Dragonfly Lake. They were a young man and woman, but they didn't look like a couple; both were wearing navy blue jackets emblazoned with Government of Canada crests and the letters "TSB." It was much too loud to talk, and Peter didn't enjoy small talk with strangers anyway, so he was pleased to leave the pleasantries at a smile and a nod, and then turn to look out the window. He couldn't stop himself from trying to puzzle out TSB, though. It sounded familiar, but he could only generate improbable guesses, like Terror Security Board, Technical Services Branch, or the one that refused to leave his head, Toxic Spice Bureau.

Northern Manitoba slid by under his window like an endlessly unrolling dark green shag carpet, liberally splashed with bright blue. Or, more accurately, an endlessly unrolling bright blue carpet, liberally flecked with dark green shag. More water than land. No two lakes, ponds, marshes, rivers, streams the same size or shape. Like the work of a fevered god. Or a god driven to a Jackson Pollock frenzy after the monotony of oceans, plains, and deserts. As Peter looked north, he marvelled that this went on for thousands of kilometres past the horizon, slowly turning into taiga, then tundra, and then the Arctic Ocean. If the line extended further across the North Pole, the same would happen in reverse, crossing into Siberia. Eventually somewhere there, on the other side of the globe, it would intersect with a road or a settlement, but before then, only wilderness, no sign of man. *How glorious*, he thought.

The flight was short, and before Peter could turn his attention to figuring out which lake they were flying over, the pilot began to bank for a landing. Now he could see that it was Dragonfly Lake. Most northern lakes look similar from the air, but Dragonfly Lake had a distinctive X shape. He smiled as the plane raced down toward the surface of the lake, the trees blurring. This was one of his favourite places on Earth, and it was where Pippin, his prize-winning sniffer dog and best friend, was originally from. He had thought about bringing Pippin, but it was too much fuss for what would be a quick visit. He would be back up here in a few days anyway, and Pippin was definitely coming along then. The plane seemed to clear the treetops by only inches, but then hit the surface of the lake with surprising smoothness, smoother than landing on a runway.

He was met at the dock by John Reynolds, owner of the Dragonfly Lodge and Pure North Outfitters. Although they didn't know each other well, Peter recognized him right away. John was a short but powerfully built man, probably in his mid-fifties, with the kind of bushy moustache people used to call a soup-strainer. He was famous for his booming laugh and his iron handshake, his stockiness and small stature belying his strength.

His grip was light today, though, and his face marked with worry. "I can't thank you enough for coming, Peter, and on such short notice. I would have just sent them down to you, but so many are sick now I need some help figuring who to send south, who's OK to stay, and who . . . who can't be saved."

"You're welcome. It works out well because I had taken these days off to work on the garden before the canoe trip, but it's raining constantly in the south. First drought, then flood. Nutty times."

"Beautiful summer up here. Hot and dry. Beautiful so long as the fires don't start. Do you want to drop your bag first? Get cleaned up?"

"No, let's go straight to the kennels. How's Atlas?"

"Still out of it. And Pretty and Gus are looking rough too. But like I said, none of them are a hundred percent."

As they walked up the dock, they passed the two passengers with the TSB jackets, who were still waiting for their bags to finish unloading.

Peter whispered to John, "TSB? Know what that's about?"

"You didn't hear? A plane went down early this morning. They're the Transport Safety Board folks."

Ah, that makes a lot more sense than Toxic Spice Bureau, Peter thought.

"No, I didn't pay attention to the news before I left. Any casualties?"

"All three onboard presumed dead. Plunged into the lake on approach. RCMP dive team just got here." He gestured out to the lake where three boats were positioned in a rough circle.

"That's terrible," Peter said, while recalling his own experience landing on the lake. He hadn't been scared, and he wouldn't be next time either. It was all simple physics. In good weather with a well-maintained aircraft and an experienced pilot, there were no random factors to consider. Luck shouldn't play a role. He would check the statistics later, but he was confident that landing a float plane on a calm northern lake was substantially safer than driving on Highway 59, which was his customary benchmark for calibrating risk. He was always puzzled by people who were swayed by anecdotes of horrible events, rather than by the statistics regarding their actual probability.

"Yeah, it is terrible. The plane was recently fully safetied and the pilot, Ned Fromm, was one of the best. Young guy, but I'd trust him to fly me anywhere, through anything, in any aircraft. He could fly a chesterfield through a hurricane if it had wings and a prop." John chuckled at his own joke.

"Who were the passengers?" Peter asked as they climbed into the truck, Peter almost forgetting to duck his head. Being tall, normally he did this instinctively, but when he was distracted, he banged his head far more times than he could count. "Your clumsiness will be the death of you some day," his mother had often warned. But so far, so good.

"There's no official confirmation yet, but the hot rumour is that one of them was Brendan O'Daly," John said as he started the engine.

"Who's that?"

"You haven't heard of him?" John threw Peter a glance. "He's that Hydro exec who quit last year to start a bitcoin company. TealCoin, he calls it . . . called it. Teal for blue and green mixed, as in the green energy from the blue hydro power. Rumour is he wanted to dam Black Eagle River to generate power for a server farm at the First Nation."

"Ah, OK. I don't follow the business news."

John grunted. "Yeah, I usually don't either, but when there's a northern angle I pay attention, plus this guy is, or was, apparently quite the character. Not the usual dull corporate hack in a grey suit and toupee. Bit of a high-roller wannabe, dating Monique what's-her-name from that band. Even got his picture taken with Elon Musk." He glanced at Peter, apparently expecting a reaction.

Peter just nodded. He found little more boring than celebrity gossip. "Was he supposed to be your guest?"

"No. I'm guessing he was booked at The Friendly Bear." John turned right onto the gravel road that ran along the lake shore toward the lodge, which Peter could now make out through the trees on the far side of the bay.

"And the other passenger? His girlfriend, maybe?"

"No idea, haven't heard."

"Any guesses what happened? Bad weather this morning?"

"No, a perfect morning. A couple of the guests were out fishing and said they saw the plane suddenly wobble badly and then clip some trees. It then came in kind of sideways and flipped right over when it hit the water."

"Pilot had a heart attack?"

"Maybe. But as I said, young guy. But that's as good a guess as any right now." John pulled into a gravel parking lot behind the lodge. "You sure you don't want to stop by your cabin first?"

"Let's go see your dogs first."

The kennels were in the trees on the far side of the parking lot from the lodge. Whereas the lodge was a beautiful log structure, the kennel was a simple plywood building with a sheet metal roof, and chain-link-fenced runs attached to the sides, each with a wide-open door into the kennel building. A large open exercise pen, also fenced with chain-link, was attached to the back of the building. No dogs were outside. To reach the kennels, they had to walk past a large ramshackle shed, a couple of muddy ATVs, four snowmobiles, several rusty metal barrels, a burnt-out truck, and a jumbled heap of unidentifiable metal and plastic objects Peter could only describe as junk. Peter mused about the contrast between the front of the lodge, facing the lake, which was a postcard-worthy emblem of the Canadian North, and the back of it, which was a much more realistic view of what most of the settled North looked like in his experience. Aesthetics generally took a backseat to the practicalities of making a living and survival.

"Hail on the roof doesn't bother them?" Peter asked, looking at the gleaming sheet metal.

"We don't get much hail up here, but no, my dogs don't get spooked easily. Is that an issue for some of your patients?" John asked as he rummaged in his pocket for keys.

"Yeah, for some it's quite bad. Any sudden loud noises like thunder or fireworks can set them off. I had one make a dog-shaped hole in the screen door and then run for miles cross-country, presumably trying to escape the noise."

"Wow, no. No worries about that here." He found the right key and unlocked the door. "Here we are, Reynolds' Runners Kennels, fastest team in Manitoba the last three years in a row."

They stepped into a bare room with shelves and cupboards on one side and various harnesses hanging on the wall on the opposite side. Directly ahead there was a wide hall lined with kennels. Peter counted sixteen, eight on each side. Each one had a stainless-steel cage-wire door and cement walls reaching about three-quarters of the way to the ceiling. There were a couple of skylights and several large fans. It smelled much cleaner than most kennels Peter had been in, and there was something else unusual that he couldn't put his finger on immediately. Then he thought of it.

"It's so quiet in here. With 11 huskies I expected some singing."

"Normally you can't hear yourself think, especially at feeding time, but right now none of them are feeling well enough," John said quietly. "Do you want to start with Atlas?"

"Yes, please. And by the way, this is a really nice kennel. I'm used to seeing much smaller cages, or for sled dogs even just wooden cubbies or hutches."

"Traditionally sled dogs are kept outdoors year-round, so most mushers don't put too much effort into kennel construction, but there are times when it's too cold even for these guys, or during storms, or when it's too hot. Old-school mushers will bring their dogs into the house during extreme conditions, but I can't really bring them into the lodge."

"No? I'm sure the guests would love it! And you probably don't have too many anyway when it's −40."

"Ha! You'd be surprised. We're one of the only all-season lodges up here, and a real winter is a big draw for some. Europeans and Japanese especially. But no, I wanted a modern facility for my team. Flexible, comfortable, humane. Ninety percent of the time they're outside in their runs, though."

Peter nodded and pointed to the first kennel on the left. "Atlas?" He made an educated guess based on how sick the dog looked.

"Yes." John opened the kennel and motioned for Peter to go in ahead of him.

A striking-looking dog lay on the kennel floor panting, his brilliant blue eyes seemingly focused on the middle distance. He did not respond to the kennel door opening and the two men approaching him. He had dark grey fur along his back, white legs, and a white mask around those eyes.

"Beautiful boy," Peter said softly.

"Yes, he is. He's my beautiful boy. My very beautiful boy."

Peter knelt down beside Atlas and stroked him on the cheek while he counted breaths. Sixty per minute. That was very high for a dog at rest. Then he examined his gums, which were dry and tacky to the touch and had a faint orange hue coming through the salmon pink. Peter developed his first suspicion. He looked at the whites of the eyes: they were vivid lemon yellow.

"Not eating or drinking, I take it?"

"No, nothing at all. Can't coax him with anything, not even moose liver."

Peter had brought a small shoulder bag from which he retrieved a stethoscope and an ear thermometer. The dog's heart sounded good, but rapid as well. The temperature was low.

"Not in the butt anymore?" John asked, obviously trying to sound jocular, but too anxious to pull it off.

"No, not initially anyway. High on an ear thermometer is real, but low sometimes isn't. Atlas's temperature is low, so I'll have to double check the old-fashioned way."

"What does low mean?"

"One step at a time, John."

John nodded. At some level Peter knew he should reassure the man, but he was too focused on his examination to worry about that.

Atlas didn't so much as blink at the intrusion of the rectal thermometer. It also read 37°C, which was low.

Kneeling beside the dog, Peter proceeded with the rest of the examination in silence and then rocked back on his heels when he was done. When John called, Peter had assumed a stomach flu type of virus, but it didn't fit with what he was seeing. Atlas was jaundiced, which usually meant liver or gallbladder disease. Viral hepatitis existed, but these dogs were vaccinated against it, and it never hit this many dogs at the same time acutely like this. He narrowed his eyes and thought hard. He would draw blood and send it back to Winnipeg, but there must be something else he could do in the meantime.

John watched him, clearly wanting to ask what, if anything, he had found, but deciding it was better to wait for the vet to speak.

Peter snapped out of his trancelike state, straightened up, and said, "Sorry, John, I was just thinking because this is an unusual case with so many dogs sick, but it looks like a hepatopathy."

"'Hepa,' that means 'liver,' right? So, his liver is damaged?"

"Yes, possibly quite badly." Then he added, "Sorry, John. Not the news we were hoping for."

"I wasn't expecting anything good. Hoping, maybe, but not expecting. Not really. But why? Any idea?"

"Well, there is a hepatitis virus, but that's not really possible here, so with multiple dogs sick, unless it's a coincidence, which I can't believe, then we'll have to look at their food and water."

John looked shocked. "It's top-quality food and I drink the same water they do."

"Let's see the others now. Pretty and Gus were the next sickest?"

"Good memory."

The rest of the dogs, including Pretty and Gus, were not as ill as Atlas, but most had some degree of jaundice. Only four of the youngest didn't, which struck Peter as odd. Even they were subdued and clearly not well, but somehow not as badly affected as the others. Peter was still convinced they had been exposed to something in their food or water. Aflatoxin, produced by a certain kind of mould, was a very potent liver poison.

"Can I see their food?" he asked when he had finished examining the last dog, old Winter. Even though Winter was much older than Atlas, he wasn't as sick, so there was not a direct age relationship to severity. Curious.

John led Peter back into the main room and opened a cupboard to reveal large bins of kibble.

"It's the Purina Pro Plan Sport, with salmon."

Peter took a handful and sniffed it. He couldn't detect any off smells, although he wasn't Pippin. He often noted with interest how Pippin became pickier with his food toward the bottom of the bag. He'd still eat it, but the enthusiasm waned as the food evidently became stale, or something like that, even though it still smelled fine to Peter. A kibble connoisseur, that Pippin.

"How fresh is this?"

"Pretty fresh. I refilled the bins about three days before they became sick."

Peter nodded. A contaminated batch of food should have made them sick right away, and on the other hand, it was also not long enough for the food to have gone off.

"You might have mentioned this before, but is Atlas your lead dog?"

"Yes, he is."

"So, if some sort of treat were offered to them, would he command the lion's share?"

"Depends a bit, but often, yes."

"Do you give them treats or extras?"

"No, not outside race season, anyway."

"Were they all together in the exercise pen the night they became sick?"

"Yes, they were. What are you thinking?"

"Someone poisoned them by tossing something tasty into the pen. Atlas got more of it than the others."

John stared at him.

"I just don't know which poison yet. The list of hepatotoxins is long. There's the aflatoxin I mentioned, phenolic pesticides, alpha-lipoic acid, cycads, phosphorus, formaldehyde, xylitol, isoniazid, castor beans, some mushrooms, various drugs . . ." Peter rattled these off, raising a finger each time until he had circled back to the first hand.

"That's not possible! Nobody would poison my dogs!" John put his hands on his hips and furrowed his brow.

"I'm sorry, John. It really looks like someone did."

CHAPTER

Two

"I'm going to send the four sickest down right away. John's chartered a plane and I've already talked to Kat and Raj about picking them up." Kat was his RVT (Registered Veterinary Technologist), or vet nurse, and Raj, Dr. Rajkumar Talavar, was a locum vet from Winnipeg Peter relied on to cover the practice when he was away. Peter was sitting in a Muskoka chair on the deck of his cabin, talking to his wife, Laura, back in New Selfoss. It was late afternoon and the breeze had died, leaving the lake velvety smooth. The only sounds were a distant outboard motor and a pair of ravens squabbling over something on the spit of land that defined the southern edge of the bay the resort sat on.

"And you really think it's a deliberate poisoning? It couldn't have been an accident, like contaminated food?" Laura asked.

"I think so. When we had that melamine contamination in dog food from China a few years ago, the onset was more gradual. This was sudden. Overnight. And he hadn't just started a fresh bag of food or introduced anything new."

"OK, but who would do such a thing? Those poor dogs."

"I don't know. John doesn't know either."

"On a different subject, I guess everyone up there must be talking about that plane that went down."

"Well, I've only talked to John so far, and he did mention it. But it turns out I flew up with two crash investigators from the TSB."

"Awful stuff. I tried not to think too much about you flying into the same lake in the same kind of plane!"

"You know that's silly."

"I do. But I reserve the right to be silly from time to time."

They were both quiet for a moment. The raven fight had broken up and one of them flew right over Peter. Its wings made a soft swooshing sound. The distant outboard motor stopped. Peter spotted the source, a boat across the bay with two fishermen in it. In the clear light he could see them casting their rods, although they were quite a distance away. Even further out, he could just barely make out the three boats he had seen earlier that were involved in the RCMP dive operation over the wreck of the plane.

"And how's Pippin? And Merry and Gandalf?" Peter asked. Merry was their tortoiseshell cat, and Gandalf, their goat.

"Great. I'm sure they miss you. Well, Pippin for sure, the other two it's harder to tell."

"I miss them," Peter said, and then added, "and you too, of course!"

"Ha! Well, it's just one night. No different than calving season."

"True. What are you up to tonight?"

"I've got to get that order of hobbit vests done. Just the buttons left to do, but then there's the trimming and the packing. I'll be busy enough!"

Laura, although trained as paleobiologist, had found her true calling as a knitter, having carved out a niche making scarves, toques, mittens, sweaters, etc., with motifs from favourite classic geek books and movies.

"No packing yet?"

"Peter, the canoe trip is still a couple days away. Plenty of time."

Peter was a planner. Some (including Laura) would say an obsessive planner. Laura was more spontaneous. What could have become a source of discord had instead gradually evolved into an inside joke between them. Just so long as Peter didn't hound Laura about getting ready for something, and just so long as Laura didn't completely forget what they were supposed to be doing or make them more than ten minutes late. Peter figured ten minutes was a reasonable allowance, priding himself on his flexibility.

"OK, fair enough. Just don't pull a Kevin."

"Ha, no, my brother got the lion's share of the Gudmundurson head-in-the-clouds genes. Besides, I've lived with you for long enough that some of you has worn off on me, for better or worse." She laughed.

Peter snorted. "Did he at least apply for the time off this time? Remember last time we tried to organize a trip with him, he had to scramble because he forgot."

Laura laughed again. "You were so mad at him! Good thing the detachment commander let him take a Friday flex day."

"Unusual flexibility for the Mounties, but it was still a nuisance. I should go now. I'm supposed to meet John at the resort restaurant for a drink before dinner."

"I hope those dogs are going to be OK."

"I think we may lose one of them, but it could have been so much worse."

"See you tomorrow. Be safe."

Peter's phone had binged with a text message alert while he was talking to Laura, so he looked at it now. It was John, saying he would be delayed about an hour, but that Peter was welcome to head up to the restaurant and have a drink on the house while he waited. Peter felt an initial twinge of irritation at the change in plans, albeit a minor one, and didn't relish the idea of nursing a beer in the restaurant alone. It would feel awkward, and strangers might feel compelled to come over and talk to him. He cheered up when he remembered he hadn't checked out the tea offerings yet. A tray with coffee and tea supplies was set on the dresser. Normally he was a loose leaf tea person, viewing tea bags the way a wine connoisseur might view boxed wine, but in this scenario, bags were highly efficient. Peter loved things that were highly efficient, so this won out over any misgivings about quality. Unfortunately, the selection of teas and instant coffee on offer was disheartening, with the exception of one bag of rooibos, a non-caffeinated South African red bush tea. Peter was relieved. This was just the ticket. And rooibos was also very forgiving. You didn't even have to time the brew precisely as it did not become bitter with excessive steeping. This was also an advantage during travel when his routines were liable to be out of kilter.

Peter filled the electric kettle while considering that the caffeine he needed on rising in the morning would still be a problem. At home he always drank tea — precisely-brewed loose leaf tea — but when on vacation his habit was to drink coffee instead. Good coffee was easier to find on the road than good tea, or perhaps he was just less fussy with coffee. But in this case, there was neither a good, caffeinated tea, nor good coffee. Maybe the restaurant was open early for the fishermen.

While waiting for the water to boil, he examined his room again. It was in a rustic log cabin style, with even the bed frame and two chairs made from heavily varnished dark brown branches and logs. There was a small stone hearth, with a large, rather luridly coloured painting of a moose silhouetted against the sunset above it. The moose was standing in water halfway up its legs and was looking toward the low red sun as if admiring it, which struck Peter as improbable. The two other paintings were smaller and less vivid, one depicting a beaver gnawing industriously on a tree and the other, a bald eagle soaring above a set of rapids. Pretty much classic tacky Canadiana. Peter supposed the American, European, and Asian tourists who came up here lapped this sort of stuff up. Maybe the Torontonians, Calgarians, and Vancouverites did too.

The water was ready, so Peter opened the sachet of rooibos and held it to his nose to inhale the smell. Lovely, just lovely. The enamel mugs had the Dragonfly Lodge logo on them. Predictably this was a stylized dragonfly. It was quite nicely done, Peter thought, but the font for "Dragonfly Lodge" used little sticks to make up the letters. Unforgivable. Cool in 1936 or 1952, but not so much now.

Peter grabbed his book along the way, a history of the Ottoman Empire, returned to the deck with his tea, and sat back down on the Muskoka chair. Since he felt in the mood for a slightly stronger rooibos, he would allow it to steep for five minutes. Ideally it should be even hotter out for drinking this tea, as it always made him think of Africa and Precious Ramotswe, the main character in Alexander McCall Smith's No. 1 Ladies' Detective Agency series of mysteries. He wasn't normally a fan of light fiction, but he had to admit these had a certain charm. They were set in Botswana, where it was almost always hot, and drinking rooibos was one of Precious's signature habits. In fact, it was through these novels that Peter had first learned about this African tea. He was initially skeptical as it wasn't a true "tea," i.e., not the leaves of *Camellia sinensis*, but he was quickly won over.

Peter picked up the book and opened it to the bookmarked page, but found he couldn't focus on it. The fratricidal machinations of the sultan's court were unable to hold their own against the questions filling Peter's mind regarding John's dogs.

When the five minutes elapsed, he took the tea bag out and blew across the top of the mug, admiring the tendrils of steam wafting away in the strong late afternoon sunlight. As he began to sip the wonderfully earthy-tasting rooibos, he considered the possible motives for a dog poisoner. This had to be about people, not dogs. Atlas, Winter, Pretty, Gus, and the rest were innocent pawns of some sort. In Peter's experience, there were few people who hated animals, especially dogs, enough to go out of their way to try to kill them. There had been that one dispute between the Olafsson brothers in New Selfoss. Les and Frank were potty old bachelors and were neighbours on the west side of town. Les had a barky poodle and Frank couldn't stand noise of any kind. Frank tried to poison the poodle with a wiener filled with sleeping pills, but the poodle had a touchy stomach and just barfed it all back up. But even there, the conflict was as much man versus man as it was man versus poodle.

No, John had to have enemies who were trying to get to him through his dogs. Peter didn't know how cut-throat the competition between mushers was, but that was the first thing that came to mind. Hadn't John said his team were three-time champions? Who was in second place? Was it always the same frustrated, increasingly angry, ultimately desperate rival? Peter pictured a bear-like man in a red and black lumberjack shirt with a gigantic black beard and little beady eyes. The beard was flecked with spit as this man raged against John's unfair victories. But, of course, he had no idea. Maybe the dogsled world was close-knit and harmonious, and giant black beard guy gave John a bear hug at the finish line and sent him home-baked cookies all the time. Ones without poison.

Or what about the relationship with that other lodge, The Friendly Bear? To Peter's mind, the "friendly" sounded more ominous than inviting, and there had been something unidentifiable and not unambiguously positive in John's tone when he mentioned that he thought the dead Hydro guy had been planning on staying there. Was Dragonfly Lake really big enough for two lodges?

Or maybe John had a demented and vengeful ex?

Or maybe John himself was not what he seemed and had a twisted dark side, seeking attention and sympathy at the cost of his dogs' lives?

Peter stopped that train of thought in its tracks and took a deep drink of the rooibos now that it had cooled a little. Now he was indulging in wild speculation with no basis at all. The rival mushers or lodge owners had at least some plausibility and supporting data, whereas the lunatic ex-wife or the psychotic John theories had both no plausibility and no data. Regardless, it was obvious more data was needed. It was, of course, the local RCMP detachment's job to gather this data and find the culprit, but with three dead humans at the bottom of Dragonfly Lake, Peter feared they would be preoccupied for some time. John's dogs weren't even dead. Not yet, at least. It would be hard to blame the police for not prioritizing an alleged animal poisoning.

Peter took another sip and looked out at the lake. He wasn't sure why looking at water was so soothing, but it was. Objectively, it was quite boring — just a smooth blue surface, fringed by trees that were no different than a billion other trees across the northern hemisphere. Yet it was soothing and weirdly engaging. More engaging at least than 16th-century Turkish politics.

Two of the RCMP boats had left the crash scene and were headed back to the dock. Peter assumed they had recovered the bodies. He wondered whether there would be any effort to raise the plane. That would be difficult, especially up here. He didn't imagine the Dragonfly Lake First Nation, which was the only actual settlement on the lake, had the right equipment for that, nor did it seem like something that could be easily brought in from the south. He wasn't sure if small aircraft were required to carry a flight data recorder. What other evidence would police divers look for? Probably not much as it wasn't a crime, so TSB (not the Toxic Spice Bureau!) probably had a list of standard mechanical things for them to check while they were down there. They'd probably take a lot of photographs.

But back to the dogs. That's what he should be thinking about, but again, without more information, there was not much point in that either.

Peter sighed. He glanced at the Ottoman book on the armrest but didn't pick it up, and then checked his phone for messages. There were none.

A light breeze picked up, riffling the surface of the lake, causing the sunlight to scatter across the surface in a thousand diamond dust sparkles. When Peter squinted, the sparkles became even brighter, shooting out narrow flares of white light. He wondered why that was. Optical physics were fascinating, but many aspects eluded him. He'd have to read up on it. He kept widening and narrowing his eyes to play with this effect when he was suddenly startled by a booming "Hey, Peter!"

Peter whirled around, almost spilling tea on himself.

It was John.

"You weren't at the restaurant, so I thought I'd come down and catch you here. Settled in OK?" John said.

"Yes, fantastic, thank you. It's really lovely."

"Glad to hear it! Ready for a drink and then some dinner?"

They walked up the path between the tall black spruces to where the lodge sat on a granite ridge. Peter loved the sharp smell of spruce needles in the cool moist shade of the path. He was about to comment on it when John spoke.

"Just before I came to get you, I got a call from a guy I know down at the dock. He does contract work for the Mounties, helps with the boats and skidoos and stuff. Guess what he said?"

Peter hated that type of question. Clearly, he would have no idea nor any sensible basis for guessing, so why bother asking? But over the years he had learned to play along with these irrational social conventions.

"I don't know. What did he say?"

"They found a bullet hole in the cockpit and in the pilot."

CHAPTER
Three

Peter had to admit the restaurant was impressive. It was the focal point of the lodge, with a vaulted ceiling and massive windows that looked out over Dragonfly Lake. It was done in the same log style as his cabin, but on a much larger scale. It reminded him of Voittu Talo, Michelle Nyquist's log mansion on the edge of New Selfoss. But whereas Michelle had tastefully merged a clean modern Scandinavian aesthetic with the old log structure, the lodge had gone all-in with backwoods Canadian wilderness kitsch. Or at least Peter considered it kitsch. There was an astonishing amount of taxidermy, from the requisite moose head above the bar through to a bear standing in the middle, beside a pillar, eternally frozen in ferocious slavering attack mode. A school of fish of various species pretended to swim across the far wall, and a small flock of snow geese suspended from the ceiling by wires pretended to fly toward the windows. The rafters were festooned with antique snowshoes, fishing rods, nets, skis, a canoe, and, in pride of place between the two enormous caribou antler chandeliers, a large vintage dog sled. Peter was relieved that there were no taxidermized huskies harnessed to it. John apparently had limits to his baroque tastes after all.

Peter's favourite pub in New Selfoss, The Flying Beaver, did have one piece of taxidermy, a beaver with goose wings, but it was for the humorous effect, not to awe visitors with the hunting and fishing prowess of previous guests.

"Wow, impressive," was the comment he settled on when it became obvious that John was expecting a reaction. "Impressive" was a word most people read as positive, but to Peter it was neutral because it simply meant it made a strong impression. That it certainly had.

"Isn't it? I'm glad you like it!"

John steered them toward a table by the window. A group of three men dressed head to foot in camouflage occupied the prime centre table.

Peter sat down and found himself eye to eye with an enraged wolverine, mounted on a shelf attached to a massive tree trunk post beside the table.

"So, murder?" Peter asked. A question from the staff about the washing machine had cut John off earlier.

"Well, suicide would be a stretch. And somebody accidentally shooting up into the air and accidentally hitting the pilot would be a stretch too. So yes, everyone assumes murder." John stated this with an air of authority he was clearly used to assuming.

"That's incredible. What are the odds of hitting the pilot when you're shooting from the ground?"

"If you've got the right rifle and you're a marksman, maybe it's not so hard. Those planes come in low and not as fast as you might think. About 70 knots usually, so highway speed for a car."

Peter did the math quickly in his head. "About 130 kilometres per hour. What highways do you drive on?" He laughed to make sure John knew he was just teasing.

"No comment!" John laughed. "Let's get some beers. What'll you have? We've got everything."

Peter seriously doubted they had "everything." In fact, that would be physically impossible, but he knew better than to point that out.

"Do you have Manipogo Pale?" It was a decent pale ale and Peter liked the reference to the legendary Lake Winnipeg sea monster.

"You bet!"

While John got up to fetch the beers, Peter surveyed the room. In addition to the camo crew beside them, there was a table with four tall blond women, probably in their forties and fifties, toward the centre of the room, and past them there were two heavyset older white men sitting with a young Indigenous man. He could hear one of the older men from across the room as he had a booming voice. American accent. *South, but not deep south*, Peter thought. And then at the far end of the room, near the door, were two younger couples dressed in expensive-looking outdoor wear, drinking Heineken.

When John returned, he picked up the thread of the conversation where he had left it. "Point being, even at 70 knots, it's not impossible. Whoever did it knew what they were doing." John took a long swallow from his beer and then wiped the foam from his walrus moustache with his sleeve before continuing. "Not only were they able to pull off a tricky shot, but they knew that was the only shot to take."

"What do you mean?"

"Most people would assume that you take down a plane by shooting at the engine or the props, but when it's on approach to landing it can just glide in without those working. You need to take out the pilot. It's the only sure way."

"That makes sense, but why?" Peter asked, not really expecting an answer.

"Not a hot clue. That'll only be the second murder ever on Dragonfly Lake."

"Second, third, and fourth," Peter corrected him.

"Right."

"And who was the real intended victim? The Hydro guy?"

"That's a decent guess, but who knows? But to kill three people to get at one, that's messed up."

They sipped their beers in silence for a couple of minutes, and then Peter inclined his head toward the men in camo.

"I didn't think it was hunting season."

"No, not for moose or bear," John said with a laugh. "These fellows are hunting mushrooms. Morels specifically."

"There's lots of those around here?"

"Apparently. Came all the way from Minsk to check out the morel scene, and then they're on to somewhere in Nunavut for Arctic char fishing and muskox hunting."

Peter made a face at the mention of muskox hunting. "Minsk? In Belarus?"

"That's what they said. Not sure where that is, though. Near Russia, I'm guessing?"

"Yes, Belarus is between Russia and Poland. The name means 'white Russia.'"

"So, they're white Russians, like the drink," John chortled. "I should get Cam to put it on the cocktail menu!" He gestured to the bartender, a young man with a shaved head and a black patch over his right eye who was busy putting the finishing touches on a tray of four drinks.

Peter ignored this. "Mushroom hunting is really big in that part of the world. It's odd they would come all the way here for it. The char fishing sort of makes sense, and I guess the muskox if you're into that, but morels grow over there too."

"They were saying we have a lot more of the really rare and expensive black kind."

"Huh. Interesting."

"Yeah, we get quite a mix in here. Those girls over there are from Iceland. The Pure North Outfitters side of the business has started running Gudrun Jónsdóttir's *Forest Heart Kingdom* tours for Icelanders—"

"That's why my wife's parents moved to Manitoba! They loved Jónsdóttir's book so much they wanted to live where it was set."

"No kidding? Crazy, eh? Anyway, we bring them up here to give a true Manitoba forest experience because things down south have changed so much since the book was written. But we also take them down to New Selfoss after to show them the sites mentioned in the books and give them the flavour of Icelandic-Canadian life."

"Makes sense, I guess."

"Normally I'd take them dryland sledding, but with my team sick . . ." He looked down at the table.

"I'm sorry, John. I'll do my best to get them healthy and running again soon."

"I know you will, but you'll give it to me straight if I need to, you know . . ."

"Let a really sick one go? I will. But let's not get ahead of ourselves. Raj will call me when they arrive and will update me on how they look. I'll let you know what he says."

"I appreciate it. Not knowing is always the worst."

"Well, if I can do anything else, let me know." Peter said this because he knew it was the socially correct thing to say in this situation, but he assumed his veterinary help, plus perhaps thinking a bit about who might have poisoned the dogs, was enough and that there wouldn't be anything else he could do.

"Actually, since you mention it, going back to what you said earlier about your in-laws and *Forest Heart Kingdom*, and tell me if I'm way out of line with this, but is there any chance at all your wife might be available and willing to show these Icelandic ladies around New Selfoss? I know it's a lot to ask and I'm sure she's busy like everyone, but I'm in a bind because on top of the dogs being sick, Pure North's New Selfoss guide just up and quit this morning. I was going to do it myself, although I'm not Icelandic, but now with the dogs sick, I really can't get away."

"Wow, rotten timing. I can certainly ask Laura. She's a professional knitter and her time is usually somewhat flexible, but it would be a bad idea for me to just assume!"

"No doubt! I'm so grateful for you even considering asking her. I'd pay her of course, plus she'd keep any tips. Icelanders are usually pretty generous by European standards. They're scheduled to head down day after tomorrow, on Thursday. Sorry for the short notice."

Peter was fascinated by how John's moustache quivered when he spoke louder and more enthusiastically.

"No, that's OK. I understand. Laura's pretty keen on her Icelandic roots, so if she has the time, I think she might be excited by the opportunity. She talks to her aunt in Reykjavík at least once a month."

"Great. And if not, I'm sure I can figure something else out."

John quickly downed the rest of his beer and ordered another. Peter was only about a quarter of the way through his and waved off the offer of a second but asked to see a dinner menu. His stomach had a built-in clock, and it was time.

"We pride ourselves on fresh and wild here," John said and pointed to a blackboard above the bar Peter hadn't noticed before — from his angle it was partially screened by the moose's bulbous nose. Peter leaned forward and to the side to get a better look.

"I recommend the moose sausage with the chef's signature curly fries, or the pan-fried northern pike with wild rice."

Peter nodded and squinted to try to make out all the details on the board. They had used multiple colours of chalk in an elaborate font, so it was tricky to read. Only meat and starch. Peter weighed how to approach this. He decided on the honest straightforward tack.

"That all looks great, but I'm mostly a vegetarian. I mean, I will occasionally eat meat if I'm, say, at a dinner party, and I want to avoid the hassle. But the fries look good. You know, a double order of the fries would be fine." His words came out more awkwardly than Peter had hoped.

John laughed. "We can't have our esteemed Dr. Bannerman just eat fries, no matter how delicious they are. The chef's a magician. I'm a pre-diabetic myself, so he does all sorts of fancy stuff for me. I love my desserts and you wouldn't even know they were sugar-free, so I'm sure he can do the same for meat-free. I'll get him to come over and suggest something for you."

Peter felt himself flushing with embarrassment. That was precisely the reaction he sought to avoid. He didn't want to make a spectacle of his dietary preferences. Years of ministering to the medical needs of animals whose owners' livelihoods depended on their slaughter had taught him to be circumspect.

"No, no, it's fine. Please don't go to any trouble on my account."

"Nonsense, it's no trouble at all. You're a guest, a very important guest. And Evan will be delighted. He gets bored with the same old, same old."

Before Peter could object further, John had gotten up and disappeared through the swinging doors beside the bar that presumably led to the kitchen. A moment later he emerged with a tall blond man, probably in his late twenties, with large black discs stretching his earlobes. He had artfully spiked blond hair and remarkably broad shoulders. Peter assumed women would find him good-looking, although he had been surprised on that count before.

"Evan, this is Dr. Peter Bannerman, our vet up from New Selfoss."

"Pleased to meet you, sir." Evan extended his hand and Peter half-stood to shake it. "I might have just the thing for you. Those gentlemen" — Evan inclined his head toward the table with the Belarusians — "gave me some morels to cook for them. There were lots left over, and they said I could keep them. Are you vegan or vegetarian? If you're not vegan, I can fry them in butter with a side of garlic-sauteed wild rice and steamed wild asparagus. Unfortunately, I used up the last of the water lilies last week."

"Wow, that sounds fantastic. But only if it's no bother. Butter is fine."

"No bother at all. Anything to help a vet." Evan rolled up his left sleeve, revealing a tattoo of what appeared to be a rottweiler's face. "That's Sage. My best friend. You guys did so much for him."

"Beautiful dog," Peter lied. It was impossible to tell from the tattoo.

"He was. I still miss him every day."

After Evan left to prepare their dinners, John attempted to engage Peter in small talk, but having struck out on fishing, golf, and the past hockey season as subjects, they lapsed into a long silence, drinking their beers and glancing around the room, John smiling at the guests when he caught their eye, and Peter carefully observing them. Humans were fascinating — sometimes annoying and confusing, but fascinating. For one thing, they had so many different facial expressions, some of them quite subtle. Reading people's faces didn't come naturally to Peter, so he had made a point of studying the subject and memorizing as many variations as he could. Cultural differences could make it more challenging, though. For example, the Belarusian facing Peter seemed upset by something, not sad upset but aggravated upset. However, this could just be a generic serious face for him if, for example, they were discussing important aspects of their morel business. He had no idea. The Icelanders, on the other hand, appeared to be open books. They were constantly laughing and smiling, and their faces seemed to indicate that this was genuine mirth and happiness, not put on for some social reason, unless Icelanders were more skilled at dissembling than Canadians.

Peter's reverie was interrupted by the waitress's sudden appearance beside John.

"John, two RCMP officers are here to speak to you. They're in the lobby."

"Oh? OK, I'm on my way. And Molly, please get Dr. Bannerman another beer. He's not on call tonight."

He winked at Peter, got up, and gave Molly a quick hug. "You're sure you're OK working?"

Molly nodded. John smiled at her, gave her shoulders a squeeze, and walked quickly toward the door. Peter noticed the bartender watching them while he polished glasses.

"Can I bring you anything else besides the beer while you're waiting for your dinner, sir?" Molly asked. She was a small woman with black pigtails and dark, red-rimmed eyes, as if she had been crying. Something about her reminded him of Laura, although Laura had red hair and was about 20 years older. He supposed it was her size and the way the tops of her ears protruded slightly. A little bit elfin, like Laura. He felt a pang of homesickness.

Peter briefly wondered whether he should ask whether she was OK, but instead he said, "No, thank you. And I don't need the beer either."

As Molly turned to go, Peter spoke again. "Actually, there is one thing. The website mentioned a library. I wouldn't mind taking a quick peek at that if you think there's enough time before dinner. The book I brought isn't working for me."

"Dinner will be at least 20 minutes, and it's a pretty small library. It's down the hall to the right of reception. I'll show you. It won't take a second."

"I'm sure I can find it, thanks. You're busy here."

"It's not that busy." Molly smiled, but it was a half-smile and she looked like she was on the verge of tears.

Peter took a chance. "Are you OK? Did you know somebody on the plane?"

Molly squeezed her eyes shut briefly and then wiped them with the back of her hand. "Yes. Yes, I did."

"I'm very sorry." Peter cast about for something else to say but couldn't think of anything, other than to ask which of the three passengers she was upset about, and that question felt too awkward.

"Thank you." Molly blew her nose and smiled. "I'll grab you from the library if the food comes early."

CHAPTER
Four

The so-called library was as small as Molly said and ended up featuring almost as much taxidermy as literature. The books that were there ran to dog-eared thrillers and fishing guides, so Peter decided to give the Ottomans another chance. He headed back to the restaurant.

John returned shortly after the food arrived and, without Peter asking, explained that the RCMP had located what they believed to be the murder weapon, a high-powered rifle registered in John's name. It had been found that morning by two kids from the Dragonfly Lake First Nation out fishing on the far side of Wilcox Point from where the plane went down. They were close to the shore there when they spotted the rifle lying in the bush. John showed the officers his locked gun cabinet in his office, at which point he discovered that the lock had been broken. Someone had taken his new 308 Sako Finnlight, which is the one that had been found, and an antique German rifle from World War Two. They had left the Winchester, the Ruger, the Weatherby, and two shotguns. John went on to describe the other questions the police asked, such as who had access to his office, where he had been last night, and whether they could see staff and guest lists.

Peter listened to all this, occasionally nodding.

When John appeared to be done, Peter asked, "This Finn rifle . . ."

"Sako Finnlight."

"Was it the most accurate and would that be obvious to anyone? Or would you have to know something about guns to know that? I don't know anything about them."

"Oh yeah, it's the most accurate. I don't know how obvious that is, though. You'd probably have to know your guns. They all had scopes mounted on them. Except the shotguns, of course." John laughed.

Peter thought this was interesting, although not in a useful way.

"And the missing German rifle, was it also an accurate one?"

John chortled. "The Mauser K98? Only the best sniper rifle in the war. It was my grandfather's. He fought with the Princess Pats in Holland and brought it back as a souvenir. That and a bunch of Nazi flags and insignias and stuff we thankfully got rid of when I was a kid."

Peter nodded. "And the police haven't found it yet?"

"Not that they told me."

"Did you tell them about the dogs?"

"I did. They asked whether any died and whether I had any proof that they were deliberately poisoned. I said not yet on both counts. They were very sympathetic but said to call if we got proof or if there was any new information, because for the time being they didn't have the resources to investigate."

Just like I expected, Peter thought.

Peter excused himself as soon as he was done eating. He planned to get up early the next morning. John was right. Evan was a magician — the meal had been delicious. As he passed their table, Peter made a point of thanking the Belarusians for their contribution of the morels. They looked delighted to be thanked. One said, "Is nothing! We are pleased! Sit and have drink with us?"

Peter declined but felt good about himself for having thanked them. He was normally uncomfortable approaching strangers, but Laura had been encouraging him for years to view it like exercise — just as a healthy person needs to regularly exercise their body and their mind, they also need to exercise their sociability. He was the 98-pound weakling of sociability, so he did need the exercise. Once every few days seemed like plenty, though.

Back at his cabin he stepped out onto the dock to admire the sky. The sun had set an hour ago, but the western horizon was still lit with pale pink. A light blue above the pink gradually became darker the higher Peter looked in the sky until it became deep indigo directly above. The black of night was still hours off. A few stars were visible, but the brightest object was Venus, a shining dot about a hand's breadth above where the sun had set. The only sound was the faint lapping of water against the dock.

A loon began to call. No matter how often Peter heard it, and it had been many times in his life, he always felt a thrill at the sound. It may be a cliché, but this was the sound of the Canadian wilderness for him, and probably for most people, he assumed. Brazil had its riotous screechy macaws. Australia its manic laughing kookaburra. But Canada had its loons. The sound was difficult to describe — a kind of plaintive warble. When he was a little kid, he had watched Bob and Doug McKenzie imitate loon calls on their comedy show. They were famous for it, but it was terrible. Even at that age, he knew it was terrible. It didn't sound anything like a loon. He supposed it was just done for the laughs, although it wasn't clear to him how this was funny. No, a loon's call was a unique sound that spoke to Peter of loneliness. But a beautiful, almost defiant, loneliness.

He sat on the Muskoka chair and listened to the call echo and fade. The surface of the lake was perfectly smooth and seemed to gather every remaining photon from the west, giving it the appearance of burnished pewter. Peter waited for the loon to call again, but it didn't, and the mosquitoes were beginning to pester him, so he headed inside.

Peter woke up suddenly during the night. He didn't need to go to the bathroom. Had there been a noise outside his cabin? He thought possibly there had been, so he sat up in bed and listened carefully.

Just when he was about to conclude that it was nothing, he heard it, a clunking sound coming from toward the lake, like wood hitting wood.

Perhaps a log had drifted in and was striking the dock?

Not a bear, or a dog killer, or an airplane shooter anyway.

Peter tried to go back to sleep, but now he was wide awake and listening.

The night was silent again. No more clunking. But his curiosity overwhelmed his rational knowledge that he should just ignore it and go back to sleep. He got up and opened the Canada-goose-patterned curtains on the window facing the lake. It was two or three days away from a full moon, and the moonlight turned the lake a pearly grey, except the shadows, which were purest black. He looked at the dock, which was shared by the four guest cabins. There was no log. Nothing. Then, as his eyes adjusted, he saw movement.

There was a canoe heading out onto the lake. He could make out a paddler moving quickly. Paddler and canoe were a single black silhouette against the dull grey gleam of the lake. They were not far from the dock yet. If they kept going in the same direction, they would pass the crash site and eventually end up at the Dragonfly Lake First Nation.

"How odd," Peter whispered to himself. He picked up his phone and checked the time: 3:47. The paddler shifted. Peter had the sense they were looking back. He wondered whether the glow from his phone was enough to make his outline visible in the window. All the cabins and the whole shore were otherwise pitch dark, after all. Peter turned his screen off.

He wondered whether he should even bother trying to get back to sleep, but he needed to be as well rested as possible for tomorrow, or, today actually, he realized. He'd read a chapter in the Ottoman book. That would do it. And it did.

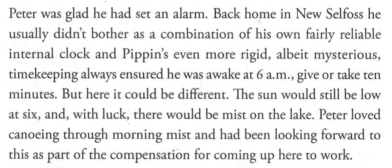

Peter was glad he had set an alarm. Back home in New Selfoss he usually didn't bother as a combination of his own fairly reliable internal clock and Pippin's even more rigid, albeit mysterious, timekeeping always ensured he was awake at 6 a.m., give or take ten minutes. But here it could be different. The sun would still be low at six, and, with luck, there would be mist on the lake. Peter loved canoeing through morning mist and had been looking forward to this as part of the compensation for coming up here to work.

The alarm had snapped him out of a dream involving his clinic suddenly being ten times larger, with lots of noise and confusion and unfamiliar people in white coats rushing about. He was happy to be woken from that, and when he pulled the goose curtains open, he saw he was in luck: Dragonfly Lake was capped with a two- to three-metre-thick layer of fog, generated as the water vapour off the lake condensed in the cool early morning air. Above this cap was clear air, with a sharp, but undulating, demarcation between the two. Strong early morning light streaming from the east made the fog glow. It was thicker in the deeply shadowed small bays and inlets and was beginning to break apart in the middle of the lake.

There, tendrils of mist danced across the surface, moving back and forth with the smallest changes in air currents. It was breathtakingly beautiful, magical even, although Peter was again reluctant to use that word.

He glanced at the coffee service on the dresser with its nasty-looking offering of some off-brand of instant. He had planned to get coffee in the restaurant with the early morning fishermen, but the mist was perfect now and wouldn't last, so he decided the instant would have to do. His plan was to paddle across the bay to the Dragonfly Lake First Nation and look in on his old friend, Lawrence Littlebear, returning with plenty of time to pack up for his flight home.

The coffee was as abysmal as he had predicted, but for this morning it was not about having a gourmet beverage experience. Peter had experienced caffeine withdrawal before and was determined never to allow it to happen again. He had debated with himself about slowly weaning himself off, perhaps by cutting back by five milligrams of caffeine a week until he got to zero, as he hated the idea of being dependent on a drug, but his real passion was tea, and the best teas often did not have a decaf version. It was a conundrum. However he reasoned that there were far worse vices and dependencies, so he more or less made his peace with needing modest doses of caffeine.

Fortunately, the coffee cooled quickly in the enamel mug, and he was able to drink it down in a few quick large unpleasant swallows. Then he pushed the canoe off the dock and glided out onto the bay. The water was glassy smooth, and the air was absolutely still. There was no sound and no movement, other than the canoe. Being the only animate object in a world frozen in place was a peculiar sensation. Peter was experienced enough that he could paddle without making a splash. He sliced into the water cleanly and then held the blade just slightly above the surface at the end of the stroke, so the drips were silent. These were long, slow strokes, but powerful enough that soon he was out in the middle of the bay, occupying a circle of clear air, surrounded by the mist that moved with him as he paddled. Up close, the mist was insubstantial, unlike the dense fog last spring with the ostriches. Peter shuddered when he thought of that day and how close it had come to tragedy. He pushed these thoughts aside and tried to focus on the calm and beauty of the lake.

His mind wouldn't let him.

It seemed to always need to feed on something, so he tossed it Atlas. Last night Raj had said Atlas was stable, but his liver values were off the charts. He recommended transferring him to Heartland Animal Medical Centre, the 24-hour clinic in Winnipeg. Peter agreed. The prognosis was grave, but they had to try so long as the dog wasn't suffering in the meantime. In Peter's judgment, Atlas was too out of it to be suffering, and Raj agreed.

These thoughts propelled Peter to Wilcox Point, the long spit of land that separated the half of the bay where the lodge was from the half that had the Dragonfly Lake First Nation community. The spit was littered with logs and boulders and featured one scraggly spruce at the very end, the kind Tom Thomson would have painted. An osprey perched at the tip of the spruce flew off as Peter approached.

With the mist gradually lifting, Peter could now make out four red buoys marking off a large rectangle in the deep water just past the spit. He assumed this was the crash site. It roughly lined up with where he had seen the RCMP boats the night before. He supposed they wouldn't be guarding a murder scene out here the way they would in the south. And anyway, how could anyone tamper with something deep under water? Even though he knew he would see nothing, Peter felt compelled to paddle directly through the rect-angle. He peered into the water from time to time, but there was nothing but black below. The only sign that anything was amiss, other than the buoys, was a wide iridescent ribbon of oil trailing off to the south.

Twenty minutes later Peter was at the DLFN dock, and, as expected, Lawrence was sitting there in a lawn chair, fiddling with a fishing lure. He likely would have been there anyway, as that was his morning ritual, but Peter had forewarned him of the visit and given him a time to expect him. Peter glanced around, looking for the mysterious night canoe, but there were several canoes among the many boats on the beach and at the dock. There was no way to tell if any of them was the one he'd seen. At least none of them had "Dragonfly Lodge" stencilled on them.

Lawrence glanced up. "It's Peter 'never call me Pete' Bannerman!"

"It's Lawrence 'never call me Larry' Littlebear!"

CHAPTER

Five

Peter and Lawrence had known each other for years, ever since Peter first took over the practice in New Selfoss from old Dr. Irwin "McSuperVet" McSorley. Business was slow in those years, so Peter offered to run spay-and-neuter and vaccine clinics in some remote First Nations communities. Although Peter and Lawrence were physical opposites, Peter tall and thin and dishevelled, and Lawrence short and heavy and well groomed, they were otherwise very much alike, down to some of their quirks and obsession with logic. Both were also huge Tolkien fans and former Dungeons and Dragons players.

Lawrence pointed to an empty lawn chair beside him and motioned for Peter to sit. "Welcome, cuz! It's been too long."

"It has."

"I'm sorry it's bad news that's brought you up here sooner than planned. How are the dogs doing?"

"Mixed. We'll probably lose his lead dog, Atlas, and the rest range from being quite sick to barely affected."

"Any idea why?"

"They were poisoned, damaging their livers, but I don't know with what yet."

"Wow, really? Someone has a hate on for poor old John, eh?"

"Yeah, that's what I'm thinking."

"Hey cousin, can I offer you some tea? I made some fresh Labrador tea just for you." He pointed to a battered thermos between the lawn chairs. Labrador tea was a plant that grew in boggy areas up here and was not strictly speaking a true "tea," kind of like rooibos wasn't, but it was not unpleasant tasting when made properly, and Lawrence knew how.

"Sure, please. I just had foul instant coffee over at the lodge this morning."

Lawrence wrinkled his nose. "This'll put you right."

They sipped in silence for several minutes, watching the remnants of the mist burn off while the first fishing boats from the distant lodge put-putted across the lake, causing long v-shaped ripples in the otherwise still perfectly flat surface.

"So, speaking of someone hating John, any ideas who?" Peter said. "You know the area much better than me."

"Hmm, well, I can't say everybody up here loves him, he can be a crusty old coot, but to try to kill his dogs? I dunno. Bev over at Friendly Bear tried to sue him a couple years back, for defaming them or something. So, there's that. And there's some in the community here who think he doesn't hire enough local people, although my favourite nephew, Jacob, is a guide there. But anyways, I can't see anyone around here hurting the dogs. Telling jokes about him behind his back is about as bad as it ever gets!" Lawrence laughed loudly enough to startle a duck who had been swimming beside the dock. The duck took off in flurry of quacking and flapping.

"Yeah, it's hard to figure out."

"More data needed," Lawrence said, flashing Peter a big grin.

"Yes, more data needed." Peter grinned back.

"And no doubt the cops don't have time for this, what with what that tragedy with Edna and the other two."

"Edna?"

"Edna Simpson, DLFN band council member. I don't think you've met her when you've been up here. A young up-and-comer, challenging the chief and the old boys."

"Serious dispute between them?"

"Not really. Just the usual political blah blah." Lawrence shook his head. "Anyways, I hate band politics. Edna was a good kid, bright future. It's a real tragedy, for the pilot and that Hydro guy, and their families too, of course."

"I can't imagine what the families are going through, especially since it's sounding like murder, rather than just an accident."

"You heard that rumour too?"

"I didn't think it was just a rumour, although I guess there hasn't been an official press release yet."

"Not that I know of. But that's definitely the solid word around here too, especially since Jonas and Ethan found that gun."

Peter nodded and they both lapsed into quiet tea drinking again. The mist was now confined to the furthest shadows, where it looked like cotton stuffed into the corners of the lake.

"Do you know if Edna and the Hydro guy knew each other?"

"She did talk about maybe getting this bitcoin thing set up here on the res, you know, for jobs and economic development. Cold weather and cheap hydro power is attractive for the massive servers they have to run. That's maybe why they were flying together. Or maybe coincidence. She has a sister in Thompson she visits a lot."

Peter was about to ask another question about this when he felt a wet dog nose press against his left hand.

"Gladys!" Peter exclaimed and turned to face the dog and give her a big scratch behind the ears. Gladys was Pippin's sister. Lawrence had wanted to name her Galadriel but was overruled by his kids. They wanted Rubble, which Lawrence thought was a Flintstones reference, but to his disappointment it turned out to be from *PAW Patrol*. Gladys was a compromise suggested by Cheryl, his wife.

Gladys was roughly the same size and shape as Pippin, but whereas Pippin was mostly black with a white chest and paws, Gladys was mostly white with a few random black splotches across her back, like a Holstein cow. They shared the same happy curled flag of a tail. Two more of Pippin's siblings still lived at Dragonfly Lake, and another had been adopted by a fisherman from Texas and apparently now lived in a mansion on the outskirts of Houston where he had his own personal dog-sized in-ground swimming pool. Or so the story went.

"And you are bringing Pippin up with you next week, aren't you? Hopefully you'll have time to bring him over for a doggie family reunion!" Lawrence laughed another one of his duck-frightening laughs, although this time there were no ducks nearby. "I'll round up my whole sled team. Pippin hasn't met most of them. Some are his cousins, and like second cousins and aunties and stuff. They'll have a blast!"

"Yes, that would be great!" Peter said, although privately he had his doubts whether even smart dogs like Pippin and Gladys cared that much about connecting with "family." They were happy to meet any friendly dog, and whether they preferred vaguely remembered family over friends was an open question. Mind you, he realized, that applied to humans as well.

Gladys completed a sniff tour of Peter's pants and shoes, padded over to greet Lawrence, and then, after turning around three times, settled down between their feet.

"Ha! Pippin does that too. He'll do a number of tight little circles before deciding on exactly which position to curl up in. But if he's truly tired, he'll just plop himself down like a sack of potatoes."

"Is he still solving crimes and saving the world from evildoers?"

"Mostly just evildoing squirrels since the ostrich incident."

"That was crazy. I couldn't believe stuff like that was going on in New Selfoss."

"I couldn't believe it either, but facts trump belief."

"That they do."

They both were quiet again. Their friendship didn't require constant banter. Peter liked to talk when he had something to say, and he liked to listen when the other person had something to say, but he especially liked peace when there was nothing to say.

A breeze began to riffle the surface of the lake just as a boat set out from the RCMP dock. Peter and Lawrence watched the boat progress toward the crash site. Peter was intrigued by the interplay between the boat's wake and the wavelets from the breeze.

Gladys perked her ears up and opened her eyes. Peter assumed it was because of the boat, but she had turned her head toward the shore. He glanced, but he couldn't see what she was looking at.

The RCMP boat cut its motor and began to drift. Silence returned to the lake. Peter could see two officers standing in the boat, looking at something in the water.

Then a gunshot split the silence.

CHAPTER
Six

F ight, flight, or freeze. Peter automatically froze. The gunshot came from behind them, on the shore, so the only way to flee would be into the lake. He whipped his head around, but couldn't see anyone, let alone someone with a gun. So, fight wasn't an alternative either.

"What the . . . ?" Lawrence shouted and jumped into the water. Just like that. Gladys jumped in immediately behind him.

It looked like fleeing was an option after all.

Peter was wearing his flying clothes, a nice set of khaki Patagonia travel pants and a blue long-sleeve button-up shirt, and he didn't want to get them wet. But he didn't want to get shot either and he supposed they were quick-dry anyway.

He jumped in.

It was startlingly cold.

Lawrence was holding onto one of the support posts for the dock, so Peter did the same. Gladys dog-paddled happily beside them, smiling an enormous doggie smile, clearly thinking, *Wow, what a fun surprise! We never go for a swim this way!*

The RCMP had obviously noticed the shot as well and had started the boat up and were racing for shore.

"It came from the bush on the far side of the community," Lawrence said, panting.

"What's in the bush there?"

Lawrence shot him a look. "Bush."

"No, I mean, a trail or a rock outcropping overlooking the lake or a stream or any kind of feature that would draw someone there?"

"Nope, just bush. Plain vanilla standard issue northern Canada bush. Sometimes the kids go out there and mess around, shoot squirrels or tin cans and stuff. That's probably all it is."

"Still . . ."

"Yeah, still. Given what happened two days ago, it pays to be careful, eh? And there's nothing like an early morning dip to clear the old noggin and give you a good start on the day!" Lawrence laughed.

Peter was beginning to shiver. In the abstract, he liked the idea of cold-water swimming and the theories behind its purported health benefits made sense to him, but he had never gotten around to trying it. The truth was, he didn't especially like getting wet, warm water or cold.

"Do you think we can climb back out now? The Mounties are almost here, so I doubt anyone would be targeting us with the police as witnesses."

"Yeah, sure. I'm going to swim to shore and get a bit of exercise — Cheryl says I'm getting fat — but feel free to haul your carcass back up onto the dock."

Peter was surprised how difficult it was to pull himself up onto the dock. The combination of his poor upper-body strength and general awkwardness made him feel like one of those elephant seals on the nature shows, laboriously dragging themselves up onto a rock. This was made worse by the acute embarrassment of doing this in front of presumably highly fit RCMP officers.

Peter was too busy floundering to notice that the RCMP boat had already pulled in on the other side of the dock. A hand reached down to him.

"Let me help you," said a bright female voice.

Peter knew it was sexist and wrong to feel even more humiliated that it was a female officer, but he couldn't help himself.

"Thank you," he said in as manly a voice as he could muster as he flopped onto the dock.

"Are you OK?" It was a blond woman with dark eyes and high cheekbones, about his age. She was squatting beside him.

"Wet and cold, but fine. Not shot, if that's what you mean."

"That's partly what I meant." She smiled at him and then straightened up. "Any idea where the shot came from?"

"I'm not sure, but Lawrence thinks it was from the bush, over there. Probably kids fooling around, he thought." Peter stood as well and pointed a dripping finger at the dense trees past the last bungalow to their right.

"Ah, the chief," the officer said.

For a brief second Peter thought she was using a wildly inappropriate racial slur, but then something dawned on him. "Chief? Lawrence Littlebear is the chief of DLFN?"

"Uh-huh." The officer gave him a queer look.

The other officer had been on his radio on the boat. Now he stepped up onto the dock.

The female officer said, "This is Constable Luke Giordano, and I am Sergeant Emily Patterson." She paused for a moment and squinted at Peter. "Hey, you're Kev Gudmundurson's brother-in-law, aren't you? The vet with the dog?"

She looked at her partner, who chimed in, "Yeah, yeah, Bannerman, right? Pete?"

Peter couldn't conceal his surprise. "Uh, yes. Peter Bannerman. Veterinarian," he stammered, feeling even colder now that he was out in the breeze. "And I do have a dog," he added before realizing how silly that sounded.

"You're kind of famous in the force," Emily said.

"Oh?"

"Good famous, mostly."

"Yeah, mostly," Luke added. The officers laughed.

"Kev and I attended the academy together and he was always better than me at everything, so I don't mind seeing him brought down a notch occasionally!" Emily said, chuckling. "He's a great guy and a good cop. It was just sweet to see him need help from a civilian to crack the exploding pig barn case."

"And that bizarre thing with the Viking artefacts and the ostriches," Luke added.

"Yeah, that was bad all round for the force, but again, good that Kev had you."

"And good that I had him," Peter said.

"Fair enough," Emily said with a smile, but then her expression turned serious again as she turned to face Lawrence, who had just walked up the dock from the beach. "Chief Littlebear, Dr. Bannerman says you believe the shot was fired from the forested area just south of the last house there." She pointed to the same place Peter had.

"Yes, that's what it sounded like to me, but I was facing the other way, so I could be wrong. You should talk to Agnes Simpson, she's in that last house. She's an old lady so she's always up early. She's probably even on her porch sorting blueberries or mending clothing or something. She's always busy, that lady. Makes me tired just thinking about what she gets up to." Lawrence laughed. "Honestly, officers, I think it was probably kids playing around or hunting. Everyone's just on edge, me included, 'cause of, you know."

"Thank you, Chief Littlebear. We'll check in with Mrs. Simpson and have a look in the forest. Will you be available if we have further questions?"

"I'll be right here in my summer office until my wife tells me I have to be somewhere else."

"Before you go, there's one thing I should mention that might be of interest," Peter said. "Early this morning, at around a quarter to four, I suddenly woke up in my cabin at the lodge. There was the sound of something hitting the dock. When I got up to look, I saw someone paddling a canoe across the lake, possibly headed this way, although I didn't keep watching to know for sure."

Emily shot Luke a look. "Someone canoeing across the lake before dawn? One individual?" she asked while scribbling something in her notebook.

"Yes, one individual. But it was only a silhouette, and by the time I thought to look, they were pretty far out already, so I'm sorry I can't give you any kind of description."

"That's OK. Thank you for the information. That could be helpful." Emily snapped her notebook shut, and then the two officers said their goodbyes and walked down the dock into the community.

"You didn't tell me you were the chief?" Peter said, still smarting at having been doubly embarrassed in front of the officers, once for his ungainly water exit and once for his ignorance of Lawrence's status.

"You didn't ask." Lawrence shrugged. "It's not a big deal, cousin. And you didn't tell me about this midnight paddler!"

"I didn't think it was that interesting until that gunshot. But you're changing the subject. Earlier you said you hated band politics!"

"I do. Hate it. It's a hateful job, but someone's gotta do it."

"So, you're one of the old boys now?"

"Cuz, if you're over 40, you're old in the eyes of anyone under 30. And I'm over 40."

"Me too. Forty-three now."

"Got you beat. Forty-four. Yup, we're old farts now. Not old farts like Silas there." Lawrence pointed to a stooped old man in a red checked shirt and a bright pink ballcap who had emerged from his bungalow and was hobbling toward the shore. "But plenty old enough, and" — he stopped and grinned at Peter — "farty enough."

"Come on, we're middle-aged, not old," Peter protested.

"Sure, keep stretching that middle, but not young anyway. Come on, let's see if Cheryl will let us dirty up some of our nice guest towels and then we can come back down to my office and chat with the nice officers when they're done. Maybe, just maybe, we can snag some carrot cake too."

They were able to dry off with fluffy white towels, although Peter didn't have a change of clothes with him and Lawrence was a completely different size, so he was still wearing damp stuff, but it was drying quickly in the sun. They also got the carrot cake. Cheryl, an effusively friendly, high-energy woman, insisted Peter take an extra piece for later. Lawrence had hit his quota for the day, so his request for another piece was refused.

Emily and Luke were back on the dock about an hour later with nothing to report. There were no witnesses, no shell casings, no footprints, nothing. Agnes Simpson had heard the gunshot too and had worried it was a suicide, so she was relieved when no body was found. Then she made the officers sit down for tea so she could lecture them on how important it was that they found Edna's killer. It turned out Edna was her grand-niece and the apple of her eye.

"Really nice lady, though," Emily said. "She's helped us before. It goes without saying, though, that we're committing all available resources to finding out who's behind downing the plane and killing those three people. Here's my card if either of you have new information."

She handed one business card each to Peter and Lawrence and then motioned to Luke to get the boat ready.

"Just before you go, Sergeant, this shot just now — do you have any guesses whether it was aimed at us, or at you, or at something else, or not aimed at all?" Peter asked.

"Dr. Bannerman, given your reputation, I'm surprised you would ask that. You know there is no information whatsoever to support or refute any of those theories. In other words, at this point, your guess is as good as mine. But you're probably safe out here on the dock right now. If anyone was being targeted, and that's quite the 'if,' then it was us, not you." She paused and then added, "Probably." She grinned and slapped him lightly him on the shoulder before turning around and climbing into the boat beside her partner.

CHAPTER
Seven

L aura sighed as she watched the arrivals screen post another delay for Peter's flight from Thompson. Mechanical issues, apparently. He had to get back, both to deal with the Reynolds' dogs because Raj was booked at another clinic tomorrow, and to get ready for their upcoming canoe trip. If he didn't have the time to properly prepare for that, he would get antsy and be hard to live with. Laura chuckled to herself when she thought about what Peter was like in that state. Funny and not funny at the same time.

Just then a text message arrived from Peter.

Apparently we're looking at another four hours.
Sorry you have to wait so long!

not your fault! I should've checked before
I left home — got stuff I can do in
town while I'm here anyway

Good, thanks. BTW, you're sure
re those Icelandic ladies tomorrow?

I can still tell John no. Especially since
your day today is messed up now.

Laura smiled at Peter's concern. It was cute that he offered, but
she knew it would be extremely painful for him to go back on what
he told John.

no, no, it's cool —
looking forward to it even

And in fact, this was true. She was looking forward to it. It felt
like an opportunity to reconnect with her parents' world and her
childhood. It would be nostalgic and fun.

OK, thanks.

enjoy Thompson airport!

:-/

Laura tucked her phone away in her purse, double-checked the
time, and decided there was plenty of time to have a late lunch in
the Exchange District, poke around some galleries, and pop into
Wolesley Wool to see if there was anything new. Peter's delayed
flight actually felt like bonus time to her, almost like a snow day.
Maybe there'd even be time to visit Atlas at Heartland. Peter would
be grateful, and it would save him from having to stop by there if
he was pressed for time. In fact, she'd skip the galleries to make sure
that happened, but she wouldn't skip lunch or Wolesley Wool.

The Ottoman history book still wasn't speaking to Peter, and he found that surfing the web on his phone during downtime made him feel fidgety and anxious. Unless there was a specific news item he wanted to follow, or something he wanted to research, mindless scrolling was just that, mindless, and mindlessness was never something Peter was interested in. You might as well be dead, or a cactus or a rock, as be mindless, was his philosophy. So instead, he counted ceiling tiles, and light fixtures, and light switches in the Thompson Airport waiting room, and calculated ratios between these and mused about the principles, if any, behind these ratios. He recognized this was a decidedly unusual way to occupy oneself, but he didn't care. Math always kept him calm and happy. He alternated this with studying the other passengers and walking laps around the room to prevent his long legs from cramping.

The only restaurant was a Robin's Donuts which usually served passable coffee. There was a certain nostalgia appeal to Robin's, which was once much more common before Tim Hortons and Starbucks began their triumphal march across the country, but today Peter avoided it out of fear of having to visit the washroom more often than absolutely necessary. He was not an especially fastidious person, but on his one toilet visit after arriving from Dragonfly Lake, he was alarmed to see a sharps container overflowing with used needles, a large "do not drink the water" sign, and a screaming baby being diapered by his frazzled father. The baby wouldn't necessarily be there still, but the unspeakable diaper smell likely would as the trash can was also overfull. He and Laura had decided not to have children. He was uncomfortable around babies, and both had agreed that the planet was full. But sometimes he wondered whether Laura was still fully on board with this decision.

This troubling train of thought was happily stopped in its tracks by the appearance of one TSB — *Not Thompson Sports Bar*, Peter thought, smiling to himself — agent and two RCMP officers in the waiting room. That piqued his curiosity, as he knew from Kevin that the Mounties had their own aircraft. In fact, he remembered the number Kevin quoted — the RCMP Air Services branch had 41 aircraft, mostly fixed wing, but some helicopters. Maybe they were just patrolling the airport, but why with a TSB agent? His question was partially answered when they went into the Borealis Airlines office on the far side of the room. Borealis was the owner of the float plane that went down. Peter moved to an empty chair nearest the Borealis office door, but of course there was nothing to hear or see, so he felt a little silly. Nonetheless, this shifted his brain from ceiling tiles and odiferous babies to murders.

In the last two years he had personally known three people who had been murdered. This was three more than his previous total. He didn't know any of them very well, mind you, but well enough. Murder had gone from being an abstract event in books and television and film to a significant part of his life. And now there were three more, although here the connection was far more tenuous — he had just happened to go to the same lake shortly after they were murdered. If he were superstitious, he'd have to start wondering whether there was something about him, but he was the opposite of superstitious, and quite happy about that.

While he waited, he googled Borealis. It was a small airline with just a dozen planes. It was based here in Thompson, with the float planes taking off from the Burntwood River, two kilometres from the airport, and they had a couple small wheeled aircraft as well. They did a lot of charters, but had some regularly scheduled flights too, including the daily to Dragonfly Lake. Their webpage featured a large memorial banner for Ned Fromm. It showed a photo of him in his dark blue pilot's uniform, with a fashionable, neatly trimmed beard, short black hair, and a friendly smile. The accompanying mini-obituary indicated that he was single, with only parents in Australia listed as grieving next of kin. In addition to flying, his hobbies apparently included bass fishing and water polo. It was vaguely interesting that he turned out to be Australian, but not relevant. Poor guy, poor parents. Imagine being half a world away and hearing that your only child — no siblings had been listed — had been shot to death.

This got Peter thinking about the other victims, so he decided he did have something useful and non-mindless to surf after all.

The lead article on the CBC page, which previously just had a stock photo of a Borealis float plane, plus a few lines summarizing the story with a promise of details to follow, now featured a photo of Brendan O'Daly, looking sunburnt in a bright yellow Hawaiian shirt, beaming at the camera, hoisting a cocktail with a wedge of pineapple in it. His vividly pink face was almost perfectly round, topped by short yellow-blond bristles. As John had said, the article detailed that Brendan had been an executive with Manitoba Hydro who quit to start up a bitcoin venture. According to the most recent update of the news article, his company, TealCoin, had been preparing for an IPO, but that was now on hold. His girlfriend, Monique Gagnon, was the lead singer of a band, The Queenston Heights, that Peter was only dimly familiar with, although they had apparently won a Juno award. She was reported to be devastated and asked for privacy. Brendan also had two ex-wives and several children. The article contained links to other articles detailing some of what appeared to be publicity stunts he was famous for, but Peter didn't follow these as they didn't constitute real news.

The paragraph on Ned covered the same ground as the notice on the Borealis website. It also had a link to a story about him helping in the rescue of German canoeists last summer with a particularly daring landing. And they mentioned that his parents owned Australia's leading greeting card company, Wombat Notes.

There was much less to read about regarding Edna Simpson. Her picture showed a young woman with shoulder-length black hair, pretty eyes, and a Mona Lisa smile. The article only described her as a rising star in Indigenous political leadership, part of a new generation. There were no links to any stories about her activities on band council. Peter couldn't help but muse that wealthy white men dominated in death as they did in life. He looked at Edna's picture and wondered which of the three victims Molly the waitress was so upset about. Edna was about Molly's age, and they lived on the same lake, so maybe they were friends. Peter wasn't clear how much interaction there was between the First Nation and the lodge. Ned was also a possibility, given that he was also in the same age range and Molly likely would have flown with him. Brendan looked like the least probable connection. Not that any of this mattered, but her sadness was a puzzle, and Peter's brain could never leave a puzzle alone.

Peter's phone vibrated.

"Hi! Any updates?" Laura asked.

"Looks like the plane's coming in, so I should be able to board in the next half-hour."

"Great! I'm calling from beside Atlas's kennel. I popped by to visit him and give you an update."

"That's great! Saves me from having to stop by on our way home. How's he doing?"

"He's sleeping now, but when I came, he was half awake and he wagged his tail a little when I patted him, even though he doesn't know who I am."

"Did you get the chance to talk to one of the emergency vets? Who's on right now?" Peter hoped it was one of the more experienced vets, and one who wouldn't be snarky with Laura.

"It's Karla, and she didn't have much time, but at least she knows me. She said his liver values were still sky high, but at least they were within the readable range now after aggressive IV treatment. She thought it was worth continuing treatment for another couple days at least, even though the prognosis was still poor."

"Good, at least there's a chance, however slim. John will be pleased to hear that." Peter shifted his phone to his left ear and covered his right ear to try to block out the baby who had begun crying again.

"Any more thoughts on how this could have happened?" Laura asked.

"Lots of thoughts, but nothing worth talking about. The how is deliberate poisoning, I'm sure of that, but which specific poison is still not clear to me. I've also been thinking about who would do something like this, and why, but haven't made any progress. Lawrence said John isn't that well liked."

"Huh. Well, I should go. It looks like one of the techs is getting ready to take some more blood from Atlas."

"OK, see you soon."

Just then the Borealis Airlines office door opened, and the three officers emerged, one carrying a Bankers Box of files. Another of the RCMP officers, a stocky middle-aged man with a grey buzz cut, seemed to recognize Peter and smiled at him. Peter had no idea who he was.

The officer stopped and extended his hand. "Staff Sergeant Todd Rehnquist. You're Dr. Bannerman, the vet with the dog, right?"

Again, "the vet with the dog," Peter thought. He stood up hastily to return the handshake, dropping his phone to the floor with a clatter as he did so. After picking it up and quickly checking it for cracks, he smiled awkwardly and replied, "Yes, that's me — the vet with the dog."

They both laughed.

"Well, that's a heck of a coincidence, because I was just thinking about you."

"Oh?"

"Well, to be honest, I was thinking about your dog, the champion sniffer. And I hear you and the dog — what's his name?"

"Pippin."

"Yeah, Pippin, and Corporal Gudmundurson, are headed up to Dragonfly day after tomorrow for a canoeing holiday?"

"Yes, that's right."

"We might want to borrow Pippin for an hour or two while you're up there. Just a hunch I want to follow."

"Sure, no problem at all. Anything to help."

"Perfect. I'll be in touch."

The RCMP had a large canine unit, with dogs well trained in drug and bomb detection, and in tracking people, or finding their remains, but Pippin's reputation for finding objects with scent on them, such as that note in the pig case or the "nithing pole" in the ostrich case, had spread through the force. He was far better at this than any of their dogs. To the best of Peter's knowledge, Pippin was the only non-RCMP dog anywhere in the country that had helped in an investigation. Peter smiled to himself. Pippin would be delighted to do it again.

On the drive home from the Winnipeg airport, Laura chatted happily about her plans for the Icelandic women. Peter was relieved that she seemed to be genuinely excited about this. He was only mildly anxious that it would interfere with her preparations for the canoe trip, but he reasoned that he could take over some of the to-do items that had been assigned to her. He had to work tomorrow as Raj wasn't available, but if he made a list and a schedule, he'd be able to get through everything that needed to be done in the evening, after work.

"And then I thought we'd have them over for dinner at our place," he suddenly heard Laura say, realizing he had tuned her out while musing over the canoe trip plans.

"Dinner? Tomorrow at our house?" So much for getting ready in the evening.

"Yes, that's what I said." She shot him a look as she merged onto the Perimeter Highway. "Pure North's itinerary calls for dinner at the Flying Beaver, which, while a great New Selfoss institution, is probably the least Auni aspect of town." "Auni" was short for Austur Nýr Islendingur, or East New Icelanders, the group that split away from the main Vestur (west) settlement across the lake at Gimli. "I have my mom's old recipes based on what they ate in *Forest Heart Kingdom*. It would be a much more fitting finish to their day."

"Like that fish stew, but with Lake Winnipeg pickerel and white fish rather than the cod or whatever they eat in Iceland?"

"Plokkfiskur, exactly! With a salad of wild greens!"

"You have time for all this? And for getting ready for the canoe trip?" Peter gripped the door handle tightly as Laura sped up to pass a semi-trailer truck. She was an excellent driver, but unnervingly aggressive by Peter's standards. After all their years together, he still hadn't got used to it.

"We don't leave until noon Friday, and I've done lots already."

Peter's eyes were glued to the road as Laura was passing another semi that was weaving a little, sometimes crossing slightly into the passing lane.

"And you've always got all the camping gear cleaned and sorted in advance because you do that after every trip, so it's ready to go for the next time," Laura said in a cheery sing-song as she darted back into the right lane, in front of the weaving semi.

Peter exhaled and nodded stiffly. "Yes, I suppose. And the food?"

"Half done!" Laura pumped her fist in the air. "Oh, and I forgot to mention, Stuart called, and he wants to do as much of the cooking as possible."

"Oh?" Stuart was Kevin's boyfriend. Peter liked him. He was a tall, cultured, polite Nigerian-Canadian accountant who lived in Gimli. He was in a lot of ways the opposite of Kevin, but somehow it seemed to work well.

"Yeah, said because he's never canoed or camped before, he wants to be an asset in some way. He's modest, but Kevin says he's an excellent cook. His specialty is Nigerian fish stew."

"More fish stew," Peter chuckled, beginning to relax now that the highway ahead was clearer, and Laura had slowed down to only ten kilometres an hour over the speed limit. "OK, maybe we've got more of the food covered than I had originally planned for."

They lapsed into a pleasant silence as the green prairie, punctuated by squares of bright yellow canola, rolled by. Laura put on some of her favourite '80s music, humming along to it, tapping on the steering wheel while Peter spent the rest of the drive home looking forward to seeing Pippin. Soon they would be in the trees, which was the first sign they were nearing home.

CHAPTER
Eight

Pippin stared at the crust of toast as if he was trying to will it up through the air and into his mouth by telekinesis.

Laura said, "OK," and in the blink of an eye, like a frog catching a fly, Pippin snapped up the crust. Then he looked at her and cocked his head. Maybe if he was quiet and polite there'd be more. Maybe.

Laura smiled at him and tossed him another crust, this time not making him wait. She was up unusually early. Peter was the consistent early riser in the family, while Laura's waking was much more variable. If she had been up late trying to finish a knitting order, she'd sleep in, but if she had something on in the morning, she could easily, even happily, get up early too. And this was one of those days. She was supposed to meet the Icelandic ladies at the East New Iceland Motor Inn at eight o'clock and walk with them to Rita's Coffee Shop for breakfast. They had a full day ahead of them, with the highlight being a hike through the forest along the New Selfoss Heritage Trail to the log cabin built by the tourist board to mimic the one described in *Forest Heart Kingdom*. In the summer it was staffed by local student re-enactors wearing period costumes, and at eleven and two o'clock every day they put on a short play centred on a love triangle in the book. It was excessively melodramatic by Laura's standards, but the tourists lapped it up.

And it was nostalgic for her, as her mother used to read to her from the book.

Pippin was still watching her. A third crust would be unusual, but not entirely out of the question with Laura. With Peter, the strict limit was one, but with Laura, three was possible.

"Not today," Laura said and reached down to pat the dog. "But I do have good news for you — you can come with me while I show the visitors from Iceland around!" Rita's allowed well-behaved dogs, and the rest of the plans were mostly outside.

Pippin panted happily and began to wag his tail. Laura had used the upbeat, something-fun-is-going-to-happen voice.

"Peter is at the clinic already, checking on those poor dogs from Dragonfly Lake, so it would be lonely for you here. And Merry has his own sunbathing and napping plans." Laura smiled over at the cat, who was sprawled out on the windowsill that caught the first warm rays of morning sun.

Laura's phone rang. It was Kevin.

"Hey sis, surprised you're up. Thought I'd have to leave a voicemail!"

"No, I'm squiring those Icelandic tourists around today."

"Ah, right. So, I haven't started packing yet — I've got plenty of time tonight — but I was thinking about it on my way to the station this morning and it occurred to me that I don't think I have a sleeping bag anymore. The last one got all wet and gross that time I tipped the canoe, remember? Anyway, have you guys got a spare? I don't know if I have time to drive into the city and buy another."

Laura groaned. It was a good thing Peter had gone into work early and wasn't home to hear this.

Peter liked being in the clinic by himself early in the morning. He loved his staff, Kat, the vet tech, and Theresa, the receptionist, but he also loved solitude and the chance to organize his thoughts and plans without external input. The first order of business was to check on Pretty, Gus, and Winter. All three dogs were awake and alert when Peter came into the ward to greet them. They were in adjacent kennels, each with an IV line running in. The clinic only had one proper IV pole, so the other two bags were suspended from hooks on the wall. As Peter couldn't offer nursing care through the night, he only hospitalized the most stable patients, and only when either himself or Kat was able to check on them late in the evening and again early in the morning.

Three pairs of eyes followed Peter as he went from kennel to kennel, checking the IV lines and looking at Kat's notes from the night before. Everything looked good. Everyone had eaten last night. Even Winter seemed to be making progress. He'd check bloodwork again this morning before updating John, but it looked like for these three at least, the damage to the liver was below the threshold where it would affect them day to day. Everyone — dogs and humans — had surplus liver capacity, which is why you could abuse your liver with alcohol for years without noticing the damage. However, losing some of that capacity meant you were more vulnerable to a worse outcome if you encountered any other liver disease in the future. John would have to be careful about what they were exposed to in order to minimize the risks.

The three pairs of eyes still following him, Peter went to the cupboard and pulled out the bag of special diet that had been opened for them. He gave each a small amount and then stood back and smiled as they attacked their food, Winter with slightly less enthusiasm than the other two, but nonetheless, he finished it before lying down again, curling up, and wrapping his tail around his nose. Gus gave an excited little yip, presumably requesting more food. Pretty just stared at him with laser intensity, as if trying to read his mind.

The next task was to check his messages. He dreaded this. He briefly wondered whether he should perhaps read up some more on liver toxins first instead, but he recognized that this was just a stalling tactic. He wouldn't find out anything new or useful about hepatotoxicity. He needed to just "eat the frog." Laura had taught him this years ago when he explained how stressed he got when he had to phone clients. Something about picking up the phone and having to talk into it always felt awkward to him. This was especially true when he didn't know what to expect. He knew this was just one of his autism spectrum traits but knowing so didn't make it any better. Theresa was good at eliciting as many details from the callers as possible, but sometimes she was in a hurry, or sometimes the caller didn't want to say. In any case, the "eat the frog" strategy was to imagine the phone calls as a frog you didn't want to eat, but you knew you eventually had to. There was no avoiding eating the frog. You could either stare at the frog all day, eating it a hundred times in your mind first, or you could just get it over with and eat it once in one quick gulp, keeping the grisly chewing to a minimum.

Peter started his computer and scanned the list of messages. Not so bad, given he had been away all week. A small frog. Raj had been good at dealing with anything urgent, but some people just insisted on talking to Peter. There was Mrs. Perkins with Chester the bulldog, who had apparently eaten a spider. And there was Mr. Arneson with Blackie the cat, who wouldn't stop licking his belly. And Ms. Ericson with Ernie the mutt, who had taken to howling for no reason at three o'clock in the morning. And Peggy Dinsdale, who refused to say why she was calling. Peter groaned lightly. Everyone believed Peggy had a crush on him. Theresa had even put a smiley emoticon at the end of the message. This was going to be even more awkward.

(Eat the frog.)

And then finally, with no patient file associated with it, a call from a "Cam" at Dragonfly Lodge with the message only saying, "Call ASAP — private."

Peter struggled for a moment to place Cam. Then he remembered. He was the bartender at the lodge. The young guy with the black eye patch and shaved head. He glanced at the time, 7:40. Probably not too early to call, he reasoned. Did calling Cam before the clients constitute stalling, or was it frog eating? Probably the former, but he didn't care. Curiosity often held the trump card for Peter.

A sleep-heavy voice answered after five rings, "Hello?"

"Hi, this is Dr. Peter Bannerman in New Selfoss. You called?"

"Oh, yeah, I did! Thanks for calling back. Hang on a sec." There were some shuffling noises in the background. "OK, that's better. Um, yeah, about John's dogs, I have some information that might help."

"Interesting, go ahead."

"I heard you were thinking it was poisoning, right?"

"I'm sure of it now."

"Well, you can be even more sure because I know where it came from."

"Oh?"

"Bartending's just a part-time gig — the rest of the time I'm the handyman around the lodge. I went into the supply shed yesterday to get some drain cleaner and I noticed the Santophen bottle was in a different spot and had been opened. I know this because we never use it anymore . . ."

"What's Santophen?" Peter asked.

"It's PCP. Something chlorine phenol."

"Pentachlorophenol?"

"Yeah, that's it. John had it for treating lumber against termites or something like that."

"Interesting. It's been banned in Canada for years."

"Yeah, I think probably that's why it doesn't get used anymore, but he likes to keep it around, you know, just in case. Especially since you can't legally buy it here anymore."

"And phenols are highly toxic to the liver if ingested," Peter said. "So that's why you're calling me."

"Yes, exactly. I thought it was weird that it suddenly got used and nobody told me, and then I had this 'oh shit' thought about the dogs, so I looked the stuff up online. Like you said, highly toxic to the liver." Cam was quiet for a moment and there was faint crackling on the line, as there often was during calls to the North. Peter was about to speak, when Cam began again, "But here's the thing, Dr. Bannerman — only John and I have keys to that shed. There was another guy, Marty, a snowmobiling guide John hired for the winter, who had keys, but he would have turned them in when his contract was done in April."

"Have you told this to the police?"

"No. They're not investigating this, and I've" — the young man paused again and cleared his throat — "I've got a record and I've done time, so I don't love talking to them. If they do start looking into this, I thought you could pass the info along and then if they want to interview me, fine, but mostly I thought you'd want to know that it might be this pesticide and that maybe you shouldn't believe everything John tells you."

Peter didn't know how to respond to this, so he just thanked Cam and they wrapped up the call with some pleasantries about his trip back north tomorrow.

After Peter hung up, he stared blankly at the computer screen for several long minutes, trying to process his thoughts. He didn't know John nearly well enough to be able to make a rational judgment about whether he was capable of harming his own dogs, but the capacity to do so was the less interesting question. The more interesting question was the motivation. What possible reason could he have for doing so? Peter couldn't think of anything other than sick attention seeking, like that Munchausen by proxy syndrome where mentally ill parents deliberately harm their children to elicit sympathy. But that was a stretch. There had to be a better, more logical explanation. He would let Kevin know about his conversation with Cam and let him decide if it was worth the Dragonfly Lake detachment's time or not.

Peter was just about to call Mrs. Perkins, who he knew was an early riser, when he found himself opening Dragonfly Lodge's website instead. He clicked on the "Meet the Team" button, and scrolled through the faces and names until he came to Marty Sullivan, a burly-looking older fellow with the kind of big bristling white lumberjack beard small birds could nest in. He had shaggy snow-white hair, a jovial smile, and crinkly eyes in the photograph, which, in combination with the beard, gave him a bit of a Santa Claus vibe. His write-up described him as Dragonfly's winter guide, an expert in snowmobile expeditions, ice fishing, trapping, hunting, and winter survival. It said he spent his summers alone in an off-the-grid cabin away from Dragonfly Lake.

He'd tell Kevin about Marty too. It might not be possible to copy keys up there, but he wondered how carefully John would have looked at what Peter presumed would be quite a big keyring when Marty returned it? There were lots of outbuildings and locked doors. Lots of keys to keep track of.

Peter mulled this over a moment longer before starting to get up with the intent of checking on the huskies again.

Stalling.

Eat the frog.

He sat back down and picked up the phone.

The phone calls to the clients all went well, even the one with Peggy, who just had a question about Emma's meds for her Addison's disease. Why she wouldn't tell Theresa that was beyond him. Maybe she liked the mystery and control that came with making him guess. Peter shuddered. She was an attractive woman, but she was definitely not his type — just far too . . . something — and in any case he was happily married. He looked at the picture above his desk of him and Laura on their honeymoon in Ireland, on the wild, wave-hammered west coast. An old couple walking by had insisted on taking their picture. They had guessed Laura and Peter were on their honeymoon. It was the only photo he could think of where his smile didn't look stupid to him. And Laura positively radiated happiness, along with that dash of good-natured mischief that had attracted him to her in the first place.

Theresa and Kat arrived, each popping their heads into the office to say "Good morning, welcome back!" and the phone was starting to ring, but it was still ten minutes before the first appointment. Peter opened the Dragonfly Lodge website again and looked at each of the bios of the dozen staff. He didn't know what he was looking for, but he felt compelled to look anyway. Most of it was boring and predictable, but Molly's and Evan's entries stood out. Molly Smithfield had been his waitress, the one who reminded him of Laura, and who looked like she had been crying. Evan Lundquist was the chef with the big black plugs in his earlobes. They both originally came from the same small town of Zealandia, Saskatchewan. Peter looked it up — it was 100 kilometres southwest of Saskatoon and had a population of 79. They were about the same age and not apparently related, so they must have been friends, perhaps one securing the job at the lodge for the other? Peter smiled because he knew how Zealandia got its odd name — it was on one of the "alphabet lines," where the railways named towns alphabetically as they established them about every ten miles. Consequently, there was also a Zelma and Zenon Park. Many were ghost towns now as the Prairies could not support the population size the early boosters dreamed of. But Zealandia was not a ghost town. Not quite yet.

Cam Schmidt's entry was unenlightening, just listing previous bartending in Winnipeg and Montreal, and saying that he was from New Selfoss. Peter couldn't recall any Schmidts he knew in town, but that didn't mean much if they didn't own pets or farm animals.

Beyond those three and John, whose bio was also predictable (from Winnipeg originally but passionate about the North), there were the housekeeping and kitchen staff, five in total, another waitress, who was also from Winnipeg, two guides from Dragonfly Lake First Nation, and Marty.

Peter was about to search morel hunting in Belarus when Theresa popped her head into the office. "Peter, Dennis is set up with Killer!"

Killer was misnamed with deliberate irony; he was the sweetest little fluffy white Maltese poodle cross, or Maltipoo. Peter didn't normally think of himself as a little fluffy dog guy, but he made an exception for Killer.

CHAPTER
Nine

The plokkfiskur the next evening was excellent. Although Peter and Laura were mostly vegetarians, they did eat fish from sustainable and ethical fisheries, and Lake Winnipeg fish was some of the best in that regard. The Icelandic women seemed to genuinely love the stew as well. Thordis and Kristjana were seated on one side of the table, with Sigrun and Helga on the other side. Peter and Laura were at either end. Pippin had decided he loved Sigrun and curled up on the floor beside her where she could rub his belly with her foot. Peter had trouble keeping the four women straight, so he avoided using their names for fear of getting it wrong. Laura, being better at such things, and having spent the day with them, seemed to know them like best friends.

"I have to say again, what a wonderful meal, what a beautiful home, and what a perfect day," the tallest one said, who Peter thought was Thordis, but possibly could be Helga. "We cannot thank you enough. Next time you are coming to Iceland, you must allow us to return the favour!"

"Be careful what you offer," Laura said with a laugh. "Because we're likely to take you up on it!"

Everyone laughed and then raised their glasses of white wine as the short-haired one — Kristjana? Or maybe this was Thordis? — proposed a toast to trans-Atlantic friendship, and then winked at Peter, adding that this included people married to Icelanders, and their cats, raising her glass to Merry, who was sleeping in the corner of the dining room, and even their dogs too, since they were now considered acceptable. Sigrun had explained earlier that dogs had been completely illegal in Reykjavík until the 1980s because of fears of tapeworms, and even today they were carefully licensed and regulated. Consequently, it was still more of a cat city than a dog city.

Later Peter and Sigrun — and Peter was sure it was Sigrun because Laura had told him about how she and Pippin had bonded — were sitting on the deck with their wine while the others were chatting over by Gandalf's pen. The goat looked indifferent to the company, but the sun was warm over there, whereas the deck was in the shade. It had been an unusually cool day for July, but Sigrun said she preferred it that way. Like the others she was blond, but she was freckled and had her hair done in pigtails that reminded Peter of Pippi Longstocking, although Pippi might have had red pigtails, if he remembered correctly.

"You are lucky to live here, Peter," she said, raising her glass to the forest beyond the yard.

"Yes, I am, but you are lucky to live in Iceland. It's beautiful there too."

"It is, but not very many trees."

"However, lots of volcanoes. Volcanoes are cool. And it's hard to have both volcanoes and trees," Peter said, taking a small sip of his wine. He did this to be sociable. He didn't actually like wine.

"True, I do love our volcanoes. And another good thing about Iceland is that we have less murders. You have many so murders here!"

"Yes, that's rotten luck that you were at Dragonfly Lake when those three people were killed. How many murders do you have in a year in Iceland?"

"In all Iceland?" Sigrun paused and thought a moment. "Maybe one? A really bad year is three."

"Ha!" Peter snorted. "So those Netflix shows exaggerate?"

"Terribly!" Sigrun laughed. "People being murdered left and right in *Trapped* and in *The Valhalla Murders*. And the Ragnar Jónasson and Arnaldur Indriðason crime novels are even worse! If all of this were true, our little country would be emptying out. Bodies overwhelming the morgues! People fleeing for safer places, like Libya or Afghanistan!"

"So, at the most three murders in a bad year in an entire country of, what, 350,000 people?"

"Almost 370,000 now."

"Dragonfly Lake is maybe 1,200 people and had three murders. And New Selfoss had four murders last year and its population is 3,152. But that was a really bad year. We go many years without any murders at all, not even half-hearted attempts, as does Dragonfly Lake. But Winnipeg has something like 40 a year, every year. It's roughly double the population of Iceland, so its murder rate is anywhere from about 7 to 20 times Iceland's, depending on whether you guys had a one-, two-, or three-murder year!" Peter laughed to underline the absurdity of the difference.

Sigrun shook her head slowly. "And to think I may have seen the murderer with my own eyes!"

Peter almost choked on the sip of wine he had just taken. "Oh? Really?"

"Yes, the jet lag is terrible for me, so I was awake early, before the sunrise when it was still dark, and I could not get back to sleep, so I thought I would take my coffee onto the dock and wait for the sun."

Peter's stomach tightened. He knew what she was going to say next.

"When I got down there, I could see someone on the lake. They were paddling a canoe toward that, what do you call it, a piece of land that sticks into the water?"

"Peninsula or spit," Peter offered, staring straight ahead, anticipating what else she was going to say.

"Yes, peninsula, we have many at home, so I should know this word well! They were paddling toward it and then as I watched I could see them turn to go around it and disappear into the bay behind the trees. It was dark, but there was a little moonlight and I have good eyes at night."

"And you think this was the person who shot the airplane?"

"That is what the police think. I told the officers what I saw when they came to the lodge, and they were very interested. They said the shot came from the same area, on the land in the bay past that . . . peninsula, about three hours later. Unfortunately, I could not even say whether it was a man or a woman or how old. Only not a child." She gave a little laugh.

The night paddler. Was it a coincidence? Peter tended to be suspicious of coincidences, especially when so many details aligned. The probability was high that it was the same person. It wasn't a certainty, just a probability. Using a canoe made sense. A power-boat would be too loud and would attract attention, and there was no way to walk through the dense bush to where the shot was apparently taken from. Even the shot yesterday morning, while not from the same place, seemed to come from somewhere that would be easier to reach by water than land. A pattern of sorts was forming in his mind. Someone from the lodge, either an employee or guest, was connected to both shootings. The dog poisoning was also at the lodge, and around the same time, so there was another element in the pattern. There seemed to be no other connection between these events besides the lodge. What were the odds of two different people with evil intent carrying out two unrelated acts in the same time frame in the same place? Two criminals out of maybe 30 combined staff and guests? The odds struck him as low. Not zero, but low. But that was the only connection between the two crimes. The key area of the pattern, marked "motive" in Peter's mind, was completely blank. A large white space. Any motives he drew in there did not overlap between attempted dog murder and actual human murder. And motivation was always key. Nothing was ever truly random.

Peter suddenly realized he had been quiet for too long. "Sorry, just thinking about something. About how sad it all is." No harm in a white lie, although he wasn't sure why he didn't share his own experience seeing a pre-dawn canoeist. "Can I offer you a refill on your wine?"

"That would be wonderful, thank you. And maybe a treat I can give to Pippin?"

At the sound of his name, Pippin, who had been sleeping between them on the deck, opened one eye and began to wag his tail slowly.

CHAPTER
Ten

"They seem like nice people," Peter said, after the Icelanders left. He settled into his favourite armchair, glancing at the fireplace. They had a beautiful stone hearth. He wished it wasn't summer. He understood why people liked the season, but it precluded a blazing fire, which is exactly what he felt like now.

"Yes, very nice," Laura said. She sat down across from him. Pippin came over to curl up on the floor beside her. Merry jumped onto Peter's lap. "I wasn't really worried that they wouldn't be nice, but a full day with cranky or demanding tourists would have made me . . ."

"Cranky or demanding?" Peter finished Laura's sentence.

"Ha! Yes, I would be cranky or demanding at least." She chuckled. "What were you and Sigrun talking about out on the deck?"

Peter recounted the woman's story of the pre-dawn paddler.

"Very interesting. So, probably the murderer."

"Unless the police find someone who says they were canoeing at that hour for fun or exercise, but who, for some reason, could not be the marksman."

Laura absentmindedly scratched Pippin behind the ear with her foot. The only sounds were the faint tick of the old brass clock on the mantel and the rumble of Merry's purr.

"I did a little digging," she finally said. "I had a fair bit of down-time today while they poked around in the museum, so I thought I'd check a few things. You know, to satisfy my curiosity."

"Oh? Regarding what happened at Dragonfly?" Peter was mildly surprised. Laura usually avoided any involvement with, or even conversation about, criminal cases Peter became involved with. She worried about him being in harm's way, and with good reason, given past experience. But, on the other hand, she also had a deeply inquisitive nature. While the two of them were often cited as examples of opposites attracting, they were in fact similar in many ways.

"Yes. I know you won't be able to resist looking into who might have poisoned the dogs, and the murder of those three people on the airplane at the same time does seem like almost too much of a coincidence," Laura said, continuing to scratch Pippin.

"Agreed."

"So, I thought I could make things a little easier and safer for you by doing some legwork, some research. Besides, as I said, I'm kinda curious about all this too."

"And you don't think it's interfering with police work?" Peter asked, fighting to stop himself from smirking at the irony, given previous conversations where she accused him of that.

Laura stopped scratching Pippin and sat forward, looking Peter in the eye. "No. If I find anything useful, I will let Kevin know immediately, and he'll pass it on to his colleagues up there. This isn't actual investigation; it's just browsing through what's in the public record."

Peter held his hand up and laughed. "No, no, I agree completely. I'm just surprised is all."

Laura shrugged. "Well, don't get too excited. There isn't much that isn't common knowledge, but I did find something kind of interesting in the online memorial for Ned Fromm."

"The pilot?"

"Exactly. The funeral home set up a forum where you can post condolences for the family to read or memories about the deceased.

Most of it was predictable. It looks like he was popular and well connected as there are a lot of entries already, and the funeral hasn't even happened yet. But one stood out. Molly Smithfield."

"Molly Smithfield, the waitress from Dragonfly Lodge?"

"That's the one. I remember you mentioning a waitress named Molly who you said looked like me, so I thought, what the heck, and looked at the lodge website to find her last name."

"OK, what did she write?"

"I don't remember the exact words, but something generic like 'miss you so much' with xoxo after."

"Hmm. That's one to mention to Kev. Don't know how it connects. I guess all the staff fly in and out using Borealis, so maybe they know each other from that. The first time I saw her, she looked like she had been crying. So that's probably why." Peter paused and smiled at Laura. "Good idea, by the way, to look at the memorial pages. Anything else?"

"I gave up on O'Daly's after the first couple pages. Blah bah, titan of industry, blah blah, cutting-edge genius, blah blah, taken from us too soon, blah blah. But I'll tell Kev to suggest they should look through it, if they haven't already, in case there's a nugget in there I didn't have the patience to find."

Peter nodded. Merry stood up on his lap and stretched. He gently pushed her back into a lying-down position as he hated the stiletto heels effect of having a cat standing on his lap.

"And Edna Simpson? Nothing of interest there?" he asked.

"Her funeral home doesn't have a memorial page I could find, so I looked her up on Facebook. Fortunately, her main page is open, so I could scroll through it. Lots of people loved her too. Your friend Lawrence posted on there."

"Oh yeah? I got the impression they didn't get along. He said nice things about her to me, but she was kind of like a Young Turk in the band council, challenging him."

"Young Turk?"

"The Young Turks were a group who rebelled against the Turkish sultan Abdulhamid II in 1908. Serious reformers trying to overturn the status quo."

Laura shook her head and grinned. "Have we talked about getting you on *Jeopardy!*?"

Peter ignored this and asked, "But what did he write?"

"Just pretty standard condolences to the family. I don't remember the exact words. There was also a short phrase in what I assume was Cree."

Peter nodded, and then glanced at his watch. It was a quarter after ten. He generally liked to be in bed by ten, but his brain was buzzing with too many thoughts. He knew himself well enough that he would not be able to go to sleep until he had resolved some of these mental threads.

"You going to bed soon?" he asked.

"Nah. I've got to finish an order and I'm not really tired anyway."

"What order? The hobbit vests?"

"No, those are done now. It's that set of Ravenclaw scarves I've also been working on for a while."

"Right, for that guy in Korea, right?" Peter recalled the subtle eagle design she used to evade trademark issues, and the fact that, at the client's request, she selected the bronze and blue colours from the books, not the silver and blue from the movies.

"Yeah. I had to redo a couple, so I'm a bit behind. I think I can finish it tonight, though, and then be able to look forward to starting something new on the trip."

Merry hopped off Peter's lap and walked over to Laura, purring and stretching her front paws up her leg, getting ready to hop up.

"No, Merry." Laura laughed. "It's amazing how you know exactly when I'm about to start knitting and pick that moment to want to get on my lap. I love you and love having you on my lap, but not when I'm knitting . . ." She shook her leg slightly and gave the cat a nudge with her hand. Merry took the hint and sauntered off to lie by the fireplace. Pippin didn't stir during this entire interaction. "What about you? Going to bed, I assume?"

"I wish, but I've got to sort a few things out first. For starters, I'm going to call Heartland and check on Atlas. I hope Karla's on. There was a message earlier that he was stable, but I want to talk to them before we head north."

"Makes sense," Laura said, distracted as she rooted around in her knitting bag.

Peter was in luck. Karla was on duty that evening. He liked all the vets there, but he was most comfortable with her, and she was also the most familiar with Atlas.

Karla sounded tired, but happy to hear from Peter. He could hear phones ringing and dogs barking in the background. "Yeah, it's a busy night. It's always a busy night," she said in response to his polite query. "Atlas was doing as well as can be expected. We did an ultrasound this afternoon and there was evidence of extensive damage to the liver, but it's far too soon to say how much of that is permanent, and how much repair and regeneration is going to happen."

"OK."

"He looks comfortable enough. For a dog used to life in the North, he appears to have settled into his new environment with equanimity." She chuckled as she enunciated "equanimity" one careful syllable after another.

"That's great."

"Sorry, hang on a sec . . ."

He could hear someone interrupt Karla to ask her a question. While he waited, he listened to the click-clack of Laura's knitting needles. It was a sound that always soothed him. The clicking and the sounds of Merry purring and Pippin snoring were the sounds of home.

"Yeah, sorry 'bout that. Looks like we've got a torsion coming down."

"Yikes. Before you go, a quick question." Peter cleared his throat. This was the main reason he had called. "I've done a search for ways to detect pentachlorophenol, also known as PCP. Have you run into this before? You guys must have to do some testing for toxins at emerg?"

"Can't say I have. I mean, usually it doesn't matter because we're going to treat it the same way anyway. In our practice at least the most common liver toxin by far is xylitol. It's in all kinds of sugar-free stuff dogs get into. We diagnose it based on the history, hypoglycemia, and other blood parameters, so we don't do any specific testing. Any diabetics at the lodge? Ha ha."

"Makes sense. Unfortunately, I didn't get there quickly enough to run acute bloods. Although the results won't impact the treatment, we want to know because we think it was deliberate poisoning and if we can figure out the toxin, we'll be that much closer to figuring out who did it."

"We, like you and police?"

"Yeah, unfortunately there was a murder up there at the same time, three people killed in that plane that went down after someone shot at it . . ."

"Right. Heard that. Crazy."

"Consequently, the Mounties are really tied up with that, and no dogs have died, so it's a way lower priority."

"So, you want to do some of the legwork for them? Make it easier for them to crack the case when they have time?"

"Basically, yes."

"What's tomorrow? Friday? Let me see what I can do. I know somebody at the toxicology lab at St. B. I've got them to run stuff on the weekend for me before."

"That would be wonderful. Thank you, Karla."

"No promises, but I'll try."

Peter heard distant shouting on the other end followed by Karla saying, "I'll be right there!"

"OK, gotta go. Have fun up north."

That went better than Peter had feared. Karla was usually accommodating, but she was also often so busy that asking her to do something extra on the side made Peter feel awkward. The conversation settled his mind somewhat, but not completely. The new information from Cam and Sigrun pinged around his brain like it was a pinball machine.

Peter set his phone down and looked up at Laura. She was still absorbed in her knitting. Both pets were still sleeping.

He considered the options for a moment, and then got up and fetched his favourite pen and his bison-hide-covered notebook, what he called Bella's book after the patient whose owner gave it to him. He returned to his armchair and opened the book. This almost always helped quiet that pinball machine. Get it all out on paper. He turned to a new page and divided it into two columns with a wobbly vertical line. On the left he wrote "poisoning suspects" at the top, and on the right, "murder suspects." Then he began to fill each column with names, drawing lines to connect names that appeared in both columns, and then putting asterisks beside some.

CHAPTER
Eleven

As Peter feared, Friday morning was chaotic. Peter hated chaos. Despised it. Detested it. Loathed it. Really, really didn't like it. His mind was orderly and his world, or at least those parts he had complete control over, was orderly. Order made life so much easier. Chaos made life so much more difficult. But Laura and Kevin didn't seem to mind. They darted about the house, suddenly remembering this, and then suddenly remembering that, but did not seem especially stressed about it. Peter, on the other hand, had checked off everything on each of his lists — packing, house preparation, flight preparation — but was still stressed because of the frenetic energy given off by his wife and her brother, who had abandoned their lists and seemed to be relying on a blend of instinct, memory, and luck.

Stuart, however, was in Peter's camp. He sat across from Peter in the living room, with his long fingers tented on his lap, drumming the tips together, except when he turned his left wrist to glance at the time, which he did frequently. His luggage was beside him and consisted of a small black backpack for carry-on, a large red duffle bag, and two blue coolers with the food he planned to cook for them. Everything was neatly labelled.

"So, camping is supposed to be relaxing?" Stuart said, with a faint lilt of a Nigerian accent. He smiled at Peter. "Are you relaxed, Peter?"

"Nope. You?"

"I am not. And those two do not look relaxed either."

The red-haired Gudmundurson siblings almost collided as they rocketed past each other. Laura would have gotten the worst of that, as she was half the size of her beefy brother, who could have easily gotten work as an extra on a Viking film, whereas "elfin" was the descriptor most commonly used for Laura, at least by Lord of the Rings and Dungeons & Dragons fans. It wasn't even Kevin's house, but still he found reason to rush about, allegedly helping Laura with various aspects of the preparations.

"But the weird thing is, Stuart, they may look like hamsters on crystal meth, but they claim that this is how their brains function optimally and while they're not relaxed, they are at peace with this. It feels right to them. Making a list and going through it methodically is what makes them jittery. Like I said, weird."

"Very weird. You see a lot of this in Lagos, but here in Canada, especially among people of Icelandic origin, I expected more calmness and deliberation. More cold-bloodedness, I suppose."

Peter laughed. He enjoyed talking to Stuart. It always took him a while to warm up to new people, but Stuart was easy for him to like. "Yes, you would think. Canadians, as you know, are a pretty mixed bunch, although we are generally calmer than the Americans."

"And more polite. All the comedians say so at least." Stuart flashed a big smile.

"That's our reputation, true. But you're right about Icelanders, at least from my experience with them, just not about Gudmundursons and the others who came in the '60s and '70s. Many, like Laura and Kevin's parents, were sort of hippies. More passionate and less calm. More spontaneous and less deliberate."

"But we love them for it."

"That we do." Peter paused to reach down and pat Pippin. "I'm going to take Pippin for a walk now. He needs to get out before all the flying starts. Did you want to come?"

"No, thank you, Peter. I am going to sit here and enjoy the climate-controlled insect-free comforts of your home while I can. And if I stare out your window, I can see the clouds and imagine happy shapes and probably manage to ignore those two. This will help as well." Stuart grinned as he fished earbuds out of his pocket. "A little peppy Herb Alpert and the Tijuana Brass is always good for what ails you!"

"I love Herb Alpert! Enjoy. I'll be back in 20."

"Take your time. These guys will need a lot longer than that."

Among the things Peter loved, walking ranked near the top. Or possibly right at the top. It was a silly apples and oranges comparison to line walking up against reading or drinking tea. But after the pandemonium in the house, stepping outside felt like turning off a too-loud radio. Suddenly, peace. Pippin seemed to feel this too. He had been notably quiet, subdued even, during all the packing commotion, but now he was energized, his tail wagging, his tongue lolling as he panted, his steps brisk. He loved walks too.

"Did I tell you you're going to do a scent hunt up north?" Peter asked. He was long since past feeling self-conscious about talking to his dog. He knew very well that Pippin didn't understand all the words, but he would get the general positive tone.

Pippin glanced up at his master and then resumed sniffing along the grassy margin of the street leading up to the house. There were no sidewalks in this part of New Selfoss, but it was a cul-de-sac, so there wasn't much traffic.

"The police haven't told me why yet, but I'm willing to bet it's to find the missing gun. They found the murder weapon, but not the other rifle, the antique German one. That's probably what the night paddler used when he shot near Lawrence and me on Wednesday morning."

Pippin ignored him.

"Or maybe they're taking the poisoning of John's dogs seriously and want you to sniff out possible sources, even though we think we know where it came from. Mind you, I haven't gotten around to telling Kevin yet, so they may not know. Do you think you could smell Santophen? Probably, eh?"

At the sound of a question Pippin looked up at Peter, but immediately recognized that Peter was still really just talking to himself.

"That would be helpful, because then we could get you to check for traces around the kennels. If it's not the Santophen, then from that list I'd be thinking xylitol, mushrooms, castor beans, and cycad seeds, in that order, based on availability and ease of concealing in dog food. I'm sure those would be a cinch for you. And then maybe we could somehow have you check the staff and guest rooms for traces, but . . ."

Peter's phone vibrated. It was a text message from Raj, who was back in the clinic that day.

Pretty & Gus looking even better today. Bloodwork almost normal. Winter still borderline, but also steadily improving. Any word on Atlas?

How weird was that? He was just thinking about the huskies and then this message came in. This was a true coincidence, although not a strange one given that the poisonings were top of mind for both him and Raj.

Yeah, I talked to Karla at Heartland last night, and he's still hanging in there. Not better, not worse. Stable. I let John know already. I'll text him about the others now too. He'll be happy.

Have a great trip!

> Thanks. Don't hesitate to call if
> something comes up. I'll only be
> out of cell range for a couple days.

Peter looked at the time on his phone — they had only been gone 15 minutes, so he decided to take Stuart's advice and go on the longer loop with Pippin. They still had an hour before they should leave for the airport and being in the house any longer than necessary would just make Peter anxious. Ten minutes would be plenty to load his own bags in the car. That's all he was responsible for at this point.

After a precisely 50-minute walk, Peter and Pippin returned home to find Kevin standing beside the car, arms crossed, grinning. Stuart was in the passenger seat and shrugged at Peter. Laura was in the back seat, grinning like her brother.

"Oh, ye of little faith," Kevin said with a chuckle. "Probably thought you had plenty of time for a leisurely pre-departure walk? Probably thought we'd still be doing the headless chicken dance, eh? Didn't think we'd be done early, did you? Even loaded your bags." Kevin folded his arms across his broad chest and gave an emphatic nod.

Peter didn't want to show his surprise, so he smiled, nodded back, and said, "Good. Thank you."

"The line-up at the Tim's at the airport is always a killer, so we'll make good use of these extra ten" — Kevin paused to glance at his watch — "no, make that nine, minutes."

Kevin was an even faster and more aggressive driver than his sister, so they were at the airport in plenty of time, especially as Peter had insisted on planning to be there early to allow for any complications regarding getting Pippin checked in. He was much too large to fit under the seat, so he had to go in cargo in his kennel. They'd see him again in Thompson when they switched to the float plane, and there he would be visible at the back of the aircraft, but for this first flight he'd be on his own in the hold. Laura worried about this, but Peter didn't. He told her repeatedly that his colleagues in the city who practised near the airport had never had a dog brought to them who had suffered any sort of trauma on a flight. And while airlines losing pets made national news, it was exceedingly rare, and essentially impossible on this flight as Calm Air, which flew to Thompson, was a small airline that had no other flights out of Winnipeg that morning. Even so, Laura spent an extra couple of minutes with Pippin, kissing him and telling him what a good boy he was, before the baggage handler, who had been standing there, smiling patiently, took him away.

"*Calm* Air, eh?" Kevin said as the plane hit another patch of turbulence. He was sitting beside Peter, in the window seat, staring straight ahead as if the bulkhead were a fascinating work of art. He gripped the armrests tightly. "Not so friggin' calm right now."

Peter smiled at his brother-in-law. *And you're not so big and tough right now, are you?* he thought, knowing it was unfair and uncharitable. Most people had irrational fears of some sort, although at the moment he couldn't think what his own were. He actually kind of liked turbulence. It was interesting to think about the physics and picture the pockets of air of varying density. He also liked it because it stopped people from walking up and down the aisles, allowing him to stretch his long legs out properly. He glanced at Laura and Stuart across the aisle. They seemed unfazed and were chatting happily about Laura's new line of Dungeons & Dragons–themed toques, featuring different character classes. Stuart didn't know anything about the game, or the fantasy world in general, and seemed genuinely interested. Then he looked back at Kevin, who was still staring fixedly ahead, squeezing the armrests as if he were planning on crushing them like a Marvel superhero trying to contain his rage. He would try distraction to calm his brother-in-law. He had been meaning to talk to him about this anyway.

"So, Kev . . ."

"Uh-huh." Spoken through gritted teeth.

"I've been meaning to talk to you about a call I got yesterday at work."

"Uh-huh." Still gritted.

The plane suddenly dropped and shuddered violently. Someone screamed in the back, and then laughed immediately afterwards. The pilot came on to apologize. He laughed too.

Kevin's eyes were bulging.

"So anyway, this call was from Cam Schmidt. He's the bartender at the lodge."

Kevin gave a tiny nod.

Peter went on. "It seems he found a pesticide missing from the supply shed. This one is a powerful liver poison. Only he and John Reynolds, the owner of the lodge, had access to that shed, and possibly a part-time guide."

Kevin nodded again, but this time he quickly glanced at Peter before staring ahead again.

Peter then went on to explain who Marty Sullivan was and that he might also have had access if he kept or copied the shed key. He rambled on a bit as he digressed into how he knew for sure that it was liver poisoning and that it was not an accident, and how he had trouble believing the timing and location of the murders on the Borealis flights were coincidental to this. He concluded by saying that he was going to leave it up to Kevin to decide what, if any, of this information the Dragonfly Lake detachment might find useful.

The turbulence had stopped by this point and the fasten seatbelt sign went off. The colour began to return to Kevin's face and knuckles.

"So," Kevin began slowly, "if I'm hearing you right, you're saying this Reynolds character may have poisoned his own dogs for some dark reason, and then also shot down the plane, for some even darker reason. Either that or this deep woods Santa Claus guy is actually a twisted dog poisoner and a murderous marksman. Or the eye patch bartender is cleverly misdirecting, and it was him who did both these cockamamie things. Have I got it? I might not have heard every word. I was a bit preoccupied."

"In nutshell, yes, although I wouldn't put John at the top of the list. He'd have to be an Academy Award winner to fake the worry he showed about his dogs."

"Hmm, well, you've been fooled by people about that sort of thing before, haven't you?"

A flight attendant came by and offered them a beverage. They both declined. Kevin pointed at the overhead bins and quipped that his stomach was still up there somewhere.

"I suppose I have been fooled before," Peter said. "But this is different. That said, I do know I need to keep an open mind."

"You don't need to do anything, pal. You don't need to keep an open mind, or keep a closed mind, or do anything with your mind regarding this. Other than trying to save the huskies and the bit of sniffer dog handling you've been asked to do. Otherwise, all of this is, ahem" — Kevin cleared his throat in stagey way — "none of your business." He flashed Peter a brief toothy smile and then added, "But thanks, I'll pass the info along to Todd and the crew up there."

Peter considered challenging Kevin and reminding him how helpful he had been in the past, even after Kevin had warned him off on those occasions. He knew that Kevin knew that Peter's brain couldn't leave a puzzle or a mystery alone, and that deep inside, Kevin had to admit to himself that this wasn't always a bad thing. Their symbiotic relationship in these cases was an unspoken reality.

But he also knew it was Kevin's professional duty to try to prevent Peter from getting involved — his professional duty and his familial duty. Laura also worried about Peter's obsession with figuring stuff out that he really should leave to the police. But he couldn't help himself. He just couldn't.

CHAPTER
Twelve

Peter and Laura got the same cabin Peter had been in a few days before. Kevin and Stuart were in the next cabin to the south. Laura was just as amused as Peter had been by the painting of the moose gazing at the sunset, as well as by the overall cheesy, woodsy vibe.

She burst out laughing and began singing the lumberjack song from *Monty Python's Flying Circus*. "I'm a lumberjack and I'm OK . . ."

Peter joined in a mock baritone, hands on his hips, swinging side to side. They remembered all the lines from the first two verses, plus the chorus, and then both flopped on the bed, laughing. Peter usually had little capacity for unselfconscious silliness and was proud of himself when he managed to pull it off. Pippin looked at them with a mixture of concern and anticipation. They were obviously in a good mood, so perhaps something good was about to happen, but they were also behaving oddly, which made it impossible for him to predict what was going to happen next.

What happened next was they all went to dinner at the lodge, Pippin included, as it had a dog-friendly dining room. As Peter stepped inside, he bumped into one of the Belarusians, who was just on his way out.

"Sorry!" Peter exclaimed.

"No, my pardons!" he replied. "Ah, is you! Man who enjoy mushroom!" The man grasped Peter's shoulders like he was meeting a long-lost best friend. For the briefest moment Peter was afraid he was going to kiss him or crush him in a bear hug.

"I did, I mean I do. Like mushrooms, that is."

"We have more! You wait! I will bring!" The man nodded vigorously, his dark eyes crinkling in evident delight.

"Oh, thank you, but that's not necessary."

"No, no, friend! Is very necessary!"

Just then Laura, who had stopped in the lobby to ask the front desk for extra tea for the room, stepped in.

"Hi! Will you introduce me to your friend, Peter?"

"Your name is also Peter?!" the man practically bellowed. Laura smiled but took a small step backwards. Peter nodded and was about to reply, but the man went on, "I am Pyotr! I am very pleasured to correctly meeting both of you. And beautiful lady is?"

"Laura. My name is Laura. Pleased to meet you as well." She extended her hand. Pyotr released his grip from Peter's shoulders and bent down to kiss the back of her hand. Laura shot Peter a look, who gave a half-shrug in reply.

"It is delighting for me," Pyotr said, looking Laura directly in the eyes. Then he turned back to Peter, placing his hands on his shoulders again. "You are staying this night? I bringing mushrooms to this place for you in morning."

"Thank you, Pyotr, that's very kind but . . ."

The Belarusian laughed in the hearty way of someone who has been drinking the better part of the evening. "You Canadians so polite! But I am insisting!" Then he narrowed his eyes and gripped Peter's shoulders tighter. "You are not wanting me to feel insulting, are you? Is gift! In my country, one does not refuse gift!"

"Well, I suppose, yes then, thank you, it is generous of you, and I do love morels, as does Laura," Peter said, his eyes darting to the side to see if Kevin was there and was watching this.

Pyotr laughed again and suddenly engulfed Peter in a hug, knocking the breath out of him. Laura put her hand up to her mouth, trying to suppress a laugh. After several goodbyes and a hearty backslap that rattled Peter's teeth, the Belarusian left. Peter could now see that Kevin and Stuart were indeed already in the restaurant. Both were grinning from ear to ear.

"Had no idea you were so good at making friends, Pete!" Kevin said, winding up his arm as if to give Peter a big Pyotr-style slap on the shoulder and then just tapping him lightly. "Always pegged you as the sullen loner type, which is an official Mountie category for civilians, by the way. Since you're not, when am I going to get my big ole bear hug?"

"Leave him alone, you cruel misanthrope," Stuart said. "I believe that is also an official mounted police category, is it not?"

"Absolutely. Cruel misanthrope and shining hero, all in one lovable ginger package."

"Let us *not* discuss your lovable package at the dinner table," Stuart replied with a wink at Kevin. "Any mention thereof would surely put our poor companions off their dinner. In fact, it would put me off my dinner as well."

"Thank you, Stuart. My brother often needs reining in. I'm glad I have an ally in that department now," Laura said. "Although teasing Peter is fair game anytime. He needs it to balance the adoration of his clients and the media." She put her arm around Peter and gave him a squeeze. "I hope that wasn't the sore spot." She giggled.

"Hey! Now I'm feeling ganged up on."

"Not from me, Dr. Bannerman. I am firmly on your side," Stuart said. "But now let us set all this cruelty and hilarity aside and turn our collective attention to the menu. My treat tonight. I insist."

Peter and Laura swivelled to look at the blackboard menu behind them. They had to angle their heads to be able to see around a stuffed great horned owl with its wings spread and a vole in its beak. The vole looked annoyed. The owl looked bored.

Peter caught Cam's eye at the bar beside the blackboard, but Cam didn't appear to register recognition. Peter thought he probably didn't want anyone else to know they had any sort of connection. Just then Evan, the tall blond chef with the dramatic earrings, appeared beside Cam. Evan spotted Peter right away and waved at him.

"That's the chef," Peter said unnecessarily, as Evan was wearing a white apron and tall chef's toque.

Evan came over and introduced himself to Laura, Kevin, and Stuart. "It's great to have you all here! Knowing you were coming, Dr. Bannerman, I have a few vegetarian options in my specials. Are any of you vegetarian as well?"

"I am," Laura said.

"I am a shameless carnivore," Kevin said, and then gnashed his teeth and made low growling sounds.

"I am a carnivore as well, but frequently full of shame," Stuart said, frowning and lowering his head theatrically.

"Perfect," Evan said. "Can I suggest to the good doctor and his partner my housemade Lviv-style pierogies, stuffed with feta from Chaeban in Winnipeg, and spinach that I grow right up here?"

"That sounds marvellous," Laura said. Peter nodded his enthusiastic agreement.

"And for our esteemed meat eaters, my special tonight is venison prime rib in a red wine sauce with locally foraged juniper berries and young fingerling potatoes from our garden." He paused. "I hope this detail isn't too distressing to the vegetarians at the table, but I'm pleased to say I hunted the deer myself, so this special could hardly be more local. Of course, the full regular menu is available as well." He swept his arm toward the blackboard.

"Works for me," Kevin said.

"Me as well, thank you so much," Stuart said.

"My pleasure. Erin is going to be looking after you tonight, so she'll be right by to inquire about appetizers and drinks."

"Where's Molly?" Peter asked.

Evan paused a brief moment and Peter thought he saw the chef's jovial host expression falter. "She's not feeling well. But I'm sure she'll be on the mend soon."

"Your regular waitress?" Kevin asked after Evan left.

"Molly's the one Peter said looked a little like me," Laura said.

"Yes," Peter said.

"Although now it occurs to me to ask whether they have middle-aged servers," Laura said. "All the staff look like they're under 30!"

"This is where you say, 'So do you, my dear,'" Kevin said in a stagey whisper, leaning toward Peter.

Peter blushed. "Of course, you look under 30 too, but I meant in size and facial features, not age necessarily. Although again, you're . . ."

Laura cut him off by laughing and raising her hand, palm toward her husband. "Yeah, yeah, I get it. Let's move on."

"So, in the spirit of moving on," Kevin said. "A little shop talk if you two don't mind?" He inclined his head, first to Stuart and then to Laura. Both shrugged. Kevin turned his attention to Peter. "Regarding your hot tip, brother-in-law of mine, the local constabulary do thank you. I was on the phone with Todd just before you guys arrived. They are already doing their due diligence with respect to Reynolds and Schmidt because of the missing rifles, but were unaware of Sullivan, so that was useful. That's all I am at liberty to say." He said the last bit with a flourish, and then craned his neck and looked around. "Where's this Erin? I'm thirsty."

Peter chewed his lower lip. He really wanted to ask Kevin whether he had discussed the coincidence of the poisonings and the shooting happening around the same time and place with them. If they expanded their investigation of the lodge beyond the missing rifle and the mystery paddler to include the poisonings, they might find clues that would ultimately help their hunt for the murderer as well.

Erin appeared and began taking drink and appetizer orders. Peter would wait and try to find the right time to press Kevin further.

Later that evening in the cabin Peter checked his email and was surprised to see a message from Dwayne Lautermilch. Dwayne had come back into his life last year during the ostrich case when they connected over metal detectors. Back in high school he had bullied Peter mercilessly, but he had somehow managed to become a pleasant and gentle person over the intervening decades. Although they were on friendly terms and even on the same darts team now, they were both introverts and long periods of time went by without one contacting the other.

> *Dear Peter,*
>
> *I hope your summer is going well. Mine is. I have interesting news for you, or at least news I hope you will find interesting. I may have found a clue to the location of Paavo Jarvinen's gold. I don't want to explain over email as it is not a secure medium, but I hope we can meet soon and then I can show you what I found. Even if it turns out to be nothing, it might be fun to do some detectoring together again. This time without crazy Vikings. Ha ha.*
>
> *All the best.*
> *Your friend,*
> *Dwayne*

Paavo Jarvinen was an eccentric Finnish lumber baron from a century ago, and New Selfoss's first millionaire. Local legend insisted that he hid gold bullion somewhere in the bush north of town when he disappeared. Hundreds of people had tried and failed to find any trace of it. Peter didn't believe it ever existed, but he enjoyed playing with his metal detector and, against all odds, he enjoyed Dwayne's company as well. Also, as Dwayne had been in prison, his email sparked a thought.

Hi Dwayne,

That's really cool. Sure, let's get together when I'm back in town. I'm up north right now, getting ready to start a canoe trip with Laura, Kevin, and Kevin's partner. I'll be back in a week.

By the way, this might be a weird question, but do you know anything about a Cam Schmidt? He's working at the lodge up here and apparently he did time. Don't know whether it was at Stony, or if it was when you were there, but thought it couldn't hurt to ask. I'll explain why I'm curious about him when we meet. As you say, email isn't secure.

Regards,
Peter

Peter woke up in the middle of the night to go to the bathroom. Laura, as usual, slept the sleep of the dead, never stirring, never troubled by any impulse to wake. Before returning to bed Peter opened the curtains and looked out on the lake. The moon had not risen yet and the lake was barely visible as a smooth black expanse, like a highly polished slab of ebony. He watched for a long time, finding himself half expecting to see a canoe out there, but he didn't. Either it was too dark to see, or there was nothing to see.

CHAPTER
Thirteen

Staff Sergeant Todd Rehnquist and Sergeant Emily Patterson were waiting for Peter and Pippin outside the front door of the lodge at seven o'clock the next morning. They were chatting and both leaning on the hood of their Chevy Tahoe when Peter walked up.

"Is Kevin joining us? I forgot to ask last night," Peter said.

"Corporal Gudmundurson is on vacation, and as you are likely aware, he is not a morning person unless he absolutely has to be," Emily said with a big grin.

"Good point! So, are we starting from here?"

"Yes, we want to try to track the other rifle."

Peter nodded. "The Mauser, right? What have you got for a scent sample for Pippin?" He tried to keep doubt from creeping into his voice. Pippin was good, the best even, but he was not magical. What kind of specific scent would a rifle have?

Todd pulled a plastic baggie out of his pocket that appeared to have a piece of cloth in it. "I hope this is big enough. John Reynolds is fully cooperating. We asked him to get his hands sweaty and then wipe them on this cloth. He told us he had been handling the Mauser just the day before the theft. It was hot that day and he says he sweats easily, so the wooden stock would be permeated with his scent. It was his favourite rifle, and he was the only one who touched it."

"But then we're looking for John's scent, and it'll be everywhere here. It would be like asking Pippin to find a specific kernel of popcorn at a circus."

"Ha! Give us some credit, Dr. Bannerman. This isn't our first rodeo. We've also impregnated the cloth with the gun oil John uses on the Mauser. I presume Pippin can target blended scents?"

"Ah, OK, that makes more sense. Yes, he can track specific mixes of smells." Then, Peter turned to Pippin, who had been sitting quietly beside him, watching him carefully as if aware that he was about to be asked to do something. "OK, Pippin. Are you ready for a scent hunt?"

Pippin began to wag his tail. His mouth opened in a big panting smile. Of course, he was ready. He was always ready.

Peter never tired of watching Pippin's nostrils flare and his upper lips bellow as he deeply inhaled the smells he was supposed to memorize. Although he understood the process better than the great majority of people, he was still amazed by it. Pippin possessed a power that was alien to humans. Sure, humans had a sense of smell too, but it was like comparing a two-year-old's vocabulary to Shakespeare's.

Pippin stood as he sniffed. Once he was done, he sat down again and looked up at Peter, one ear erect and one flopped, waiting for the command.

"What a sweet dog," Emily said. "I don't suppose I should pet him when he's working though, should I?"

"Actually, it wouldn't matter. You're not supposed to touch service dogs and police dogs, but Pippin is neither, he's just a talented pet."

"A very talented pet." Emily reached down and gave Pippin a scratch behind the ears.

Pippin ignored Emily and kept staring at Peter.

Once Emily was done, Peter commanded, "OK, Pippin, seek!" Pippin immediately began swinging his nose from side to side. He trotted in slow, ever-expanding circles in front of the lodge.

"Are you assuming the gun thief left through the front door?" Peter asked. The front door was only notionally "front," as the lodge was oriented to the lake, but the reception desk was here. The door faced a small parking lot, landscaped with tamaracks and junipers, that connected to Dragonfly Lake's only road, running to the main docks, on to the First Nation, and then The Friendly Bear Lodge beyond that. Peter assumed this door was mostly used when guests checked in or out.

"No, not necessarily, but we have to start somewhere. There are two other doors, so if he doesn't pick up anything here, we'll move on," Todd replied.

"What about inside the lodge?"

"We've searched it thoroughly. A rifle is difficult to hide. So, we assume it is being kept somewhere else."

After ten minutes of watching Pippin carefully sniff, Peter declared the front door area to be clear of any scent. Pippin would have kept sniffing all day, going in larger and larger circles, if Peter hadn't called to him with a "Good boy, stop." Pippin immediately sat down, as if a button had been pressed, and looked at Peter with a neutral expression.

They followed Todd and Emily to the second door, which was the one the guests who stayed in the lodge building itself used if they wanted to go down to the lakeside. The same sniffing and slow circling procedure followed while the three humans stood by and watched. Occasionally Pippin would briefly move out of sight in a denser part of the woods that covered the slope between this guest entrance and the lake, but he always appeared again moments later, still on track, nose still down, tail still up.

"How much does it matter that the scent could be up to a week old?" Todd asked while chewing on a blade of grass he had just plucked.

"It matters, but not too much with such strong smells. Oil and human sweat are fairly potent. The relatively humid air of the boreal forest is good for holding scents too, and it hasn't rained since the theft, so that helps a lot. Rain badly messes up scent tracking as it can both dilute the scents and make them run together with other scents, confusing the smell picture."

"Like leaving out a watercolour painting in the rain."

"Exactly like that." Peter was impressed by the Mountie's insight. He often used the analogy of vision himself when explaining to clients how important smell was to dogs. A dog sniffing on a walk in the park was like a person gazing at a series of paintings in a gallery where many of the paintings were by friends.

"It hasn't rained in weeks, so we should be good that way," Todd concluded.

But again, ten minutes elapsed without Pippin showing any sign of having picked up the scent, so they moved on to the third door, which Peter hadn't seen yet. It was on the far side of the lodge, by the kitchen, and was used by staff to access a large cabin that served as a bunkhouse for them, as well as a couple picnic benches where they could take their breaks, and the vegetable garden Evan, the chef, had mentioned.

Once again, Pippin set off, but this time within seconds he gave a short, sharp bark and began to trot quickly away from the lodge, down a narrow path that looked more like a deer track. He disappeared into the forest, with the three humans right behind him. The track wound through the trees, at first seeming to head inland, but then veering toward the lake. They could see glimpses of the lodge to their right. At times the ground was spongy and damp, and on two occasions they had to clamber over granite outcrops where there no longer was a visible path. At these points Pippin slowed down and began to circle again. Peter knew scent was also harder to pick up on the rock. But both times Pippin soon found a spot on the far side where the trail continued, or at least the scent trail did, as there was no longer any kind of a footpath, whether for deer or humans.

Peter heard movement in the bush to the side. Pippin was right in front of him and stopped, suddenly tense and alert.

Peter also stopped and strained to listen.

He was just about to say something when the sound stopped. The two officers would have heard it too and would have reacted if they were concerned. Just an animal, he supposed. Still, he felt unsettled and a little nervous.

And then they were on the lakeshore. The big windows of the lodge's dining room glinted up ahead on a large granite outcrop commanding the best view of the bay. The cabins would be just out of sight, on the far side of the outcrop.

Pippin didn't stop. Not even for a second. On reaching the water he immediately turned right and continued down the shore, nose still down, tail still up. It was hard to follow him without risking getting wet feet as there wasn't a beach here, just a jumble of logs, rocks, and eroding forest bottom earth. As Peter picked his way along, he heard a splash, followed immediately by Todd uttering a curse under his breath. Emily was agile, though, and quickly passed Peter, a big grin on her face. "I love this this kind of stuff," she said.

Soon they reached a pebble beach with a small dock at the far end. Canoes were lined up, upside down on the beach. Pippin was sitting primly on the dock.

"Has he found something?" Todd asked when he caught up, boots squelching.

"I don't think so. It looks like this is just the end of the scent trail," Peter said.

"So, we can assume they sailed away?" Emily asked.

"Seems that way," Peter said, petting Pippin and offering him a small chunk of his number one absolute favourite treat, liverwurst.

"And never to return, or do we know? Maybe they used the exact same route through the woods on the way back?"

"He can't determine which direction a smell went, only which path it took, so in theory, yes, the Mauser could have been carried back and forth to the water many times."

"According to Reynolds, none of the canoes are missing," Todd added. "So, either they're using their own canoe and are away right now, or they are here and used a lodge canoe before."

"Or they used a lodge canoe before but are not here now because they left by some other means," Peter said, still petting Pippin.

"Good, Bannerman," Todd said. "Your brother-in-law was right about you. Maybe you should have become a cop." Peter couldn't read from his tone whether he was teasing him or was serious.

"Oh no, I don't like violence," was the first response that came to his mind. He immediately regretted it.

Emily guffawed. "Do you think we do?"

"No, sorry, I meant . . ." He didn't finish his sentence because he noticed something across the lake. A column of smoke was rising from beyond the shore, near Wilcox Point, but further inland. "Hey, look at that." Peter pointed at the smoke.

"Huh," Todd said. "That's near Shankie Lake. Em, do you want to radio MWS? See if they know about this."

"MWS?" Peter asked.

"Manitoba Wildfire Service. They've been hopping all summer, but mostly far east and south of here, along the Ontario border. But we've been waiting for the other shoe to drop here. It's been so friggin' dry."

Emily walked down the beach while talking on her radio. When she returned, she looked grim. "We're the first to call it in, but they're really stretched, and they won't be able to bring water bombers in right away. There's a massive burn threatening St. Theresa Point and Wasagamack. Full evacuations. They're going to talk to DLFN, see if their volunteer crew can access it."

"Shankie Lake, that's where we're supposed to be canoeing today," Peter said.

"Portage into Shankie and then the loop through Koch-Schulte, Rampitsch, and Bredin, and then down Walker Creek back into Dragonfly?" Emily asked.

"That was the plan, but I guess we can do the long portage into Parsons instead, across Tomusiak, and then that other long portage into Bredin to complete the loop from that side," Peter said, shielding his eyes against the sun as he stared out at the smoke. There was now another smaller column beside the first one.

"It's a brutal portage from Tomusiak into Bredin," Emily said. "But that makes sense — the fire looks to be on the far west side of Shankie and it shouldn't be able to jump the lake. Plus, the wind's out of the southeast and is going to push it the other way, unfortunately toward the community."

"But keep a sharp eye out," Todd added. "These buggers can change in a heartbeat. This is small still and hopefully DLFN will put it out, so we're not going to close the backcountry yet. Do you have a sat device or something in case we need to put out an alert?"

"Yeah, Kevin has one of those Garmin things that does satellite navigation and can send simple text messages or call in rescue if you push the special little red panic button."

"Well, don't do that unless your tent is actually on fire, or your head is in a bear's jaws because it'll call us, and we expect to be busy at that point."

"Or it might bring in the SAR Techs from 17 Wing," Emily said.

"The military search and rescue guys?" Peter asked. "Yeah, Kevin was hoping for that."

They all laughed.

CHAPTER
Fourteen

"I have to confess, I kind of love that smell," Kevin said as they paddled away from the Dragonfly Lodge dock.

"What smell? You mean the forest fire?" Peter asked. Their canoes were parallel, and Kevin and Peter were each in the stern, with Stuart in the front of Kevin's canoe, and Laura in the front of Peter's, although they planned to mix it up through the trip. Pippin sat in the middle of Peter and Laura's boat, tail up, mouth open, tongue dangling, eyes narrowed against the sun. The happiest dog alive.

"Yeah, it smells so . . . woodsy. I love campfires, so this gives us a bit of that campfire vibe all day long."

Peter thought his brother-in-law was probably joking, but he wasn't completely certain. Kevin was well known for his deadpan. Peter was less confident in his ability to pull it off, but he tried. "Sure, what's not to love about the destruction of habitat, threatening homes, pumping more carbon into the atmosphere, general disaster chaos . . ."

"Exactly. And as a bonus feature, we get to enjoy this badass portage! Woohoo!" Kevin let go of the top of his paddle to pump his fist in the air.

Stuart turned around and, ignoring Kevin, looked at Peter across the three-metre gap between their canoes. "Precisely how difficult is this so-called badass portage, Peter?"

"It's actually not terrible. It's about one and a half kilometres, but John said the main issue is that it doesn't get used much since most people prefer the hundred metres into Shankie. The bad one is the almost three K from Tomusiak to Bredin, supposed to be boggy."

"Let us focus on one challenge at a time. I am certain I can manage one and a half kilometres with my strong Viking partner. And then for the other one, we shall see," Stuart said with a smile, and then turned back to his paddling. Although this was his first time in a canoe, he was managing his forward stroke well, even putting in a little hook at the end to avoid striking the gunwale.

"I'm still banking on buff SAR Techs rescuing us before we have to tackle that other three-K portage," Kevin said, grinning. "But if we do have to, no worries, Pete will haul everything through the buggy bog for us. He loves that sort of thing. Aren't you always skiing in blizzards and hiking in rainstorms and messed-up shit like that, Pete?"

"Hey, I like challenging weather, not necessarily challenging terrain or challenging insects!"

"OK, guys, focus," Laura said. "Where's that portage? I don't see the triangle yet."

Portages were usually marked with white wooden triangles, but the less-used ones sometimes lost their triangles, or the white paint faded, or brush grew in front.

They had been paddling faster and faster in an unspoken competition between Peter and Kevin, but now they slowed down, all four of them scanning the shore.

"There it is," Stuart called. The triangle was barely visible behind a young tree that had grown in front of it. As they approached, they could see that the portage, while narrow and overgrown, had been recently used. There were scrape marks from a canoe on the beach and several branches were broken at the entrance to the path.

It took them the better part of a couple hours to haul the canoes over to Parsons Lake and then shuttle back for the rest of the gear. Kevin insisted on carrying his canoe by himself, reasoning that carrying it with Stuart would lead to arguments and he didn't want to spoil the holiday with that. He started belting out Stan Rogers's "Barrett's Privateers" as he portaged, claiming it was to keep the bears away. Peter suspected it was also because he loved the sound of his own baritone voice and wanted to impress everyone with his jaunty voyageur style, though he couldn't get through a line of the song without interrupting it with a loud curse as mosquitoes swarmed around his head. With his canoe hoisted over his head, he didn't have a free hand to slap them. And he had declined the repellent everyone else used as they got ready to portage. It apparently didn't fit with his voyageur self-image. After ten minutes of this Kevin dropped the canoe and bellowed, "Muskol! Now! Arrgh!" He waved his hands around his face in a high-speed blur. Kevin was much quieter for the rest of the portage.

As they began reloading their canoes on the shore of Parsons, Peter spotted a canoe in the distance.

"Look, a canoe," he said, pointing. "We didn't see it before — it was probably behind that island when we came down."

The other three stopped what they were doing and squinted out over the lake. Stuart rummaged in his pack and pulled out a pair of binoculars.

"Great! I'm glad you brought those. I thought about it, decided not to, and then promptly regretted it," Peter said.

"I'm hoping to see a golden-crowned kinglet on this trip," Stuart said as he adjusted the focus on the binoculars.

Peter didn't know Stuart was such an avid birdwatcher. He liked birds well enough himself, and always enjoyed seeing them, but he didn't make a point of seeking out specific species. He gave the tall Nigerian an appraising look. He was apparently full of surprises, which both intrigued Peter and, if he was honest with himself, unsettled him a little.

"OK, it is a green canoe. Not one that belongs to the lodge. It is a single man paddling," Stuart said.

"Hmm, funny coincidence. It's not a popular route."

"But with the fire near Shankie Lake, maybe other people had the same idea we did," Laura said.

"Fair point," Peter agreed. "Can you see anything else?" Peter was going to add "like a rifle," but didn't want to sound anxious.

"Not much, just that this man has a large white beard."

Kevin and Peter looked at each other.

"Really, a large white beard? Like Santa Claus?" Kevin asked.

"Yes, now that you put it that way, just like Santa Claus. But no red suit. He is wearing brown. And no red hat with a white pompom, just a camouflage-coloured cap. Do you know this man?"

"Maybe know *of* him. A guy named Marty Sullivan worked as a guide at the lodge last winter, and he has a Santa Claus beard. Lives out in the bush somewhere, although I don't know where. Could be out this way."

"The way his bio read, I assumed it was much further out, but I could be wrong," Peter said.

"Who knows?" Kevin said as he took the binoculars from Stuart. "Each lake is just a stepping stone. Put them in the right sequence and you can go as far out as you like. All the way to the Arctic if that's your jam."

"Do you think he's seen us?" Peter asked.

"Maybe, but I doubt it. He's close to the shore, so he's got to watch where he's going. No reason to look back," Kevin replied.

"Why are you guys so interested in this backwoods Santa?" Laura asked. "Is he a suspect?"

"Dog poisoner, just maybe," Kevin answered, handing the binoculars to Peter, who had his hand outstretched for them. "Triple murderer, probably not. Not my case, though."

"You don't think the dog poisoner is also the murderer? You really still think that's a coincidence?" Peter asked while he pulled the binoculars wider. He hadn't realized before how closely Kevin's eyes were set together.

"Like I said, not my case, so I'm just guessing. And I'm on vacation, so I'm going to stop guessing."

"Hey, he's pulling onto land. I don't remember a portage there."

Laura was in charge of the map. She took it out of its waterproof Ziploc and unfolded it. "No, no portage marked there."

"Maybe he's making camp early, which sounds good to me," Kevin said. "We should stop gawking and get a move on. I'm getting hungry for Stuart's gourmet dinner creation tonight."

Laura and Stuart returned to getting the canoes ready, but Peter continued to stare through the binoculars. "He stashed the canoe and walked into the woods with a big pack. Looks like there's a dog with him. Small one or a puppy."

"So, maybe his cabin is there somewhere. And he likes dogs after all. We all do. Who cares? If it makes you feel better, I'll tell Todd what we saw when we get back."

"It's weird, though. Wouldn't his cabin be on the water?"

Kevin sighed and pulled the binoculars away from Peter, who was scanning up and down the far shore. "Like I said, Pete, who cares? We're on vacation. The evidence that he tried to do in the huskies is flimsy, like toilet paper in a sauna . . ."

Laura chortled.

"Like that one? I just made it up on the spot. And it's extra special weird if he shot down the plane, because that Icelandic lady saw the canoe coming from the direction of the lodge, not the Parsons portage."

"I suppose," Peter said, frowning and still looking to where he saw the man disappear. There was an exposed ridge of granite above that spot. He wondered whether he might catch sight of him walking up there. Peter wondered what was on the other side of the ridge.

"Stop supposing and start paddling." Kevin laughed and gave Peter a slap on the back.

Peter watched for a moment longer, but the man didn't reappear. He handed the binoculars back to Stuart and trotted over to his canoe, where Laura was waiting.

CHAPTER
Fifteen

Peter loved small island campsites. He not only loved the practical advantages — far fewer bears, far fewer people — he loved the idea of being granted temporary overlordship of a miniature kingdom. He raced through the camp chores of helping put up the tent, filtering water, and organizing the campsite, so he could get to his primary objective as quickly as possible, which was to explore. The island they chose was the last in a chain of four ever-smaller ones, halfway up Parsons Lake, beginning with the larger island they had seen from the portage. On their way, they paddled close by where the bearded man had pulled in. They saw nothing to indicate he had ever been there. He had stashed his canoe well.

While the others lounged on a flat shelf of granite that served as a beach and enjoyed their drinks — rye whisky for Kevin, lemonade from powder for Stuart and Laura, and water for Pippin — Peter gave a cheery wave and headed off down the west shore of the island to see how far he could get. It was not very far. The granite shelf gradually sloped up to a rocky point. Once Peter was over that and back down to the waterline, he could see that the way forward was obstructed by fallen trees. He doubled back, passing the others, who were now deep in conversation about fishing, it seemed, and went the other way. This time Pippin bounded up and followed him. Peter assumed that there had been no snacks offered with the drinks, and that Peter's walk looked more interesting to the dog than the boring blah-blah.

On this side of the island there was a path of sorts through a dense spruce forest carpeted with thick moss. At times the path dipped down to the water's edge, and at other times it ran along a small cliff, where the forest suddenly ended in a ragged edge, like a cookie snapped in half. The water was only three metres below, but large algae-covered boulders broke the surface. A fall, while not fatal, would be unpleasant at a minimum, and quite possibly result in a broken ankle or wrist. Peter wasn't afraid of heights, but he wasn't fond of them either. Looking down from high up was no trouble when there was no risk of falling, but the absence of a rope, railing, or best of all, a big wall with a window unnerved him.

Just as Peter was contemplating this, his foot slipped on a loose piece of moss. He grabbed a small spruce to prevent himself from going over the edge. Pippin, sure-footed as always, cocked his head and looked at his master, who was now gripping the tree tightly. Peter debated about going on. The path was still recognizable, but barely, as if only small mammals typically went further. It seemed even deer gave up at this point. To his frustration he could now see how close he was to the north end of the island. It had become cloudy. The colours were muted and dull, but the now grey water at the north tip beckoned. Even if he couldn't circumnavigate the whole island, he could at least claim to have walked from the southernmost extremity, by the campsite, to the northernmost. The others wouldn't care in the slightest, but others not caring never bothered Peter.

The westering sun suddenly pierced through a gap in the clouds in full strength. Peter looked at the path again and squinted to try to make out its course. Then he caught sight of something glinting near the north point. Was it metal or glass? He wasn't sure. He tested the footing on the next part of the path, but he could feel it begin to give way. Peter muttered a quiet but forceful "Drat!" Pippin looked up at him again. This was doubly frustrating now! Not only would he be unable to walk the island end to end, but he wouldn't be able to reach whatever was catching the sun. But the exploration hadn't been a complete failure. At least he now had a good sense regarding the topography of the island, and he also had a story to tell the others about how he almost fell to his doom and how there was a mysterious object near the other end of the island.

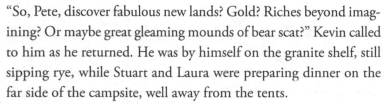

"So, Pete, discover fabulous new lands? Gold? Riches beyond imagining? Or maybe great gleaming mounds of bear scat?" Kevin called to him as he returned. He was by himself on the granite shelf, still sipping rye, while Stuart and Laura were preparing dinner on the far side of the campsite, well away from the tents.

"Absolutely! All of the above."

"Have a seat, have a snort, and do tell," Kevin said, pouring a glug of whisky into an enamel mug and handing it to Peter. Peter sniffed it suspiciously. He considered himself to be a discerning whisky aficionado, and experience had taught him not to trust his brother-in-law's taste, but as they were on vacation and everyone was in a good mood, Peter decided not to say anything beyond "thank you!"

After he described what happened and what he had seen, Kevin laughed and said, "Well, given that I outweigh you by at least 50 pounds, I had better not go on this rabbit trail! Mind you, when I need to be, I can be as nimble as a ballerina." He put his arms above his head to form a circle and turned from side to side, laughing again. "So, this shiny thing, what's your theory, Pete? You know I'm always dying to hear your theories."

"Although it's in a weird place, I'd have to say garbage. Maybe aluminum foil from some campfire meal, somehow blown in there."

"So not husky poison or a sniper's scope?" Kevin said, grinning.

"Brother-in-law, dear, my mind has many tracks, not just one. That would not be logical. In fact, either of those theories would be so illogical as to be farcical."

"Good. Glad we're on the same page there. More rye? It's that Costco stuff from the States. Pretty good, eh?"

Peter suppressed a grimace. He had been waiting for an opportunity to surreptitiously dump his whisky when Kevin wasn't looking. "Yeah, it's . . . interesting."

"Right? No need to drop a hundred bucks on snob water. This has got all kinds of flavours. All kinds. So, another splash then?"

Peter tasted malt and he tasted alcohol. So, two "flavours." That was it. But he sensed that Kevin was in one of those states where he might be willing to talk about police work with him, so he said, "Sure, why not? The devil rides tonight! Isn't that what you say?"

"That is *exactly* what I say!" Kevin slapped Peter on the back hard enough to make him cough, and then poured an alarming amount of rye into his mug.

Peter decided to test his luck. "Speaking of theories, totally off the record, of course, just us two brothers-in-law chewing the fat, what do you really think is going on at Dragonfly?" Peter held his breath. He knew Kevin always felt conflicted between his irritation at Peter meddling in his work and his natural volubility. Duty versus chattiness. Officer versus buddy.

Kevin was quiet for a moment, and Peter worried that he had misjudged the situation, but then he said, "Oh, I got my theories, all right. How couldn't I? I'm a cop, right? This mind" — Kevin tapped the side of his head with his free hand while the other one reached for the bottle of rye — "never stops. Constantly analyzing. Constantly theorizing. Constantly questioning. For example, who's Santa Claus, really? Why is he here? And that's just for starters." Kevin took a big swallow. "Just for starters," he repeated, nodding his head.

Peter knew not to interrupt him, even though he had several questions.

"I might have told you guys that 'I don't care 'cause I'm on vacation,'" Kevin continued, "but I was lying. I do care. Even on vacation I care. Just can't stop that cop mind. Can't. Stop. It. Don't want to either." He nodded in the exaggerated way of someone who is unaware of how drunk they look.

There was another pause for another big drink.

Peter waited again.

It was a quiet evening with only the occasional distant caw of a crow and the murmur of conversation from Stuart and Laura. Glancing northeast, Peter saw the smoke had increased substantially since he had last looked. What had been two separate plumes was now an ominous wall of solid grey above the treeline, with a faint tint of orange along its bottom edge. It still looked many kilometres away, and the steady southeast breeze should push it even further away, but Peter swore he detected a faint tang of smoke.

"So which theory do you want to hear first? Attempted canicide? Or actual homicide?"

"While the latter is admittedly more dramatic, the former, the 'canicide' as you put it, is obviously much more in my bailiwick."

"Bailiwick, canicide, listen to us two. What a pair of refined, eloquent gentlemen we are," Kevin said, affecting a comic British accent, as he regarded the contents of his mug with a look that indicated he was surprised by how little was left.

"So canicide it is. My money, dear brother-in-law, is on the Russkis . . ."

"Belarusians."

"Tom-ay-to, tom-ah-to."

"Not really, but proceed, I won't interrupt again. Scout's honour."

"Scouts aren't all that honourable, but yes, if you could refrain from interrupting with your know-it-all-ness, that would be grand. So, the *Belarusskis* make the most sense. They had ample opportunity and — now I know this probably doesn't pass your science brain test — but my cop instincts say not to trust them. And that's not because they're foreigners! You know I'm not like that." Kevin drained the rest of his mug in one gulp. "It's just my gut, and my gut is usually right on the money. But the big reason is means. Liver poisons aren't just lying around everywhere, so suspicion must immediately fall on those who do have access. Didn't you say that mushroom poisoning could cause the liver damage? And these guys are all about mushrooms, right?" Kevin inclined his head toward Peter. "Now you may speak."

"That *could* be the means," Peter said, trying to keep skepticism from creeping into his voice. "Fly agaric mushrooms are probably present here. In fact, I've been keeping an eye out for them. And I suppose they had the opportunity, but what about motive?"

"Ah, motive. Often dark and inscrutable on first glance! You amateurs are all about motive, but we pros worry about that last. Something always bubbles up when you dig a bit. But I'm not in a position to do the digging."

"So, just generally speaking, what are the basic motives for crime? Greed? Hate? Love? Revenge?"

"Yeah, those, and a bunch of others such as anger, insanity, jealousy — although I suppose that's what you mean by love. There's also crimes committed to hide a secret, and those meant to protect someone or something. I'm sure there's more, but this rye, although totally excellent, is making me forget some . . . stuff." There was a hint of slur in Kevin's booming voice.

"Any casual thoughts on which of those could possibly apply here?"

Kevin tried to take a drink from his empty mug. He set it down and scratched his bushy red beard. "Hard to see a money or sex angle, so it would have to be something in the hate, revenge, or anger line. Once this gets investigated, they'll look for how the Russkis, pardon me, Belarusskis" — he grinned at Peter — "know Reynolds and whatever communications there were between them. I mean, isn't it odd for those guys to come all that way just for mushrooms. Trust me, it's fishy. Pretty damned fishy." Kevin picked up the half-empty bottle of rye, and then, after a long pause, put it back down, sighing.

"OK, reasonable points, I guess. And the homicide?"

Kevin took a deep breath and turned to look Peter directly in the eye. "I'd be taking a hard look at old Reynolds himself."

"Dinner's ready!" Stuart called in a singsong, while banging a pot lid with a wooden spoon.

CHAPTER
Sixteen

The obe eja dindin, which Peter learned was Yoruba for "fried fish king" stew, was, as Kevin had predicted, excellent. The fish was first fried, hence the name, and then stewed with tomatoes, onions, garlic, ginger, red bell peppers, chilies, and basil. Stuart had asked in advance how spicy he should make it: "baby spicy, Canadian spicy, normal spicy, dragon spicy, or volcano spicy?" Kevin loudly pushed for "volcano spicy" but was outvoted. Stuart made it "normal spicy" but gave Kevin a small bowl of chilies to add. After a couple of spoonfuls, Kevin declared that it was very tasty this way and he didn't want to be a show-off by piling more chilies in. He drank a lot of water.

While they ate, Kevin rambled on about fishing. The fish in the stew was apparently smallmouth bass he had caught earlier in the day, and which he declared to be perfect for the purpose. He had also caught pickerel but wanted to save it to pan-fry with butter for breakfast. Pickerel was too delicate for any sauces and shone on its own. Kevin was partway into a dissertation on why they were called pickerel in parts of Canada and walleye everywhere else, when Peter interrupted him.

"Sorry, Kev, I just wanted to point this out — have you guys noticed that the breeze has suddenly died?"

"Now that you mention it, yes," Laura said.

"I hope the wind does not change direction when it resumes," Stuart said. "At home, when the southwesterly wet trades suddenly stop, there will be a pause, and then the northeasterly harmattan will begin. It is a strong, hot wind. Dusty. Sometimes terrible. But that is Africa."

They all scanned the skies, looking for clues, but other than the emergence of the first stars, the fading light from the departed sun in the northwest, and an unnerving faint orange glow in the northeast, there was nothing to see.

"So, as I was saying," Kevin resumed, with a touch of impatience.

Peter interrupted him again. "Actually, Kevin, let's maybe pick up where we left off tomorrow morning. With the wind stopped and the sun down, the mosquitoes are going to be on us right away. We'd better get into our tents."

"You make it sound like the zombie apocalypse is coming," Kevin said. He cupped his hand to first one ear and then the other, each time leaning in that direction. "Nope. Not hearing the shuffling of rotting feet or the spine-tingling call of 'brains, brains, brains.' Besides, aren't we going to have a campfire? Make s'mores? Sing politically incorrect campfire songs? Tell zombie stories?"

"Kevin," Laura said, adopting her stern older sister voice, "number one: a campfire when everything is crispy dry and there's a fire so close that we can see the smoke is stupid and" — she cleared her throat dramatically — "totally illegal."

"Oh yeah, I forgot." Kevin sounded genuinely sheepish.

"And number two: Peter is never wrong about the mosquitoes. It's eerie, like he can read their teensy tiny, eensy weensy two-hundred-neuron minds." Laura put her arm around Peter, who was sitting directly beside her, hugged him to herself, and gave him a peck on the cheek.

"Actually two hundred *thousand* neurons, or even a little more," Peter said.

"Of course you would know that," Kevin said.

"I think he is right," Stuart said. "I do not mean about the size of a mosquito's brain, although I have no doubt he is right about that too as evil does require some space, but about them coming. Listen again, everyone. Be very still."

Peter smiled. There it was — the unmistakable Evening Song of the North. At first almost imperceptible, it was now building rapidly. The sound came from all directions. It was an unvarying, extremely high-pitched whine. Almost electronic sounding. He estimated they had five minutes to get into their tents before becoming coated in blood-sucking insects.

"Oh shit," Kevin said and sprang to his feet.

They had had the foresight to completely clean up the cooking area and haul the food high up into a tree right after supper, so all there was to do now was to empty their bladders, brush their teeth, and dive into their tents. Kevin skipped brushing his teeth. Laura and Peter rushed through theirs, leaving Stuart as the last one outside.

Peter and Laura heard him say "Oh my" several times, accompanied by the sounds of skin being slapped repeatedly, and then the sound of the other tent's zipper opening quickly and Stuart tumbling in.

They spent the next ten minutes hunting mosquitoes that had snuck in with them, squishing them against the inside of the tent, sometimes leaving gory little splotches of red. Wherever a headlamp beam shone on the wall of the tent it silhouetted dozens of mosquitoes outside hurling themselves at the nylon, enraged and ravenous and highly frustrated.

"This is insane," Laura muttered. "Remind me again why we're canoeing in the middle of the summer?"

"It's the only time everyone could get off, and it's not always this bad. But you're right, spring and fall are much better."

"Ha! There! Got you, you little bastard." Laura hissed in triumph as she killed another mosquito. "I do believe that's the last one."

"Hope so. But back to 'why now,' you also have to remember it's only around dusk and sometimes dawn that it's really bad. During the day, so long as you stay out of the bush, it's usually OK. And middle of the night is fine too if you need to pee or something."

"Good, because I didn't bring a wide-mouth bottle."

"A wide-mouth bottle?" Peter asked, and then immediately regretted it as he suddenly understood her meaning. "Oh, gross."

"Ha! You think that's gross, Mr. I'll-just-take-a-leak-behind-the-truck?"

"That's different."

"Uh-huh . . ."

Peter was awoken during the night by a noise outside the tent. Laura was still asleep. At first, he thought it came from Kevin and Stuart's tent, but once he oriented himself, he realized the sound had come from the opposite direction. It sounded like a grunt. He strained to listen, but now there was only silence, punctuated by slow, quiet breaths from Laura.

Then it happened again. Definitely a grunt. Not loud, but distinctive.

Human? Animal? Marty Sullivan? A bear? Peter had no idea. He also had no idea what he should do. The smart thing was to stay in the tent and wait until whatever it was went away or gave more clues regarding its identity.

But Peter's bladder felt close to bursting. It probably wasn't that full, but it was also impossible to ignore. And he figured the odds that the grunter was actually dangerous were low. There was no reason whatsoever for Marty Sullivan to be on this island in the middle of the night with hostile intent. It made no sense.

And if it was a bear, Peter could easily scare it away. He remembered a large stick lying near the tent. Wave the stick. Make noise. Scare the bear away. Pee. Be a hero.

Classic win-win.

But the shape Peter saw when he crept quietly out of the tent was human. A bearded human.

Sullivan.

Then the shape shifted slightly.

It was Kevin.

Peter felt the tension leaving him like the air out of a party balloon. The tension was quickly replaced with anger. What was Kevin doing stalking around the tents in the middle of the night, grunting!

Kevin heard Peter approach and turned to wave at him.

"What the blazes are you doing up now? And why the grunting?"

Kevin chuckled. "If you really must know, all that whisky loosened my bowels. I was taking a dump." Kevin paused and adjusted where he was sitting on the granite. "I would avoid that patch of bush if I were you," he added quietly, waving to a spot off to their right.

"Oh, sorry. I guess I'm feeling a little jumpy. And you're . . . not done yet? That why you're still up?"

"No, I just wanted to look at this." Kevin pointed up at the sky where the Milky Way stretched like a shawl of diamonds from the southeast to the southwest. Peter nodded and gradually turned his head to take in the whole sky. The northeast corner was obscured by smoke, but the remainder had a crystalline clarity that made Peter feel like a wondering child.

"Let me show you something, Kev," he whispered.

"Yeah, sure."

"We're going to take the canoe out. You'll love it."

A few minutes later they were paddling noiselessly toward the middle of the lake. The air was absolutely still and neutral in temperature, neither warm nor cool. The water was obsidian, perfectly black, perfectly flat, perfectly reflective as if polished continuously.

"Stop paddling," Peter whispered.

Neither of them needed to say anything more. They were drifting through outer space. Stars above and stars below. All was silence and beauty and wonder.

CHAPTER
Seventeen

Pippin barked.

The bark entered Peter's dream. He had been dreaming about a cat the size of a brontosaurus roaming the streets of Winnipeg. Pippin suddenly appeared at Portage and Main to stop Dino-Kitty from chasing cars like they were mice. He crouched down in front of it, made hard eye contact with it, and barked.

Then Pippin barked again, louder.

Peter woke up to find himself tangled in his half-zipped sleeping bag, completely muddled as to where he was and what was going on. The tent's pale green nylon glowed in the soft pre-dawn light.

Pippin had been sleeping at their feet, but now he was standing, alternating barking at Peter and Laura and staring out the screen of the tent's door, nostrils flaring.

Laura woke up now too. "Wha . . . ?" she said, rubbing her eyes, hair-tousled.

"I don't know. Pippin smells something."

"I smell it too," Laura said. "It's smoke."

Peter was out of the tent in seconds, closely followed by Pippin and Laura. Stuart and Kevin had just emerged from their tent and were standing in their underwear, staring at the blood-red sun rising behind a curtain of smoke that was now considerably closer than it had been the night before. A steady hot wind was blowing out of the northeast.

"The fire jumped Shankie," Kevin said, his voice even and flat.

"And jumped Bredin," Laura said. She was beside Peter now. "It looks like it's just over that ridge now."

"The wind changed," Stuart said. "It is a good thing Pippin woke us all up."

"Shit," Kevin said.

"The portage is probably OK still," Peter said, pointing south in the direction they had come from the day before. "We'd better pack up and go pronto. If the wind changes even a little, we could become trapped here."

Kevin ducked into his tent and re-emerged a few seconds later holding his Garmin satellite transponder. "I'm going to send Todd a text to tell him we're OK and are headed out." After fiddling with the device for a moment he said, "Looks like they sent out an alert an hour ago. I had it turned off to save battery. Sorry, guys."

"Doesn't matter, Kev, we're good," Peter said. "But we need to move. Now."

Whereas it had taken a banter- and laughter-filled hour to set up camp, the four of them took it down in ten terse minutes, shuttling gear back and forth to the canoes at a jogging pace, casting glances to the northeast. Pippin sat patiently on the granite shelf, watching the smoke thicken and the occasional tongue of flame shoot into the sky beyond the crest that divided Parsons Lake from Bredin Lake. The wind was picking up. The smell of smoke had become pervasive.

Peter briefly thought about coffee but dismissed the idea. It would be his first morning in a long, long time without at least a little bit of caffeine, but he reasoned that he had enough adrenaline on board to compensate for the time being. And if Kevin was giving up breakfast — Kevin never gave up breakfast — Peter could give up caffeine for one morning.

Once they were on the water they fell into a powerful paddling rhythm, the canoes rocking side to side slightly with each of Kevin's and Peter's strokes, the two of them being the strongest paddlers.

"I wonder about Sullivan," Laura said as they came in sight of where the man had landed the day before. The ridge he had climbed was now choked with smoke. Fingers of flame shot up from behind it.

"Gosh, yeah, I hadn't thought of him," Peter said. "That whole area looks like it's burning now. I hope he has some sort of signalling device."

"Did he seem like the type?"

"No, not really." Peter turned to face Kevin and Stuart's canoe, which was beside them and slightly ahead. "Hey, Kev!" he shouted. "Maybe you should alert Todd that we spotted Sullivan here yesterday!"

"Good point!" Kevin shouted back as he leaned into a couple powerful strokes. "Either to arrange a rescue," he panted. "Or an arrest! Maybe the fire didn't jump two lakes! Maybe someone set it!"

Peter hadn't considered that. It made sense. He hated it when someone else thought of something clever before he did, especially when in retrospect it was obvious. He was about to shout back that he was thinking the same thing when he noticed something.

Smoke was also rising from near the portage.

They were at the portage in 15 minutes. The smoke was now so thick that the path leading back to Dragonfly disappeared into it behind the first set of trees. It reminded Peter of that dense fog last spring, only this time with a hot wind and the overwhelming smell of burning pine.

"I think the smoke's just blowing in from beyond the ridge. I don't think it's actually burning here," Kevin said as he jumped out of his canoe and helped Stuart drag it onto the shore.

"Are you sure?" Peter asked.

"I just said, 'I think,' not 'I know.'"

"No need to get testy."

"Stop it, you guys." Laura wrinkled her nose at the smoke and squinted into the forest. "Let's figure this out. With this wind, the smoke is going to arrive before the fire does, and there wasn't any smoke here half an hour ago, so Kevin's probably right."

"But perhaps a new fire began here from an ember blown by that wind," Stuart said, standing beside Laura, also squinting into the smoke-choked woods.

"That's what I was thinking," Peter said. "But we can't just stand here either. If the fire isn't on the portage trail yet, it soon will be. We could backtrack a little and find a place to camp on the southwest shore in the hope that the fire won't reach there, but under these conditions that's a faint hope. It would only buy us a few hours."

Kevin held up his Garmin and pointed at a red button on the side. "Should I press it?" His face was flushed, and he was breathing hard.

"I don't know, Kevin," Laura said. "Isn't the emergency button meant for life-and-death situations? I thought it automatically triggers a rescue mission. I mean, do we really need that yet?"

Kevin took a couple of deep breaths and nodded. "Yeah, you're right. Sorry. Don't know what came over me. I, of all people, should know not to abuse an emergency response system. Given how effing huge this fire is, there have got to be people in much dicier situations than us."

Stuart put his arm around Kevin's shoulder and winked at the others. "But you so wanted to be rescued by a cute SAR Tech with a brush cut, bulging biceps, and a come-hither twinkle in his eyes. I am so sorry you will not have that opportunity."

Kevin looked at his feet and let out a couple stagey sobs. Then he looked up and hardened his face. "OK, folks. Here's what we're going to do." Peter had seen this sudden transformation before: Kevin the impetuous Viking or the rollicking ham, to Corporal Gudmundurson, the confident, in-charge, and in-control Royal Canadian Mounted Police officer. "The canoes are the most important items to get across, and we need to be able to move as fast and light as possible, so take two minutes to repack your most vital gear into small daypacks. The tents, sleeping bags, stove, and most of the food will have to stay behind. If the trail isn't too bad and the situation stabilizes, we can run back to grab that stuff . . ."

"My brand new five-hundred-dollar MEC tent," Peter interrupted, sounding mournful.

"Doesn't do you much good if you're a pile of ash and bones," Kevin replied. "There's no way to know what the situation is over on Dragonfly, so we have to be ready to hit the water on the other side fast. Put the stuff we're leaving behind out on those rocks, as far away from the trees as possible." Kevin pointed to an outcropping protruding into the lake beside the portage. "When this is all done, we can come back for your brand new five-hundred-dollar MEC tent, and the rest of the stuff, if we can't zip back and retrieve it after taking the canoes across."

"And grab a T-shirt from your packs and soak it with water," Laura said. "We can put them over our faces if the smoke gets too thick or we encounter any flames."

Peter was astonished by the suggestion that they might walk through flames. "Surely, we turn around if there is actual fire?"

"I think it depends, right, Kevin? If it's a small fire and it looks clear beyond, we should try to push through," Laura said.

"Yes, I agree," Kevin said. "It'll be a judgment call. But let's not waste time debating what those judgment calls might be. Let's just be ready for anything."

Stuart was already dunking a shirt in the lake.

"Do you want to text Todd again?" Peter asked as he rooted through his pack for essentials.

"Good plan. We won't be able to get a satellite signal in the trees. But typing on this thing is stupidly hard, so I'll just tell him the basics. No time to peck out an explanation about Sullivan."

Minutes later they were ready to go. As on the island earlier that morning, Pippin sat at attention, staring to the northeast, where the fire was most active. He let out a woof just as they were getting ready to pick up the canoes. Pippin had at least a dozen different bark tones, probably more. Each meant something different. This was the "I see, hear, or smell something you should pay attention to" bark.

Peter glanced toward him and immediately saw what Pippin had barked at. "Fire's crowning!"

The other three swivelled to look. Not more than five hundred metres away, across on the eastern shore of the lake, balls of flame leapt from treetop to treetop, causing each successive tree to ignite like a roman candle.

"Oh my," Stuart said.

"Christ on a stick," Kevin breathed, and then, in full voice, called out, "OK! New plan! We're only taking one canoe, the seventeen-footer. It's got a twelve-hundred-pound capacity, so we'll be fine. Pete, you and me on the canoe. Stuart, you've got the paddles. Laura, you've got the emergency gear and Pippin."

"Pippin's got himself," Laura said. "But understood. I'll keep an eye on him."

Kevin laughed. Peter could see that, despite the gravity of the situation, he enjoyed the adrenaline surge of a crisis.

"OK, campers, let's go!" Kevin shouted.

Only a dozen steps up the path the lake disappeared behind them in a blue-grey fug of smoke. Visibility worsened the further they moved into the forest. The trees loomed up around them like in a fairy tale. Or nightmare. Only the ones immediately around them were clearly visible. Anything further away was only shadows and silhouettes.

Kevin, who was in the lead, carrying the front of the canoe, stopped. "I can't see the path. I can't friggin' see anything. We could end up blundering right into the fire."

Peter strained to listen for crackles, but it was eerily silent all around them, like a cosmic pause before a massive exhalation.

"Let me and Pippin go ahead," Laura said. "He might be able to find the way."

"Won't the smoke screw up his nose?" Kevin asked.

Peter answered, "It'll have an impact, but it's really just another layer of scent." He paused to cough. "When he concentrates, he can mentally edit this out and follow the underlying scents, which are still there. Like you following a dotted line across a busy painted canvas. We'll tell him to 'seek home,' and he'll find the path we took yesterday. For him it's the first link in the long chain leading back to our house in New Selfoss."

"That is amazing," Stuart said from behind them. And then he began to cough as well.

Laura and Pippin moved to the front of their little parade. "OK, Pippin, seek home!" she said.

CHAPTER
Eighteen

The portage was one and a half kilometres long. It had taken about 40 minutes to cross before, but Peter hoped they would be faster this time since their loads were lighter and they hadn't been in a particular hurry yesterday. Now it felt like every minute mattered. Deep in the smoke-bound forest they had no idea how the fire was behaving, but it was best to assume that it was moving quickly toward them. Fortunately, Pippin was moving ahead with confidence. Nose down and tail up. Faster than he sometimes was on scent hunts. Peter was grateful Kevin had taken charge. One canoe and essential gear only made sense, although he still felt a pang of sadness about his tent, and even more so about his sleeping bag, which had been with him on so many special trips. Despite his highly rational nature, he could sometimes become sentimental about some of his favourite possessions. He was embarrassed to admit this, so he hadn't said anything about the sleeping bag.

Peter was shocked out of his musings by a bang.

It sounded like a small explosion, followed by a rapid series of sparking and crackling noises. Like fireworks. It was ahead and above and slightly to the left. He looked up, but the canoe blocked his view.

"That tree!" Laura shouted. "Look out, the crown just exploded! Oh no! There's more! Stop, guys!"

"LetsputthecanoedownPete," Kevin said, breathless, the words rushing out of his mouth and mashing together.

Once his field of vision was clear with the canoe out of the way, Peter was dismayed.

Not ten metres ahead of where Laura and Pippin had stopped, several trees were engulfed in flames. This must have happened in seconds. There had been no indication of fire in the immediate area and now suddenly there was this hellish conflagration. A wave of heat hit them, causing all four of them to step back. Pippin stayed put, sniffing the ground intensively in an arc around him.

"It's blocking the trail," Laura said, panting, and wiping soot from her face.

"You OK?" Peter asked.

"Yeah, yeah. Just shaken up."

"We cannot go this way," Stuart said. "Is it the only path?"

"There's nothing else on the map," Laura said.

"Back to Parsons? Maybe wait it out on the water?" Peter suggested.

"Not a terrible idea," Kevin said, rubbing his beard, looking a little forlorn now that he had lost his momentum. "But not a great idea either. If we use the canoe as a heat shield, plus those wet shirts, we could probably sprint through that."

"*Probably?*" Peter asked, incredulous at the suggestion.

Just then a flaming tree crashed down ahead of them, and several more caught fire. The heat was becoming intolerable. All of them were coughing in the thickening smoke. All of them except Pippin, as the air was clearer closer to the ground.

"OK, maybe not," Kevin said.

Then Pippin let out a short sharp bark and began trotting off to the right, perpendicular to the path.

"What's he doing?" Kevin asked as he swivelled to watch the dog.

"I guess he's found an alternative route," Peter said.

"Really? There?" Kevin stared where Pippin was disappearing into a dense thicket of smoke-shrouded trees. There wasn't even a deer track, but there was no undergrowth either, so at least it was passable.

"I trust him," Peter said and positioned himself to pick up his end of the canoe.

"Me too," Laura said.

"We have no time. We have no choice," Stuart said and then doubled over with a short but intense coughing fit. When he recovered, he looked at Kevin and said, "Pick up the canoe."

Without a word, Kevin did as he was told, and they set off to follow Pippin.

They moved as quickly as they could but maneuvering the canoe under branches was difficult. And the ground was uneven. Peter and Kevin stumbled frequently, Kevin cursing under his breath, Peter hoping fervently that Pippin knew what he was doing. The dog would disappear into the smoke up ahead, and then stop and wait for Laura, who was in front, to catch up. Peter was able to faintly make Pippin out when this happened. From his silhouette he pictured him with a big doggie smile, his ears erect, and his eyes wide and shining. Whether the dog had a sense of fear in this situation was unclear to Peter. If he did, then adventure and duty were likely overriding it. After ensuring that he had been seen, Pippin would trot off again into the grey, nose down, tail up.

"Aargh!" Kevin shouted as the bow of the canoe snagged on an especially unyielding branch. "Back up, Pete! We're totally snared here! This is friggin' nuts. We'll have to carry it low by the gunwales."

With much grunting and swearing, and some ineffectual efforts by Stuart and Laura to help, they disentangled the canoe and lowered it to the ground. In the brief moment of silence that ensued, Peter could hear the fire crackling and roaring behind them and to the left. He turned to look, but there were no flames visible, only the dense grey pall. He looked up and could see the tops of the trees swaying in the wind, which, if anything, seemed to have become even stronger. It would push the fire right on top of them soon. It was difficult to get any sense of orientation, but he noted that they had been steadily climbing. The ground had changed from forest bottom soil to more and more granite. The trees were thinning.

"He's taking us to the high point," Peter said.

"That stone rise we saw south of the portage from the Dragonfly side?" Kevin asked.

"Yes, I think so. We should be a bit safer up there, and then we can scramble down to the shore."

Kevin just grunted in response. Carrying a canoe by the gunwales at knee level was much harder work than carrying it over your head, and it kept banging against their legs.

Peter had been right. Within a few minutes he and Kevin joined Stuart, Laura, and Pippin at a small rocky summit marked by an inukshuk.

They set the canoe down. Peter leaned forward, put his hand on his knees, and panted to catch his breath. "There's . . . a . . . reason . . . portages . . . always . . . follow . . . the . . . lowest . . . route . . . possible."

"As does fire," Laura said. "Look." She swept her arm all around her.

They were just above the tops of the tallest trees and had a 360-degree view of the area. The air up there was still smoky but at least they could make out the pale blue of the sky above the smoke when they looked straight up. They were on island in an ocean of dense smoke. None of the lakes around them were visible, only a few treetops here and there. Flames were the only other thing in sight as they shot through the smoke to the northeast, no more than five hundred metres away, entirely covering the area where

Peter guessed the portage was. The wind was steady and hot, like a hairdryer turned to max.

"Which way to Dragonfly?" Kevin asked, looking from side to side, with his hand flat above his brow like a visor in the manner of a ship's captain scanning the horizon, as if that might somehow cause the smoke to become transparent.

"That way," Peter pointed to where Pippin was staring. It was a steep drop-off into a ravine choked with juniper and dogwood. He pulled out his compass, happy that he had remembered to bring an old-school navigational tool with him, as he didn't trust the smartphone compass in these conditions. "Yeah, it makes sense."

"And how do you propose we get the canoe down there?" Kevin asked.

"It can't be that far," Peter said, peering down into the haze. "We'll lower it by the painter."

"Painter?" Kevin's look could be interpreted as either annoyance or confusion.

"Fancy word for rope tied to the bow," Laura answered. "Don't waste time, dear," she said, not unkindly, to Peter and tapped him lightly on the shoulder. "And we should tie the extra rope to the painter. We don't know how far down the bottom is."

"And us? Down by 'painter' too?" Kevin asked.

"We can proceed this way," Stuart called from a short distance to their right where he was testing his footing on a series of washing-machine-sized boulders that lay jumbled past the edge of the little summit they were on. "Then we can make our way back to the canoe and continue down the hill."

The four of them looked dubiously at the dense smoke-choked bush below them, and then Kevin shrugged and said, "I don't think we have a choice. That seems to be a theme today. Painter away then."

Peter scrambled down the boulders Stuart had found. With his gangly arms and legs, and his somewhat distracted approach to any physical endeavour, he was normally awkward and prone to clumsiness, but somehow adrenaline or fear had turned him into a kind of Spider-Man flawlessly executing the moves needed to get down without twisting an ankle. He was surprised at himself but didn't have time to think much about it. Pippin was right behind him. Stuart was already at the bottom while Laura stayed at the top with Kevin. They slowly pushed the canoe over the lip of rock, stern first. It made horrendous squealing, scraping, and banging noises as it descended, like something one might hear from the far side of a junkyard fence.

Peter heard Kevin mutter, "There goes the damage deposit." This was immediately followed by a strange sound, like a muffled roar, and then a much louder "Oh shit!"

The rope went slack. The canoe tumbled the remaining few metres, barely missing the two men and dog at the bottom of the cliff. It crashed into a large, jagged rock with a sickening crunching sound before it stopped moving.

Peter just had time to shout an annoyed "Hey!" before he noticed Laura and Kevin swarming down the boulders, rapidly pulling off their own Spider-Man moves, although Kevin missed the last step and landed with a loud "oof." He limped toward Peter.

"The fire! It suddenly came up the other side!" Kevin's beard was flecked with what looked like small chunks of charcoal. His eyes were wild.

"From over where we climbed up?" Peter asked.

Laura said, "Yes. There was a huge gust of wind all of a sudden. You wouldn't have noticed down here. It blew embers at us like a hurricane of fire." She looked like she was on the verge of tears, but at the same time, her face had a hard seriousness Peter rarely saw.

"Firestorm," Stuart said, eyes wide, looking all around.

"Exactly."

"The canoe's toast," Peter said.

Kevin shook his head as if trying to loosen something. "Doesn't matter," he said. "We just need to get to the water now. We'll figure things out from there."

Pippin was already exploring the dense dogwood that covered the slope. He quickly settled on what looked like a faint animal track. They followed, trying to watch their footing at the same time as trying to move as quickly as possible. Peter went first, trying to hold branches aside so they wouldn't snap back and strike Laura, who was right behind him. He could hear Kevin grunting and swearing. Kevin was at the back and in danger of falling even further behind. The air had quickly become much hotter. The wind was whipping the treetops around wildly above them.

Hurricane indeed, Peter thought. *Hurricane of fire.* He had recently read something about large wildfires creating their own weather. The tremendous heat could generate winds, even tornadoes, and entire weather systems, including ones with massive special clouds called pyrocumulonimbus that could spawn lightning and thus even more fire. This thought was both exciting and horrifying — one part of his brain saying, *Cool!* and the other, *Oh no!* It wasn't the first time Science Nerd Peter and Survivor Peter had found themselves in conflict. Survivor Peter was winning today, though. He didn't bother to stop to listen for thunder.

The track widened and the going became a little easier. Peter could hear Kevin begin to catch up. He reasoned that the trail was probably made by moose — he remembered Lawrence called dogwood "moose candy." The dogwood was much too dense to see where they were going, but it was downhill and that was all that mattered right now. As they descended the smoke became thicker again and all of them were coughing.

"Put something over your face, like a bandana, or pull your shirt up," Laura said. She was right, Peter's lungs felt heavy, and his chest tightened with every breath. His tongue felt like he had been licking an ashtray.

And then, suddenly, they were on flat ground and out of the dense shrubbery. The lake couldn't be far away now. They were amongst tall jack pines and birch trees. The smoke was thick. The air was still. Peter reasoned that they were in the wind shadow of the hill. It was silent other than the hard breathing and coughing of the group.

Pippin stopped and began to circle slowly, nose down, nostrils flaring. Then he suddenly looked up and stood stock-still, as if staring at something unseen.

"What's he doing?" Kevin said, panting.

Before Peter could answer there was a sudden blast of scorching wind from the left, bending the trees like blades of grass.

That instant, a wall of bright orange pulsing flame appeared, as if conjured out of the smoke by a malevolent being bent on mass destruction. A pitiless god of the apocalypse. It was the height of a six-storey building and wider than they could see.

It was rushing toward them with breathtaking speed.

Later they would argue about who had shouted "Run!" and who had been fastest, but it was hard to tell as they had fanned out. And about what route they took, other than just away. And about how long they ran, was it seconds or minutes, though it felt like hours. And about who first noticed that Peter wasn't with them anymore. And about who turned back to find him.

But the fire was too intense. There was no way to find him.

All of them later noticed that they had singed eyebrows, so perhaps they all had gone back.

Pippin wasn't with them anymore either.

All was flames and smoke and embers and wind and noise and confusion and desperation.

CHAPTER
Nineteen

Peter had tripped and fallen. And then the fire was all around him, surging past on both sides. He was face down in something wet and squishy. He had blundered into a patch of shallow bog, and then hit his head on a branch. That's why he had stumbled so badly. Being tall was a curse sometimes.

He remained face down and felt his hair. It was not on fire. He felt his backpack and pants. Also not on fire.

The bog was a tiny oasis in a scorching desert of fire. It was so hot, so unbearably hot. Peter had the bizarre thought that this is what a pizza must feel like as it lays in one of those wood-fired ovens.

Where are the others? Where's Pippin? Oh my god! Am I the only survivor?

In spite of himself, he listened for screaming, but all he could hear was the end-of-the-world sound of the fire roaring all around him.

Should he stay and hope that he would remain safe, and the fire would burn itself out around him? Or was that more dangerous? Maybe it would consume all the oxygen here and he would suffocate? Or it would become so hot that it would evaporate the bog and then burn him alive like a medieval martyr?

He didn't know.

His logical faculties were failing him. Generating a clear thought felt like lifting a two-hundred-pound weight with his pinky finger.

And then, although he was not conscious of making a decision, he pulled the wet T-shirt out of his backpack, draped it over his head, and began to crawl out of the mire on all fours.

Low was best.

Wet was best.

For good measure he rolled around in the muck to coat himself all over in mud.

But which way? He was entirely disoriented. It was completely flat here, and the sky was an invisible abstraction. There were no clues where the lake might be.

He began to crawl in the direction where the fire looked slightly less extreme, where there were possible gaps between the flames. Possible gaps.

Then he heard something that did not sound like burning or crackling or blowing.

He stopped crawling and listened as intently as he could.

There it was again. A bark. Faint, but clear and unmistakable.

Pippin!

Peter felt a surge of elation and had to stop himself from standing up and running toward the bark. Running toward . . . where? Where had it come from? Not straight ahead, it seemed.

Peter strained to listen again.

There was a third bark, and then a fourth and fifth. All faint, but unmistakably from the opposite direction Peter had been crawling toward.

He turned around and shouted, "Pippin! Pippin! I'm coming!"

More barks.

Peter pulled the wet T-shirt lower in front of his face and began to crawl as fast as the soft, wet soil would allow him. He tried to establish a rhythm of lifting the shirt every three steps, or shuffles, so he could see where he was going, inasmuch as anything was visible.

It looked like solid flame ahead. It looked impossible.

The bog water became steadily warmer and soon it felt like tea that had just barely cooled to drinking temperature.

I'm going to boil my arms and legs, he thought, but just then he crawled onto dry ground that felt like a cookie sheet fresh from the oven. He had fortunately worn his long-sleeve T-shirt that day. It was wet with bog water. Peter pulled the sleeves down to cover his hands in an attempt protect them from the heat of the ground.

Shuffle, shuffle, look.

Shuffle, shuffle, look.

Pippin was barking constantly now, so it was not difficult to keeping moving in the right direction. Quite aside from desperately wanting to see his dog, wherever Pippin was barking from did not seem to be on fire because the barks were resolute rather than distressed. Peter knew the difference.

Shuffle, shuffle, look.

He was right up to the edge of the fire now. Flames darted and jabbed toward him. The heat was incredible. He wondered whether his nylon backpack would melt onto him.

He had to stop. Crawling into fire was madness.

Then there was a crash and a loud bang. He was showered with glowing embers from behind. Peter leapt to his feet and whipped around, brushing the embers off. An enormous old birch tree had burst into flame and fallen into the bog right where he had been lying.

The fire-free circle around him was only a handful of metres now. He could feel the mud drying on him second by second from the heat.

It was a vision of hell. Peter felt he had stepped into a medieval painting depicting the torments the wicked would encounter in the afterlife. Only the devils with pitchforks were missing.

The fire had become so loud that he couldn't hear Pippin anymore.

Maybe something had happened to him.

He shoved that thought aside forcefully.

There was no way to know how wide the fire was on any side. There was only one thing to do. Peter took several successively deeper breaths and then with the last one filled his lungs as full as they would go, held his breath, threw the still-damp, but now very warm, T-shirt over his head, and sprinted, head down, arms crossed in front of him, directly into the flames. The T-shirt fell off. He felt a sharp sting in his eyes. But still he ran. Faster than he had ever run in his life.

Peter had never liked the word "miracle." In its literal sense, there was no such thing in his opinion. Everything had a cause, or series of causes, that could be illuminated by science and calculated by mathematics. Sometimes the science wasn't good enough yet, or the mathematics too complex, or the key data hidden or inaccessible, but everything had a concrete natural cause, not a wispy supernatural one. But in the figurative sense, it was OK to use the word as shorthand to describe something highly improbable that nonetheless occurred anyway. Something highly improbable *and* desirable, to be clear.

So, when his survival was subsequently described as a miracle, Peter didn't argue. Somehow, he had managed to select the only section of the ring of fire that was only a few metres thick. Somehow, with his head covered and down, he did not run into a tree or trip on a fallen log. Somehow, the flames he ran through only injured his eyes, and singed his hair and clothing.

But his eyes. They burned, especially when he opened them to more than a squint. And his vision was like looking through soap film.

The backpack was ruined and the zipper had melted so that it could no longer could be opened, but that was a trivial problem. Peter quietly thanked merino sheep as he checked himself over. He was a devotee of merino wool for outdoor clothing, even in the summer. In addition to marvellous temperature control and comfort, a bonus feature was that it had natural fire-resistant properties, although he had never imagined he would end up putting that particular property to the test.

When he burst through the flames, he felt beach sand under his feet.

He had made it to the lake.

Where was Pippin?

Where were Laura, Kevin, and Stuart?

His eyes were still heavily blurred. He dropped to his knees and exhaled in a long, ragged breath. He blinked several times and tried to look up. A low, dark shape was moving quickly toward him, yipping.

Pippin!

When Pippin reached Peter, he began to lick his face vigorously.

Then Peter became aware of another presence. He gave Pippin a hug, and, shaking slightly, stood up. He took a few deep breaths, wiped his eyes, and tried to look around him.

Down the beach a short way and a few metres offshore there was a shape in the water. Maybe a log?

Then the log moved and waved at him.

It was a person in a canoe. A waving vertical shape attached to a horizontal shape.

Was it Laura or Kevin or Stuart? But where were the other two? And where did the canoe come from? Why weren't they greeting him loudly?

Peter blinked several more times and squinted hard. His eyes wouldn't stop tearing, and his corneas felt like they had been scraped with sandpaper.

The person in the canoe had a large white smudge roughly where the lower half of their face would be. It was a beard. A large white beard.

CHAPTER
Twenty

"**T**hat's a good dog," the man said.

"Um . . . Yes, he is . . ." Peter wiped his eyes again and tried to steady himself. He was still shaking. The fire continued to rage in the forest behind him. Pulsing gusts of blast-furnace heat swept through him and on out over the lake. The man in the canoe sounded oddly calm and unfazed by the unfolding apocalypse. Peter waded further into the water until it was knee deep, which was as far he could go where Pippin could still stand. Fortunately, it was shallow, so this was a good distance from the fire. Still hot and terrifying, but it no longer felt immediately life threatening.

"Good idea," the man said. Then he pointed at Pippin and added, "Is he for sale?"

That was such an unexpected question, and the whole situation was so surreal, that it took a long moment for Peter to respond. "What? No. He's my dog. A family pet. Not for sale."

The man shrugged and repeated, "That's a good dog."

"Are you Marty Sullivan?" Peter asked, finally able to generate a clear thought.

The man cocked his head and narrowed his eyes. "Do I know you? You don't look familiar."

Peter forced a laugh so he would sound friendly and unthreatening. "No, you don't know me! But I'm a guest at Dragonfly Lodge and John told me about you. I just put two and two together. My name's Peter Bannerman."

The man burst into a hearty belly laugh. He even sounded like Santa Claus. This had to be Sullivan. "Bannerman? The vet? In that case, yes, I am Martin Sullivan, at your service! I love animals, dogs especially, so I love vets."

"Oh, great," Peter said, not knowing how else to respond. "Have you seen my wife and friends? We got separated in the fire. And I injured my eyes. I'm having trouble seeing very clearly."

"You all came down from the hill? You came the hard way, through the swamp. I expect the others took the easy way and ended up around the point." The man indicated a short rocky spit that marked the south end of the beach. "If they didn't get burned up, that is. Fire's too loud to hear anyone screaming." He said this in a jovial way, so Peter assumed it was a joke, but he was taken aback by how tasteless it was. Sullivan went on, "But that means it's also too loud to hear them calling for you. I'll paddle round and have a look."

"Yes, please. Thank you. I'll stay here."

"You do that!" Sullivan gave another hearty ho-ho-ho laugh and then paddled off with startling grace for someone with an almost spherical abdomen.

Peter looked around him. Even with his damaged eyes, he could tell that the sky and the other side of the lake were obscured by smoke. Grey water fading into grey air. The smoke was much denser on shore, where he had just come from. Peter could see fire everywhere on land. Flames often shot past the treetops. Sometimes fiery embers would fly into the lake, forcing Peter to dodge or flinch. They hit the water with a hiss and quickly turned from red to black.

This is what the end of the world looks like, he thought. *Exactly like this.*

Pippin looked untroubled. He lapped some lake water and then sniffed a little in each direction, turning slowly, before evidently deciding there was nothing worth smelling.

They stood quietly in the lake, Peter feeling his heart rate gradually returning to normal. He splashed cool water into his eyes, and that helped a little, but they still stung, and the world around him was distressingly blurry. He had been chased by human killers twice, once through a blizzard and once through a dense fog, but being chased by a firestorm was even more terrifying. He considered that maybe his current perspective was biased because time had mellowed his memories of those previous near-death experiences. But then he concluded that, no, this was worse because with humans there was always a hope, however faint, that they could be reasoned with or would have sudden clear recollection of a mother's admonition not to hurt other people. A fire, on the other hand, was a literally heartless force of nature, solely governed by physics and chemistry and meteorology. At least he couldn't get angry at the fire.

After about ten minutes, Pippin turned to stare at the spit of land Sullivan had disappeared around. He let out a soft woof and continued to stare, tail down, ears erect.

Sullivan, or a smudge Peter assumed was Sullivan, reappeared moments later and gave Peter a big wave. He shouted something, but the fire was still too nearby and loud to make it out. Peter cupped his hand to his ear and shrugged.

Sullivan shouted again when he was halfway to Peter. This time he could hear him. "They're there! A big guy with a red beard, a tall Black man, and a short red-haired woman!"

"Yes! That's them! That's Kevin, Stuart, and Laura, my wife!"

Pippin seemed to understand that important information was being exchanged and glanced back and forth quickly between the two men. Sullivan was now near enough that they could stop shouting.

"Your wife was crying. Happy crying, I think," he said. Then ho ho ho again.

Peter reached out for Pippin, both because he wanted to pat him and to steady himself because he felt his knees wobble a bit.

Disaster averted.

He couldn't believe it. The luck. The crazy, unearned, unimaginable, stupid luck. What were the odds of all of them surviving what they had just been through? He didn't have the mental energy to calculate them at the moment, but they had to be low. But sometimes you do roll double sixes.

"How do they look? Are they OK?"

"I'm sure they've all had better hair days, but nobody looks too scorched. Maybe just lightly toasted. You look like you got the worst of it, Doc." That laugh again. "I told them I'd bring you and the dog around and then we'd figure out how to get all of you characters over to the lodge."

Peter nodded and began to wade toward the canoe.

"No, Dr. Bannerman," Sullivan said, laughing. "We'll load you two on the beach. Kinda tippy out here. We can stand the heat for a minute." He scanned up and down the shore. "There." He pointed to an area where the fire looked quieter and wasn't shooting flames right over the beach.

Once Sullivan's canoe was in position on the beach, Pippin leapt in and immediately began making excited whining noises. When Peter got into the canoe, he saw why — there was a fuzzy shape curled up among the old canvas duffle bags. He squinted hard. It was a puppy, just waking up. It yawned and stretched and yipped happily when it saw Pippin, who was gently sniffing it.

"Who's this?" Peter asked.

"Her name is Dancer," Sullivan said, beaming at Peter. "Isn't she a beaut?"

"She is! I guess she's a . . . what? I can't really see."

"Mongrel. One hundred percent pure mongrel from the Canadian bush. I only get mongrels."

It had been a long time since Peter had heard the word "mongrel" used unironically. Mixed-breed, cross-bred, mutt, even Heinz 57, but not mongrel. It somehow sounded negative coming out of most people's mouths, but out of Sullivan's it came across as a term of endearment.

"Well, whatever she is, she's lovely."

"Hope she ends up as smart as yours. What's his name?"

"Pippin."

"Peregrin Took's nickname from Lord of the Rings?"

"Yes, actually." Peter tried not to sound surprised that Sullivan recognized the reference. Most people did not.

Sullivan grunted in what sounded like a satisfied way and then fell silent.

"Do you have others? Dogs, I mean?" Peter asked.

"Oh yeah."

Peter waited for Sullivan to expand on that, but he didn't. He just paddled and hummed quietly. Peter tried to help with the paddling but felt feeble in comparison to the larger man's powerful stokes.

They soon rounded the point of land. Peter could make out three silhouettes in the shallows. Laura, Kevin, and Stuart! One short, one round, one tall. The silhouettes began waving enthusiastically when the canoe came into sight. Peter could hear them shouting. Pippin let out several happy barks in response.

The reunion was tearful and ebullient. There was so much backslapping and hugging and kissing that Peter began to feel embarrassed in front of Sullivan, who remained in his canoe, chuckling. They agreed, however, to share all their stories in more detail later as an immediate departure plan was the priority. The fire was becoming more intense and even in the lake, at some distance from the flames, the heat was uncomfortable. Also, in this area they were no longer in the wind shadow, so the water was choppy, and they were showered from time to time with embers and ash.

"Your eyes, Peter, they're scary red and you're squinting," Laura said, leaning in close.

"I might have gotten ash in or even seared the corneas when I ran through the flames."

"You ran through . . . ? Never mind." Laura shook her head quickly. "Stories later. There's eye ointment in the little first aid kit."

"Yes, please. Good idea. Antibiotic and steroid. It'll help a little."

"I can take two of you to the lodge, plus the dog," Sullivan said while Laura applied ointment to each of Peter's eyes. "The two tallest should stay behind." He pointed to Peter and Stuart. "They can wade further out."

"Not the best swimmers?" Laura asked. "Because that would be me, and Kev I suppose. And Peter's hurt his eyes."

"Unless you've been to the Olympics, it wouldn't make a difference," Sullivan said and laughed one of his belly laughs.

"I will be fine here, thank you," Stuart said.

"And I don't need to see anything just standing here, especially as I have a seeing-eye human with me."

"When I drop them off, I'll wait to make sure the lodge can send a powerboat back for you guys. If not, I can paddle back, but I'd rather not."

"It must be exhausting. We're so grateful for everything you're doing for us," Laura said.

"It's not that. I just want to push on past the lodge, southwest, to the Black Eagle River system. I need to get my cabin ready if the fire makes it that far."

"We thought your cabin was somewhere near Bredin," Peter said. Black Eagle River sounded familiar, but he couldn't recall why.

Sullivan didn't seem to hear the question, because he raised his paddle in the air and shouted, "OK, folks, let's go before the world ends. There are better places to watch that happen."

Sullivan brought the canoe in to shore, as he had done before, and Kevin clambered awkwardly into the bow seat while Laura and Pippin found spots amongst the duffle bags with Dancer. A round of goodbyes and kisses and see-you-soons and be-safes followed before Sullivan indicated that they really did need to go.

Peter and Stuart watched the canoe glide into the smoke, rapidly becoming fainter and fainter until it suddenly wasn't there. Once it was gone it felt like it had never existed. They were alone, two men standing hip-deep in Dragonfly Lake as a firestorm obliterated the land.

CHAPTER
Twenty-One

W hen the dark smudges that represented Peter and Stuart disappeared and the world shrank to only the canoe and the perimeter of deep grey around it, Laura felt icy worry rise in her again. Icy despite the scorching wind pushing them across the water. This time the worry felt different. Before, when Peter had not made it to the beach with the three of them, and she had no idea where he was, the worry was clad in terror. Her mind had been a jumble of worst-case scenarios. All she could do was scream for him and struggle as Kevin stopped her from running back into the burning forest again. Now the worry was melancholic, shot through with desperate sadness. Peter was smart and resourceful, and he was a survivor, but he was not immortal. This fire was like nothing she had ever seen before. She could make no comparisons. She had no way to guess what would happen next. Sullivan had said they could wade out at least another dozen metres before the water would become too deep, but she wondered how far flames could shoot from the shore or whether the smoke could become so thick that it would choke them. She decided not to ask. Instead, she petted Pippin and Dancer and tried to turn her mind to more productive thoughts as the canoe raced along. With Sullivan and Kevin paddling and the wind behind them, they were moving so fast that it felt like flying, especially since above and below and to all sides was an undistinguishable grey. They may as well have been in a cloud. A cloud that reeked of campfire. Laura didn't think she'd ever be able to have a happy association with that smell again.

Once she was able to suppress thoughts about what might be happening to Peter back at the invisible shore behind them, the next inescapable thought was about Sullivan. Was he not a prime suspect in the dog poisoning and possibly even the murders? In rearranging the duffle bags to make some room for her, the muzzle of a rifle had been revealed. This did not seem to faze Sullivan at all, and he made no moves to conceal it again. She didn't know anything about guns, so she had no idea whether this was likely to be the missing German one, or whether you could even tell from the muzzle alone. She considered that most backwoods types probably carried rifles with them, but still, it was unnerving. Kevin had seen it too. They exchanged glances and he gave the slightest nod in Laura's direction. She felt better knowing her police officer brother was in the canoe with her, but still, the whole scenario felt ridiculously sketchy. Between this, and leaving Peter behind, and the surreal flight of the canoe through the endless grey, the whole thing was like an out-of-body experience.

But Laura prided herself on her practicality. *Bring this back to earth*, she thought. *The least I can do is try to get some information.*

"Mr. Sullivan," she said finally, after at least 20 minutes of silence had elapsed.

"Marty."

"Marty, Peter mentioned to me that you had other dogs. You must be worried about them. Who's looking after them?"

"Did I tell him that? Oh, I suppose I must have," he laughed. "I can't get used to the idea that they're gone."

"Gone? I'm so sorry. How did they die?"

"Two died a while ago. Old age, I guess. But Comet was young. Happened just a couple weeks ago. Just dead one morning. I think he was poisoned." Laura suppressed a gasp. She wondered whether Kevin heard.

"That's awful. How? By who? Do you know?"

"I don't, but I have my suspicions." The joviality had gone from his voice, replaced by something halfway between sadness and bitterness.

"Have you talked to the police?"

Sullivan snorted. "They don't even care about John's dogs and he's a big wheel, so I can hardly expect them to listen to me."

"That might not be fair," Laura said, as gently as she could. "They're very busy, but they do care. I don't know whether you're aware, but my brother is an RCMP officer." She reasoned that it didn't hurt for Sullivan to know that. She was surprised, though, by his expression of sympathy for John's dogs. This didn't match the mental picture she had been assembling.

"No offense, Officer!" Marty shouted to Kevin at the bow.

"None taken!" Kevin shouted back. "I'm in civvy mode anyway. On vacation!"

Laura smiled to herself. Peter had told her about Kevin's drunken speech of never turning off his cop brain. She knew that about him anyway. Even when they were teenagers, he was always good at making everyone believe he was a harmless joker and even a bit dim, all the while carefully taking mental notes and surprising her later with his observations of other people or situations she assumed he had been oblivious to.

"Some vacation!" Marty said. "Was Mephistopheles your travel agent?" Ho ho ho.

"Ha! My brother-in-law organized it, so close enough!" Kevin shouted.

"Hey! That's not very nice," Laura interjected, but joined in the laughter of the other two. He wondered whether Kevin was trying to get Sullivan to lower his guard.

"The good doctor doesn't seem very satanic. And anyone who loves dogs is all right in my books," Sullivan said.

"Cute pup you've got there," Kevin said. "Were you taking her to Parsons Lake to train her or something?"

"Sorta. I was showing her parts of my trapline. Only trap in the winter, of course, but I felt like getting out for an overnight paddle and couldn't leave her behind anyway."

"Overnight paddle into a firestorm," Kevin said. Laura marvelled at his ability to pitch his tone perfectly so the statement sounded innocently bemused rather than incredulous, as it would have sounded if she had said the same thing. Or downright suspicious if Peter had done so.

"Yeah, go figure, eh? It looked small and far off to the northeast when we started."

They lapsed into silence. Nothing around them had changed. It was still a world that consisted only of smoke and water. The canoe had continued to move with supernatural speed, so Laura was surprised they hadn't reached the lodge yet. She wasn't nearly as good as Peter with dead reckoning and mentally calculating time and distance, but in recalling the paddle out the day before, and the relatively greater speed, it seemed odd. She pulled her phone out of her pocket and checked to see if the GPS, or anything else useful, was working, but it wasn't. She looked around for the position of the sun, but there wasn't even a slightly brighter patch in the grey. The entire sky was uniformly pearlescent with an eerie and diffuse faint glow.

The two paddlers powered the canoe ever forward, Sullivan in the stern making occasional slight course corrections, based on what, Laura had no idea. She wondered what Kevin was thinking, and she wondered how Peter was doing. She petted Pippin, bent down to his ear, and murmured, "Do you know where we are?"

He wagged his tail and licked her cheek.

CHAPTER
Twenty-Two

Peter considered that his wife and dog had just been paddled off by an armed potential murderer. But Kevin was with them, and whatever differences they might have, Peter had confidence in his brother-in-law's ability to handle himself. An overweight part-time trapper, part-time guide Santa Claus lookalike would be no match for a highly trained and seasoned officer of the Royal Canadian Mounted Police. And Sullivan wasn't at the top of Peter's suspect list anyway; there were too many improbabilities at play. So he allowed the anxiety to wash through him and dissipate. This felt good.

He was also pleased with himself that he no longer felt afraid of the fire. It would be pointless. Fear's evolutionary purpose was to promote caution when caution was warranted. It was to prevent people from endangering themselves. That was all perfectly sensible, but he *knew* it would be foolish to walk into the burning forest; he didn't have to also *feel* that. He supposed all emotions had reasonable historical underpinnings that had served humans well in the distant past before the prefrontal cortex fully evolved, but at this point they just got in the way and clouded thought to frequent detriment. For example, standing out here, now shoulder-deep in the lake with searing blasts of hot air reaching him, would prompt fear in most people, but he knew the probability of actually being burned in this situation was low, so why bother feeling afraid? And even if you did feel afraid, what useful action could that prompt? Swimming? That would be counterproductive as it would actually have a significantly higher probability of resulting in death.

They had both been quiet since the canoe left. Peter thought this would be a good opportunity to connect with Stuart one on one, but he couldn't think of anything to say. And he then got caught up in his musings about the futility of emotion. Also, Stuart seemed preoccupied with thoughts of his own, so he didn't want to intrude.

"I remember when I was a boy," Stuart suddenly said, startling Peter, "my grandparents lived near the lagoon, east of Lagos. We spent many of our school holidays there. My grandfather would take my sisters and me fishing in the lagoon. We had to wade out and then stand there very still with our long bamboo fishing poles. The water was warmer than this and the bottom was muddier, but this reminds me of that." Stuart paused and smiled at Peter. "It reminds me especially because the farmers nearby would burn debris, sugarcane stalks I think it was. It smelled different, but sometimes it was very smoky too, like this." Then he asked Peter, "And do you know what else here reminds me of that time?"

Peter pictured the brilliant equatorial sun, and tall palms, and smiling children, and silvery bright tropical fish flopping in wicker baskets. He couldn't imagine what might be similar to here. "No, what else?"

"The fire is making it so hot here now! It is always this hot in Nigeria! There it is like living next to a fire every day!" Stuart laughed loudly, almost losing his footing as he did so. Peter laughed too, reaching over to steady him. "That is why I like it so much in Gimli," Stuart went on. "It is rarely so hot. But sometimes I do still like a little bit of the heat, just for a short time, for the reminder of my childhood. Those were good times."

"That does sound nice, fishing with your grandfather. I don't have anything from my childhood to compare to this situation or to your memory. We went on a lot of camping trips, but we never went fishing and, now that I think of it, rarely spent time at a beach or in the water. My parents liked the mountains, and we all liked to read. That's mostly what I remember. All of us — my mom and dad and brother and me — huddled around a lantern in a big canvas tent, each lost in their own book."

"That sounds nice, Peter. I dreamed of camping in Canada when I was a boy, which is a strange dream for a Nigerian boy. Most dreamed of becoming soccer stars in Europe. But I read that book Laura was talking about, *Forest Heart Kingdom.* Our English teacher was actually Icelandic."

"That's so bizarre!"

"In my experience, Peter, it is generally a bizarre world. But that is what I like about it so much."

Peter had just opened his mouth to agree when a sudden gust of wind showered them with sparks and embers. This had happened before, but this time the fusillade was so intense that Peter sucked in a deep breath and dove under the water. He heard Stuart do the same. Peter opened his eyes under water and, to his astonishment, saw baseball-sized chunks of burning wood hitting the surface. His vision was blurred, both from the water and the injury, making it an especially dreamlike sight — something from another state of consciousness, from another world and life entirely. The thwacking noise of the wood hitting water seemed to be coming from all around him and accentuated this feeling. He was only able to hold his breath 30 seconds, although it felt like ten minutes, so he was quickly back at the surface, gasping, ash-flecked water streaming off his face. Embers were still in the air, but the worst of it seemed to have passed. Stuart emerged a few seconds later.

They looked at each other, wide-eyed, and shook their heads.

"How long do you think it will be before the boat comes?" asked Stuart.

"There are a few variables, but yesterday we took about an hour to cross the lake to the portage, which is a similar distance. But they have a strong wind behind them, and two strong paddlers motivated to go fast, so I expect they'll be at the lodge in half that time. If they don't get lost in all that smoke. Then allow for ten or fifteen minutes to find John, talk to him, and for a motorboat to be made ready, assuming one is available, and ten minutes for it to cross and find us. So, an hour or slightly less."

Stuart nodded and looked at his watch, a fancy-looking analogue one, evidently waterproof and shockproof. "It has been an hour now since they left."

Peter was astonished. He didn't wear a watch on this trip, but he always had such a good sense of time. It felt like much less time had passed. The lack of visual cues and the absence of any activity, other then the quick dive just now, had distorted his perception.

"We'll hear it before we see it," Peter said before realizing how unnecessary the words were. He applied some more ointment to his eyes. They still burned, but perhaps a little less. And the world was still a gauzy, filmy smear, but that seemed to suit the circumstances.

The two of them stood out there for another hour, occasionally trading stories from their past, but mostly quietly peering into the smoke and straining to listen for anything other than the crackle and rumble and whoosh of the forest fire behind them. Once they heard an engine sound, but it quickly became clear that it was in the air and far to the north, likely a water bomber, Peter thought. And twice more they had to dive under to avoid being pelted with grenades of red-hot charcoal. This also had the advantage of washing off some of the campfire smell that had saturated Peter's hair and skin. His nostrils stung. He doubted he would be able to smell anything other than charred pine and birch for a long time to come.

"I hear something," Stuart said after an especially long period of silence.

Peter listened carefully. He heard it too. "Yes, you're right! It's coming from the south, though, not from the direction of the lodge."

The sound grew louder. Soon a dark shape was visible through the smoke. It was definitely a boat.

Peter and Stuart began to wave their arms above their heads frantically and shout, "Over here!" even though the boat was following the shore and would practically run into them unless it made a sudden deviation out onto the lake.

As it approached, Peter could make out two smudgy figures, one of whom eventually resolved itself to be Evan, the chef at the lodge, unmistakable, even to Peter's degraded vision, with his elongated earlobes and spiky hair. The other appeared to be one of the Indigenous fishing guides, whom Peter hadn't been introduced to yet.

They cut the engine and drifted up to Peter and Stuart. Peter was surprised by how anxious they looked. He expected expressions of delight and relief.

"Where are the others?" Evan asked.

CHAPTER
Twenty-Three

"**W**hat do you mean? Didn't Laura and Kevin send you?" Peter tried to quell a bubble of panic rapidly expanding in his stomach.

"No," Evan responded, looking confused. "Did you just have one canoe left and you couldn't all fit, so they went without you?"

"We lost both our canoes, but when we got here, Marty Sullivan was here. He offered to take two of us, plus Pippin, to the lodge, and then a boat would get sent back for us."

"Marty? Sullivan? Really?"

"Yes. But how did you guys end up coming here?"

"John was worried when he saw how much the fire had grown overnight. The MWS put out a bulletin that pretty much everywhere you guys were planning to paddle was burning badly. He sent us to search along the west shore in case you showed up there and needed help."

"Thank you, thank you so much," Stuart said, extending his hand to shake Evan and the other man's hands.

"OK, let's find a good spot to come in closer to shore, and then we can load you guys and get you back to the lodge. This is Jacob, by the way." The other man smiled, waved, and said, "Hi!"

"Can we look for Laura and Kevin first, though?" Peter asked as he waded alongside the boat on the way to the widest part of the beach.

Evan glanced out to the lake and then looked back at Peter, his face grim. "In this smoke, Dr. Bannerman? It would be like looking for a flea in a fog bank. Sullivan's really experienced, so even if he misses the lodge crossing the lake, he'll know how to follow the shore to find it. It just might take a while in these conditions."

That made sense to Peter. He was grateful for the rational explanation. "Is there any fire near the lodge?" he asked as he climbed aboard.

"Yeah, just this morning there's a fresh one just off the road to the main dock. Most of the rest of the staff are out trying to fight it. John would like to evacuate, but the float planes can't land in this smoke."

"Do you know how they're doing over at the First Nation?"

"I talked to my uncle . . ." Jacob answered.

"Lawrence!" Peter said.

"Yes, and he said they're hanging in. They cut a firebreak and the wind change helped them but it's still really dicey." He paused to hand out life jackets. "And Friendly Bear is toast."

"Toast? As in burnt down?"

Jacob revved up the outboard motor just then, so Evan shouted, "To the ground!"

"Wow! Anyone hurt?"

"Not that I know. They evacuated to DLFN."

Stuart was sitting on the bench beside Peter, both of them facing backwards to be out of the spray as the bow slammed across the waves. He leaned over toward Peter so he wouldn't have to shout as loud. "Where is Friendly Bear?"

Peter pointed back the way they were coming from. "That way. Just inside the southwest arm of Dragonfly."

"Makes sense." Stuart nodded.

"Sort of. But that means it's a massive fire. By water it's not far, but by land it's done a lot of jumping."

"Or new fires starting?"

"Yes, that might be more likely."

They lapsed into silence because it was too difficult to talk over the high-decibel drone of the engine and the sound of the boat rhythmically smacking the water like an aluminum fist trying to subdue the unruly lake. Even though it hurt his eyes, Peter kept scanning the blurred horizon on both sides, occasionally peering ahead, shielding his eyes with his hand against the spray. He knew it was silly to expect to see the canoe, but it felt even sillier not to try.

Eventually the waves settled, and the ride became quieter and smoother. Evan nodded and smiled at Peter. "Better now. This might sound weird, but I kind of like this," he said, sweeping his arm at the grey gloom all around them.

"Oh?" was all Peter could think to say in response.

"I don't mean the destruction of nature or the death of animals by fire and smoke. I hate that. But the vibe. The end-of-world vibe. I've gotta admit I like it." He paused, appearing to weigh his next words carefully. "We all know the world is going to shit anyway, right? So why not bring it on. As long as you're doing what you love and you're with the people you love. Down in flames and passion. Why wait until everybody hates everything and everyone and it's all just crumbling bit by bit, you know?" He paused again. "That would be way worse."

Stuart glanced at Peter. Jacob appeared to be focused on steering the boat.

"That's an interesting perspective. I'm not sure I agree, but I think I see what you mean," Peter said.

"Sorry, Doc, crazy days like this just bring out the crazy philosopher in me! I'm just shooting the shit. Metaphorical fires, right? Real fires hurt!" Evan laughed. "OK, Jacob, let's give 'er and get these gentlemen home."

Just when Peter was about to wonder whether they had gotten lost as well, Jacob gunned the engine for about ten minutes and then suddenly cut the engine. Peter and Stuart turned around to see the lodge looming up out of the haze. The smoke varied in density, being thickest near the water and again higher up, at treetop level, giving the lodge the appearance of floating on a cloud, like a fairy-tale castle. Peter had allowed himself to hope Laura would be there at the dock, waving and calling to him, having arrived in the interval since Evan and Jacob left. But there was no Laura at the dock, nor even John or anyone else from the lodge. It was empty and smoke shrouded. Now that the boat was no longer making a hellish noise, Peter became aware of another mechanical sound. He quickly saw what it was. A large orange pump was thrumming on the beach, a hose running down into the lake, and another one up toward the lodge.

"Yeah, we're getting ready for the worst-case scenario," Evan said as he steadied the boat against the dock with one hand while helping first Peter and then Stuart climb out with the other. "We're going to start hosing the lodge down. We'll get a second pump going right away too. Should have enough diesel to last three or four days."

"Is that going to work?" Peter asked. He thought about how quickly that bog dried out. "Where we just came from, the fire was hot enough to evaporate water in seconds."

Evan shrugged. "Won't hurt anyway. Beats standing around getting ready to roast marshmallows. The big thing is keeping the roof wet, so flying embers don't spark something. But yeah, if there's a wall of fire racing toward the lodge, it's pretty much game over no matter how wet we get it."

"Do you know where John is?"

"Nope. Probably in eight places at once right now." Evan finished tying up the boat, and then looked up at Peter and grinned. "You guys good now? Find your own way? Jacob and I also got eight places to be."

Peter squinted at the three fishing boats and couple remaining canoes and wondered whether there was enough space for all the staff and guests in the event of an emergency evacuation. But that's not the question he wanted to ask Evan before he left.

"Sure, we're good. Thanks again for saving our bacon," Peter said.

"Before it got cooked?" Evan laughed. "No sweat, Doctor."

"Before you go, a quick question. What do you think of Sullivan?"

"Quick question with a long answer." Evan turned to Jacob and said, "Go on ahead, I'll be right behind you."

"Thanks, Jacob!" Stuart said as the man waved goodbye and trotted up the dock.

"Yes, thank you," Peter added.

"I'm not sure what to tell you," Evan said, turning back to Peter and Stuart. "He's a strange one for sure. Kinda plays up the Santa thing, but I've seen him get mad in a very un-Santa-like way before too. But harmless, so if you're worried about your wife and stuff, I wouldn't worry about that. Just seems to get steamed about weird conspiracy theory type stuff. You know the type?"

"I do," Peter said, not feeling reassured.

"Kinda like those old guys at the coffee shop who complain about the government all the time and listen to talk radio but can always be counted on to help out their neighbours and drive blind people to the hospital and shit like that."

Peter chuckled. He definitely knew the type. Rural Manitoba was full of them.

"A kook for sure, but if I was going to get lost in the woods, he's the kook I'd want to be lost with. Knows his shit out there. Your wife's in good hands, Doc. They'll be fine. Really gotta run now, though."

Evan strode off after Jacob. Peter and Stuart watched him go before both turning to look back out at the lake.

Peter found John Reynolds in the parking lot at the front of the lodge. He was directing a couple of workers to begin shutting down the lakeside cabins by turning off the breakers and moving the bedding and towels up to the main lodge. Peter had approached from behind and waited for John to finish before stepping into his view.

"Dr. Bannerman! I'm so relieved! But what happened to your eyes?"

"Just inflamed. I might have trouble reading the menu tonight, but they'll be OK."

John nodded. "Is everyone else OK too?"

"It's just Stuart and me. Marty Sullivan picked up Laura, Kevin, and Pippin in his canoe a couple hours before Evan and Jacob showed up. I expected them to be here well before now."

John furrowed his brow, his moustache twitching. "Sullivan? Really? We don't see much of him in the summer. He sometimes gets supplies sent here that he stops by to pick up, but it's been weeks. But you're right, it should only take Marty 20 minutes to cross the lake with that tailwind."

"Got lost in the smoke is the leading theory right now."

"Sure, makes sense. He's a bit wacky, but nobody knows the area better, so he'll find his way back here soon enough, you'll see."

That seemed to be the consensus, and Peter didn't have a good reason to argue with it.

"I hope so. Changing the subject, I see you're closing up the cabins?"

"Yeah, we're moving everyone into the lodge. It might be a bit squeezy, but we can't defend the cabins too. If that new fire breaks through, it could rip along the shore first. Having everyone up here gives me one less thing to worry about."

"OK. And what about evacuation?"

John shook his head. "Not with this smoke and this wind. Planes can't come in and we can't get everyone safely across the water to the community either, plus they've got their own problems and they're already looking after everyone from Friendly Bear already."

"Evan said it burned down. That's awful."

"In a flash. Bev was on the radio saying that it had to be arson."

"That's insane," Peter said.

"Insanity looks like it's contagious these days."

CHAPTER
Twenty-Four

Peter showered quickly, just getting the worst of the dirt and debris off. He knew he'd smell like smoke for days regardless, so he didn't try too hard to make that go away. Then he went down to the restaurant to join Stuart. The restaurant was packed with guests milling about, currents of conversation about the fire loudly criss-crossing the room. He noticed that the Belarusians were there, as well as the Midwest American fishermen. This seemed odd until he realized it had been less than a week since he first arrived. Time had become rubbery and strange. And then there was the fact that nobody could leave today. Molly was there as well and came up to him.

"I'm so glad to see that you're all right, Dr. Bannerman! How are the others?"

Peter gave her a quick summary of the situation.

"I'm sure they'll turn up right away. Marty may be strange, but there's no one better when it comes to being in the bush or on the lake. You must be so worried, though."

"I have to admit, I am." More out of unexpected instinct for the moment than any plan, Peter then said, "And how about you? You seemed really upset before we left. I hear you lost someone close to you on that plane."

Molly smiled at him. "It's kind of you to ask. Yes, Ned. Ned the pilot was my boyfriend. We hadn't been dating long, but he was . . ." She smiled again.

"It's OK. You don't need to explain. I'm sorry for your loss."

"Thank you. And I hope your wife and friends and dog are back soon."

Molly turned to take an order from the fishermen.

Acknowledging his worry openly made his emotions suddenly feel raw, and potentially unmanageable. Peter went to the bar and ordered a Manipogo Pale more or less as a reflex action, but he just stared at it when it was poured. The day reverberated in his head like a carnival from hell. But one fact stood out. He didn't know where Laura and the rest were and what was happening to them. They could even be dead. It was the first time in his life he didn't know if someone close to him was dead or alive.

Then, as if conjured by his thoughts, he saw Laura.

He almost dropped his glass.

She had just stepped into the room from the lobby, looking as dishevelled as he had ever seen her. Face streaked with soot. Hair like a cartoon character who had stuck her finger in a light socket. Her clothes were wet and muddy. Kevin was just visible behind her, talking to John. Pippin rocketed across the room and was at Peter's feet before he could react.

Peter set his glass down on the counter and ran over to hug Laura. He wasn't normally a hugger, but nobody watching would have been able to tell. They squeezed each other hard for a long minute. Then Peter turned around and dropped to his knees to hug his dog, who had followed him. "Pippin, Pippin, Pippin, my boy, how are you?"

Pippin licked his face with the vigour of a mother washing her newborn pup. People stopped what they were doing and looked, making "ooh, aah, isn't that sweet" noises.

Then Peter heard Kevin grunt, "All right, you two, get a room." He laughed as Peter stood up and slapped him on the back. "Now I finally get that hug I've been wanting, don't I?"

Stuart rushed up to join them, and soon it was a group scrum with Kevin lifting each of them in the air in turn. Pippin circled them rapidly, his tail wagging as hard as it ever had. He would have barked too, but he knew he wasn't supposed to indoors unless it was an emergency.

After multiple criss-crossing reassurances to each other than they were all OK, they agreed Laura and Kevin should get cleaned up first and then they could each tell their stories over drinks and food. Peter explained that the four of them were sharing a room now, to which Kevin replied, "I call top bunk!" Peter further explained that there were no bunks, just twin beds, and mattresses on the floor. Kevin pumped his fist and declared, "Floor! In that case I call floor!" They all stared at him. "Because it's cooler and more adventurey," he said. "That's why."

After they left, Stuart picked up a week-old Saturday *Globe and Mail* from the end of the bar and brought it over to the table where Peter was sipping his beer. Stuart leafed through the paper until he got to the crossword puzzle. "Nobody has done it yet!" he said, beaming.

Peter grinned at him. "Doesn't look like much of a crossword crowd."

"This is the perfect thing for me right now. It helps me be calm," Stuart said. Peter noticed, however, that Stuart's hand shook when he picked up a pencil.

Peter flipped through the other sections of the paper but felt fidgety. He rechecked his email and messages, but there was nothing new, so he reread the note from Raj that the dogs were all doing well except Atlas, but even he had improved a little. Then he checked again and in the intervening seconds an email had arrived from Dwayne.

Dear Peter,

I hope you are OK. The news is full of stories about the fires up there. Apparently the other lodge burned down. I'm glad it wasn't yours.

I did not serve time with a Cam Schmidt, but I checked with a lifer who is a friend of mine and who would know everyone at Stoney. He said he knew Schmidt but he had nothing much to report about him. He was there on weapons charges and assault and kept to himself mostly.

Looking forward to when we can get the metal detectors out! If you're busy when you get back, hopefully by fall?

Your friend,
Dwayne

Peter typed a quick thank you and considered how much he was looking forward to detectoring again. In fact, he was looking forward to anything that wasn't what he was doing right now.

He surfed the news for a bit, which was dominated by the fires. Nothing was being reported about them that he didn't already know. He had brought the Ottoman book with him, but that appealed even less than it previously did.

He looked around the room, swirling the beer in his glass absent-mindedly. He was anxious and jittery. Everyone else looked anxious and jittery too. Stuart was staring blankly at his crossword, as if catatonic. The light was dim and diffuse for a July mid-afternoon because of the smoke. Peter assumed they were keeping the lights off to save on generator power as the Hydro lines were down. It lent an odd otherworldly atmosphere to the room. Not day, not night, not morning, not evening, but something else. Maybe this is what it was like on Jupiter, Peter thought.

He swirled his beer some more and tried to guess what had happened with Sullivan. Laura and Kevin had offered no hints. Both were wet and dirty, but then so were he and Stuart when they arrived. But they had good reason to be wet, having stood in the lake for two hours; the others did not. Had Sullivan tossed them overboard? That was silly, and probably not even physically possible in a canoe. Had they capsized? That made more sense. If so, why?

This was all speculation without information, something that irritated Peter when others did it, so he stopped.

And what about Dwayne's information regarding Cam? Weapons charges were certainly interesting. And maybe he was deliberately misdirecting when he told Peter to not believe everything John said. But despite what Kevin said about motives, the fact that Cam had no plausible motive to shoot the plane, or hurt the dogs for that matter, still seemed important. Plus, Peter had a good feeling about him. He knew he shouldn't trust such feelings, but it was still there.

He continued to look around the room, distracting himself by spotting taxidermy he hadn't noticed before. He had to close his eyes frequently to rest them, but they were better than they had been. There was an annoyed-looking lynx in the far corner. And two muskrats were nailed to a post beside the neighbouring table, facing upwards as if they were longing for the ceiling. Muskrats didn't climb, Peter thought.

Just then, Pyotr the Belarusian caught his eye. He and his two friends had been facing the other way, hunched over some documents, but now that he noticed Peter he waved and shouted, "Peter! You have adventure! Come tell!"

Peter couldn't think of an excuse not to. *In fact, it could be interesting*, he thought. They were still suspects for both the poisonings and the murders, although by the slimmest of rationales.

He walked over and endured a round of bone-crushing hand-shakes before sitting in the chair Pyotr had pulled out for him.

"You have not been meeting my friends before!" he boomed. "This very smart guy here is Yuriy! And this very strong guy is Kirill!"

"Pleased to meet you all," Peter said.

"I am making joke! Kirill is smart also and Yuriy is strong also. Only I am weak and dumb!"

Much laughter ensued. Then Peter noticed a half-empty bottle of vodka in the middle of the table beside a stack of papers with Cyrillic writing. This alarmed him. The beer alone had already made him a little loopy.

Pyotr noticed his glance and said, "You want? I get glass! Is too early for us, but we have guest earlier. Is Belaya Rus brand. Very good! Is . . . cooked . . . ? How you say?"

"Distilled?" Peter ventured.

"Yes, distilled! Is distilled six times." Pyotr counted out five fingers on his left hand and then held up his thumb on his right. "And is make from best grain and water so pure, is like a . . . how you say?" He paused and scratched his chin. Peter had no idea what he was trying to say. Pyotr beamed, having evidently remembered the word he was looking for. "A virgin! Is like a virgin water!"

"That sounds good, but no, thank you. I've had a beer already and such an exhausting day that I think a vodka will put me to sleep!"

"Wise man. Our guest not so wise. Drink in middle of day make man dull. One or two drink in night all man need. Then have good rest."

The other two Belarusians nodded gravely in agreement with what Pyotr said, although Peter was unclear how much English the other two understood.

"Tonight, maybe we drink toast to your escape from big fire! How you escape from this? Can you tell now?"

"You bet." Peter figured he still had half an hour before Laura and Kevin returned, so he went through the whole story in detail.

Pyotr had to translate some bits, but they made for an appreciative audience. They all leaned forward, eyes big, exclaiming at intervals, thumping the table at other times. When Peter was done, each one stood up to shake his hand, crushing his fingers again.

"This is wonderful story, Peter! You are hero! Only wrestle bear make story complete!"

"Ha! Well, the wildlife all fled the fire, so there were no bears to wrestle."

"Is joke, but if you see bear you maybe speak to it and not wrestle it because you are animal doctor and have special way with animal."

"Um, maybe."

Pyotr nodded and then pointed at Kirill, a short, wide man with a mop of black hair. "He wrestle bear many time!"

"Really?" Peter tried to picture this but could only generate slapstick images.

"Yes, he live in Siberia in winter. Tough as . . . what is English expression?"

"Nails?"

"Yes, tough like nails!"

"That's impressive." Peter smiled at Kirill, who smiled and nodded in return, and asked, "In Siberia by yourself?"

Kirill nodded vigorously. "Yes. By self. With dog."

"What kind of dog?" Maybe Kirill had a sled team. Maybe this was a thread that connected to the events here, however improbable that might be.

Kirill furrowed his brow and said something to Pyotr in Belarusian. They spoke back and forth a little, then Kirill turned back to Peter and said, "Big dog."

This line of questioning wasn't going where Peter had hoped. He tried another tack. "And what do you do there?"

There was another rapid exchange of Belarusian between Kirill and Pyotr. Pyotr answered. "He trap small animal for his furs and he shoot big animal for his meats." Pyotr made a shooting motion at the moose head above the bar, using his left arm as a pretend rifle. "Kirill is very great shooter. In army he was, how you say, marking man?"

"Marksman?"

"Very great marksman!" Pyotr made more shooting motions, this time with sound effects. Kirill joined in.

The American fishermen at the next table stopped talking and turned around to look.

Peter kept his face blank.

The conversation veered into Yuriy's own time in the army. According to the anecdotes told with great animation, this appeared to mostly involve the soldiers playing hair-raising pranks on each other and on the less popular officers.

After the laughter died down, Peter turned to Pyotr. Hoping to hear something more comprehensible, he asked, "And you, Pyotr? Any funny army stories?"

Pyotr gave him a thin smile and said, "No, nothing funny. Only boring office job in army." Peter saw Pyotr wink at Yuriy and Kirill.

Everyone was quiet for a long moment. "But Peter, my friend, I almost forgetting something," Pyotr suddenly said. He reached under the table and pulled out a camouflage-patterned backpack. He rummaged around in it for a moment and then produced a crumpled brown paper bag, which he handed to Peter with a big smile.

It was full of mushrooms. Not morels, which had a distinctive corrugated appearance Peter was familiar with, but rather a clutch of smooth round brown ones. Very generic looking.

"Not sure what name is in English. We say 'borovik.'" Pyotr loudly kissed the tips of his fingers like a cartoon chef.

CHAPTER
Twenty-Five

"The Belarusskis gave you mushrooms? And you're actually going to eat them?" Kevin said. He smelled of soap and smoke, and his hair was wet. His eyes were still red from the smoke irritation, although not as cherry red as Peter's. Peter was amused to see that Kevin had braided the tip of his red beard. Laura was evidently still getting cleaned up. Stuart was sitting by himself near the window, doing a crossword.

"I think so. I mean, why would they bother to poison me even if they were behind the other dastardly deeds?" Peter glanced over to where the Belarusians sat, across the room and well out of earshot. They were now in conversation with the Americans, evidently about guns as Pyotr was doing the mock rifle thing with his arm again.

Kevin grunted and shrugged. "I just don't trust them."

"And you? You going for the Durin look?" Peter asked, smirking and pointing at his brother-in-law's new beard braid.

"The dwarf from *The Rings of Power*? Ha! Sure! Why not? He's a cool little dude, isn't he? I'm the supersized Viking version is all." Kevin flexed his pectorals and set his face into a fierce grimace.

"But without the weird Scottish accent."

"Durin has a weird Scottish accent? No, without that. I don't do accents. Or kinky dwarf things, whatever those might be."

"Ha! And how long will the force let you keep that braid?"

"About three seconds. It's a vacation braid." Kevin glanced around until he caught the eye of a waitress. "And now I need a vacation beer or three. You too?"

"Had one already. And one is it for me today. So, not feeling too rough from last night?" Peter asked, recalling that less than 24 hours ago Kevin had downed the better part of a bottle of whisky.

"Super-sized Viking dwarves have legendary constitutions. Legendary. Especially when they're on vacation. I think Tolkien mentioned that." Kevin grinned and then turned his attention to Erin, the petite blond waitress with horn-rimmed glasses from the other night, who had appeared by his side with a notepad and raised eyebrows.

"Ah, hello. A big Barn Hammer Lumberjack Double IPA, please, followed 15 minutes later by another big Barn Hammer Lumberjack Double IPA. And after that . . . wait for my signal." Kevin winked at her.

After she left Kevin turned to Peter and leaned forward. "Nice waitress. Speaking of waitresses, when I got back from our, er, adventure, I saw who I assume must be Molly: short, black pigtails, ears kinda like Laura's?"

"Yeah, that'd be her."

"Well, I saw her arguing with the bartender . . ."

"Cam?"

"If you say so. Guy with the eye patch."

"That's Cam."

"OK, well, they were arguing down the hall from our room. Couldn't tell what it was about, but this Molly was crying, and the bartender guy looked really mad. The only word I caught was the name 'Evan.' I pretended that I forgot something in my room, so I turned around."

"That's the chef. The guy who rescued us earlier."

"Oh yeah? I gotta hear that story yet, and you gotta hear ours. But when Laura comes down. Anyway, seems the staff don't all get along. Big surprise. Never worked anywhere where the staff all got along."

"But . . ."

Kevin raised his hand and interrupted Peter. "There's my beer!"

"Thank you!" Kevin raised his glass to the waitress. "This is going to be the best-tasting beer of the summer!"

"You're welcome, darlin'," Erin said, smiling at Kevin. She brushed his shoulder lightly with her hand as she turned to go.

"Uh-oh, you gave off too much of a hetero vibe." Peter chuckled.

"Doesn't matter what vibe I give off — queer, straight, something in between — it's just my pure elemental animal magnetism. People can't resist it. It's like a superpower."

"Must come in handy in your police work."

"You don't know the half of it. Cheers!"

Peter raised his empty glass. "Cheers!"

Laura appeared a few minutes later with her knitting bag and a paperback. Her red hair was wet and loose around her shoulders. She gave Peter a peck on the cheek and then settled into one of the two spare seats.

Stuart had just come over from where he had been sitting in an armchair by the window. His crossword was folded under his arm, and he had a pencil behind his ear.

"May I join the party?" he asked. "First one question, though." He unfolded the crossword. "Three-letter word for 'extinct flightless bird,' second letter 'o.'"

"Dodo!" Kevin exclaimed.

"*Three-letter*," Stuart said. Then he looked at Kevin as if seeing him properly for the first time. He wrinkled his brow, leaned over, and whispered, "*That* is disappearing right away."

"Oh, come on! It's my vacation Viking braid!"

"What you call it is no concern of mine. I only know that it is unsightly and unsuited to man who expects to be seen in my company. It looks like a rat has burrowed into your beard and has left its tail hanging out."

Laura guffawed, and Peter snorted and said, "Moa. Three-letter extinct flightless bird."

"Perfect. You are very good!"

Kevin ignored the change of subject and protested, "Rats don't have red tails!"

"That is your principal objection to my critique?" Stuart said, arching his eyebrows.

"OK, OK. We'll talk about it later. Switching channels now." Kevin took a deep drink from his beer and cleared his throat. "Laura and I are dying to hear what happened. How did you guys get here before we did? We arrived expecting to call the cavalry for you only to find you snarfing beers at the bar already."

Peter and Stuart laughed and then took turns explaining everything from having to dive to avoid being bombed by embers, to how Evan and Jacob had been out looking for them.

When they were done, Peter turned his palms outward toward Kevin and Laura and said, "Now your turn."

"You'll probably tell it better, sis," Kevin said. "Just don't make me look like a total dumbass."

Laura smiled and patted her brother on the shoulder. "Well, the big thing after we left you guys was how long it was taking. With both Kevin and Sullivan paddling, and with that strong tailwind . . ."

Just then, as if on cue, a blast of wind rattled the windows, startling everyone. The smoke was thicker now and had taken on an odd yellow tinge. The lake was not visible except for a narrow fringe at the shore below the lodge. An anxious murmur ran through the room, but Kevin picked up the story.

"Ha, the wind gods are listening! Like I was saying, with all of that, I assumed we'd be across to the lodge much faster. Sullivan seemed to know what he was doing, because he would check his compass from time to time and adjust the direction of the canoe. After what seemed like a ridiculously long time, I finally asked him what was going on."

Erin appeared and asked if anyone would like to order anything. Laura and Stuart asked for coffees. Peter said, "No, thank you," and Kevin pointed at his empty beer glass, glanced at his watch, and said, "Just in time!"

"Of course, darlin', and anything to eat? The kitchen is closed on account of the boys being out with John fightin' that fire, but we have snacks and fruit, and I can make simple sandwiches."

"No, thank you so much. You're very kind," Kevin smiled and winked at her. "You're busy enough. We're OK waiting for supper, assuming that there will be supper?"

"Oh yes, we'll surely figure something out by then. Don't you worry, darlin'."

"*Darlin'?*" Stuart asked, in a surprisingly good imitation of a Newfie accent after she left.

"What can I say? I'm just a lovable guy," Kevin said, puffing his chest out.

Laura rolled her eyes. "I'm just going to ignore all that and move right along unless somebody objects." She paused for half a beat, and then continued. "So, as I was saying, I asked Sullivan where we were. He laughed his weird Santa laugh and explained that he had decided not to take us directly to the lodge. He had noticed new fires on the east side of the lake. How he noticed that through all that smoke is beyond me, but I didn't question him. Anyway, this meant he wanted to get to his cabin as quickly as possible. It would potentially be in the path of an east side fire."

Laura paused to take a sip of her coffee, which Erin had brought much faster than she expected.

"His portage to Black Eagle River was quite a distance up the shore from the lodge, so he had adjusted our course in that direction. He said he wanted to go fast and light, so he was going to stash most of his bags and leave us with the canoe. He had another one on the other side anyway because it was a really long portage through rough terrain. Only he ever used it."

"Sorry to interrupt," Peter said. "Did you get any idea what was in those duffles? Looked like a lot for a little paddling trip with a puppy."

"No, no idea. But then we don't know how long he planned to be away anyway. I did notice him stash a jerrycan that looked empty, the way he pulled it out of the bottom of the canoe like it was nothing."

"Really? Did it smell like kerosene or something else flammable?" Peter asked.

Kevin answered for Laura. "Pete, the whole friggin' world smells like something flammable or flaming right now. Even the insides of my nostrils smell like smoke. My brain probably smells like smoke too. So no, neither of us detected any smell associated with the jerrycan."

"Fair point," Peter said.

"Anyway," Laura continued, "he was brisk and businesslike and was up into the bush with a small pack and Dancer before we could have any sort of conversation. He just pointed down the shore and said it should take us about an hour. He'd come for the canoe some other time. And then . . . are you sure you want me to tell this part, Kev?"

"Yeah, yeah. The truth will get out eventually anyway. Not my proudest moment."

Stuart raised his eyebrows. Peter said, "Oh?"

"I got in first, and set myself up in the bow, and Pippin followed and sat behind me. There's no beach there, just a rocky shore. With the crazy wind, the waves kept slamming the canoe against the rocks. It was super rough. I held on to a nearby rock as best as I could to steady the boat. Then I looked over my shoulder just in time to yell, 'Stay low and toward the centre,' when my darling brother did the opposite."

"I was anxious to get going!" Kevin said, red-faced. "And my brain was all messed up from the crazy day. Anyway, I took a big step into the stern, but I was off-centre and standing tall, so it instantly pivoted."

"And dumped Pippin and me into the water."

"And me."

"Good thing Kevin was able to grab the canoe before it got swept down the shore."

"One good thing I did."

"So, anyway. We all got wet, but we didn't lose the canoe or paddles."

"Or Pippin," Peter added.

"Or Pippin. And a couple hours later, we were here. Sullivan way overestimated our canoeing prowess and speed."

"But we are so thankful you all made it without injury," Stuart said, raising his coffee cup for a toast.

Before they could make the toast, there was a cacophony from the doors to the lobby. Barking, shouting, slamming, stomping, more barking.

John, Evan, Jacob, another man, another woman, and seven huskies burst into the restaurant.

CHAPTER
Twenty-Six

A ll five people were soot-stained and wild-haired. The dogs were extremely excited, yipping and leaping up at nearby tables. Everyone in the restaurant stopped what they were doing to watch what was going on.

John gestured to Cam, who was behind the bar, and shouted, "Cam, come round up the dogs and take them to the conference room." And then turning to the woman who had come in with him: "Nicole, you help him." Then he climbed onto a chair and cupped his hands around his mouth like a megaphone. "Can I have everyone's attention, please!"

A lot of shuffling and scraping of chairs and murmuring followed. Peter signalled to Pippin to stay put under their table, where he had been napping quietly until all the commotion started. He knew Pippin would be interested in following the huskies.

"I hope the staff have been treating you well! I do apologize that we have been unable to offer a full kitchen or any of the fishing or outings Dragonfly Lodge has built its reputation on. As you have likely noticed, we have a bit of a 'situation.'" John used air quotes.

Nervous laughter all around.

"The lodge is perfectly safe. We will continue to hose it down, and we have the advantage of a high position. The fire near the road is, however, too big for us to deal with."

Gasps.

John held up his hand. "But like I said, it does not threaten the lodge itself. I repeat, it does not threaten the lodge itself. Friendly Bear was much lower, closer to the trees, and closer to the main fire. The boys and Nicole and I have dug a firebreak, but we can't protect the cabins or the outbuildings too, *if* the fire moves that way. This is why the dogs have been brought in. It'll be fine, but we just want to be as safe as possible. I'm sure the Wildfire Service will be on top of this as quickly as they can, but they're putting everything they've got over at DLFN right now to try to save the community. We *will* get you folks out of here at the very earliest opportunity." John took a deep breath, surveyed the room, and raised his arms in the air. "In the meantime, I'm declaring an open bar with all the drinks on me." He pointed to one of the Americans, a portly middle-aged guy with a blond buzz cut. "We're in no danger of running out of Moosehead, Ted!"

Guffaws from Ted. More nervous laughter from everyone else.

"And the meals tonight are complimentary too! And if there's anything else we can do, anything at all, just holler!"

Stuart leaned over the table and whispered, "Open bar? Is that really a good idea under these circumstances?"

Kevin leaned forward and said, using a caricature of a conspiratorial voice, "Might help with the murder investigation."

"How so?" Peter asked.

Just then, one of the huskies broke away from the group being herded across the restaurant past admiring guests to the doors of the conference room at the far side. It ran up to Pippin, who stood up to greet the dog. They stood nose to nose, both tails wagging, and then moved alongside each other so each could sniff the other's genitals. They turned in slow circles, sniffing deeply, until Cam came running up.

"Sorry, Doc. Daisy got away! Not so easy herding seven excited huskies. They haven't seen this many people in a long time!"

"No trouble! So, you're the dog whisperer?" Peter asked.

"Not exactly, but I'm John's go-to guy when he needs help with them. Nicole and Molly are good with them too."

After Cam gently pulled Daisy away from Pippin, Kevin cleared his throat and answered Peter's question. "Drink loosens tongues. It's that simple. If I could pour tequila shots for suspects I'm questioning, I'd do it. But *apparently*, it's against regulations or something." He shrugged dramatically, palms up in the universally recognized "beats me" gesture.

"Funny, but seriously, Kev, you think the murderer is here and they are going to talk just because there's free beer? And even if they did, are we going to necessarily hear it?" Peter asked.

"I've seen it happen before. It's not just the booze, but the end-of-the-world vibe. It's very . . . confessional? Is that the right word?"

"Close enough. I see what you mean, but it still seems like a long shot."

Laura had begun knitting but was paying close attention. Stuart glanced nervously about and made a "shhh" sound when one of the Americans — the one who was not Ted — walked by to look out the window.

"He can't hear us," Kevin said. "It's too loud in here."

"Maybe." Stuart pursed his lips before going on. "But the other thing is that you have been saying this is your vacation and that you are not a police officer when you are on vacation. Why are we speaking of this at all? Is it not the business of the local police?"

"Excellent points, Stu. I did say that. But like I told Pete last night, I was fooling myself. I gotta accept who I am. And in this specific situation, the local cops are over in DLFN. They're up to their eyeballs with the fire. So, I am *it*. I'm 'the law' here."

"Even off duty?" Stuart asked, eyes narrow.

"Yup. I still have all the same powers of search, arrest, etcetera. Not that I want to use them, but they're there if I have to."

Stuart sighed. "OK."

"It would only be to protect you guys, and everyone else here."

"So, Kevin," Laura said, not looking up from her knitting, "how do you know the murderer is even still here?"

"I don't, but to quote your esteemed husband, the probability is high. Don't you agree, Pete?"

"On a balance of probabilities, yes. We can be reasonably certain that the murderer came from the lodge because that Icelandic woman, Sigrun, saw someone canoeing before dawn toward the area where the shots were fired from."

"There could be another explanation for the pre-dawn paddle," Kevin said. "But Todd interviewed everyone here and nobody claimed to have done that, so someone is lying."

"Meaning," Peter said, taking the thread over again, "it was lodge staff or a guest. The staff are all still here, and most of the guests are too. People usually come up Sunday to Sunday, so everyone who was here the day of the murder, except the Icelandic women, is still here. Today would have been departure day." Peter paused to pour himself a glass of water from the jug on the table.

Kevin pulled a napkin toward him and asked for Stuart's pencil. "So, that's John, Cam, Evan, Molly, Erin . . ." He hesitated, scratching his beard. "I forget now, what was that girl's name with John just now? And the Indigenous guy?"

"Nicole and Jacob," Peter answered. "Should you really be writing those names down?"

"I'm not." Kevin held up the napkin, which had the letters J, C, E, M, E2, N, and J scrawled on it, barely legible, especially to Peter's still somewhat blurry vision. "But pencil on napkin is shit. I'll just remember. Or Laura will. She's got one of those steel-trap memories." Kevin crumpled the napkin and stuffed it into his pocket.

"Uh-huh," Laura said, still not looking up from the beginnings of something tubular and dark blue. *Maybe a sweater sleeve*, Peter thought.

"So, anyway, that's seven staff we know the names of, and how many more?" Kevin asked, looking at Peter.

"Well, there's the other man who was with John fighting the fire. He's from the kitchen, as is Nicole. I don't know his name. There's another fishing guide besides Jacob. And I think there are two housekeepers, both women on work permits from, I think, the Philippines."

Kevin was counting on his fingers. "Eleven staff? And how many guests?"

"The three Belarusians, the two Americans, and those two young couples, who sound Canadian. Not sure where they're from."

"So, nine guests, plus us, but I'm not counting us. Not as suspects, anyway. Ha ha!"

"Twenty potential suspects then?" Laura asked.

"Twenty-one. Don't forget Santa Claus," Kevin answered.

"Let me understand you correctly," Stuart said, frowning, leaning forward, pressing on the table with the palms of his hands. Peter noticed that his Nigerian accent was more obvious when he was upset. "Are you telling us we are trapped in this wilderness hotel with a murderer?"

"In short, yes. Sorry," Kevin said, reaching over to rub Stuart on the shoulder.

They were all quiet for a moment.

"That is a lot of suspects," Laura said, nodding slowly as she knit.

"But we can winnow down that list pretty quickly," Peter said, trying to keep his excitement from becoming obvious given how Stuart felt. The way Laura grimaced at him made it clear he hadn't succeeded. He couldn't help himself. Even when Peter was a boy, his father had called his brain a "puzzle-seeking missile." He asked the same "why" questions other little kids did, but unlike most kids, where one "why" triggered further whys like a series of dominos, after the first why Peter would propose a theory as to why that was. Soon he even stopped asking the first why and started the conversation with a theory, but only after he had weighed the question carefully in his mind and settled on the most plausible explanation. "I think the sky is blue because . . ." and "I think that hole in the yard is from . . ." and so forth.

"Absolutely," Kevin agreed. "We can start by determining who can paddle solo and who can handle a rifle. These things may not be immediately obvious, but with smart questions and a bit of deduction we can get there."

Laura looked up from her knitting and asked, "What about those poor huskies? Do we also need to consider who is willing to hurt animals?"

"Good point, sis. That's Peter's theory too; that it's probably the same person. I'm not so sure, but if we say it is, then you're right. It would put animal lovers like Cam, Nicole, and Molly lower on the list."

"And Mr. Reynolds," Stuart added, his face and hands more relaxed.

"Maybe, although Pete and I have another theory about that." Kevin smiled at Stuart, obviously pleased that he looked calmer and was taking an interest.

"Speak of the devil," Laura whispered out of the side of her mouth and jerked her head to where John was approaching them.

"I just wanted to stop by and see how you folks are doing," John said, looking around the table, smiling broadly, his bright white teeth contrasting his coal miner face.

"Good. We're good, John," Peter said.

"And I wanted to check in with you on my pups, Peter. Any news?"

"There was a message from my colleague. They're doing really well. Atlas is still touch and go, but the fact that he's stable is good news. Every day he doesn't deteriorate is a day where his liver is repairing itself."

"It can do that?" Stuart asked.

"Yes, one of the few organs that can."

"Then there's hope for you after all," Stuart said, touching Kevin's hand and grinning.

They all laughed, albeit in a fatigued way. John thanked Peter and was about to move on when the American who had been standing by the window shouted, "Look at this!"

Peter had been half ignoring the view as it had been nothing but yellow-grey smoke for hours, but when he turned to look, he could see what the American was referring to.

To the east, and higher in the sky, the smoke had darkened to almost black, with reddish patches. Forks of lightning jumped from one part of the cloud to another. The cloud changed shape and billowed toward them as if in a sped-up time lapse film.

"Pyroclastic storm," Peter said.

CHAPTER
Twenty-Seven

"Meaning?" Kevin asked, still staring at the window. Most of the guests and staff were making their way over there.

"The cloud is called a pyrocumulonimbus or cumulonimbus flammagenitus —"

"Sounds like a weird sex thing for pyromaniacs, flamma-genitals whatever," Kevin said.

"Ha," Peter said, his tone flat. "No. It all just means a storm generated by a fire. The fire creates so much heat and wind that it makes its own weather. 'Flammagenitus' translates to 'generated by flames.' 'Pyroclastic' translates to 'made by fire.' As is often the case in science, one term is Latin and one is Greek, so you can get different words that have very similar meanings."

"Cut to the chase and spare us the nerd languages."

Peter sighed. "Margaritas antes porcos."

"OK, now you've completely lost it," Kevin said. "Margaritas and pork? Sounds delicious, but what's that got to with anything?"

"It's Latin for 'pearls before swine.' But OK, cutting to the chase, as you say, this is on balance probably a bad thing."

"On balance probably?" Laura asked. "There's a potential upside?"

"If it brings a lot of rain, it could help douse the fires, but the new ones it sparks with lightning strikes will likely outweigh that.

And it will produce crazy winds that will push the fires faster and send damaged trees flying."

"Damaged trees flying . . ." Stuart looked out the window, squinting as if trying to spot charred logs hurtling toward them.

The sky darkened rapidly. The caribou antler chandeliers winked on, flickered off and on briefly, and then remained on. Most of the guests had gathered by the window to watch the storm approach.

"But we're still safe in here?" one of the young Canadian men asked John.

"Is safer than outside!" Pyotr, who was standing next to him, said with a laugh. Even his laugh seemed a degree less hearty than it had been.

"Yes, certainly safer than out there, but very safe in here regardless," John answered. "We get big thunderstorms all the time and we have state-of-the-art lightning protection."

Peter recalled seeing a pair of lightning rods and a wire running along the top of the roofline.

"Hopefully it's a soaker!" John added. "That would be just what the doctor ordered."

The Canadian looked mildly skeptical but nodded and returned to his table.

Then the storm was upon them. It hit the lodge with the abrupt fury of a boxer charging out of his corner. The big picture windows began to shake with wind gusts that had to be at least one hundred kilometres an hour, in Peter's estimation. Lightning shot down directly in front of the lodge, near the shore, and a split second later, a deafening clap of thunder made the room rattle.

Someone screamed.

The lights flickered again.

More lightning and thunder. Now from all sides.

Then there was the sound of something smashing in the kitchen.

Everyone backed away from the windows. Some people, including Peter's table, sat down at their table, but many stood in the middle of the room, milling about, talking nervously.

"There is not very much rain," Stuart said, pointing at the window. He was right. There were some streaks of water running down the glass, but not nearly as much as Peter expected with a storm of such ferocity. And mixed with the bit of rain, white and grey flecks were also sliding down the window. Ash.

The storm was suddenly quieter. Everyone looked at each other.

The lull lasted maybe ten seconds and was followed by a series of thunderclaps so loud that Peter could feel them deep inside his chest. His ears rang. The wind picked up again. The windows shook and the chandeliers swayed. Beer glasses rattled behind the bar like they were in the back of a truck on a gravel road.

T.S. Eliot was wrong, Peter thought. *The world does end with a bang.*

Then there was another loud sound, even louder, like thunder, but in a different pitch, somehow sharper. It occurred to Peter that it sounded like an explosion.

Immediately after this sound, the lights went out. And the pumps, which they previously could still hear snatches of through the din of the storm, suddenly fell silent.

Definitely an explosion then, or a direct lightning hit on the generator.

Despite being late afternoon with west-facing windows, it was dim in the room due to the double obliteration of the sun by smoke and storm.

John stood up on a chair again and shouted, "Nothing to worry about! We're going to go check the primary generator, but if there's a problem with that, we have a secondary generator."

"Did any of our headlamps make it into our emergency bags when we left Parsons?" Laura asked. "I left mine behind."

"Same," Peter said.

"Me as well," Stuart said.

"I brought mine," Kevin said. "But then I dunked it when the canoe tipped, so I doubt it works."

"Well, we have our phones. How's everyone's battery?" Peter asked.

They all took out their phones to check, Laura noting that the wi-fi was down, which made sense as it ran off the satellite receiver, which would also be powered by the generator. Nobody had much charge as they had just been camping and hadn't considered it a priority to plug in when they returned to the lodge. Stuart had a small, fully charged power bank, though.

"There'll still be enough light to see our beers and stop us from walking into walls until late," Kevin said.

"Yeah, sun goes down around ten up here this time of year, and dusk drags on for another hour or so after."

"No worries, then," Kevin said, folding his hands behind his head and leaning back.

"Except that there was an explosion," Stuart said. "I feel that is a worry." This could have been read as sarcasm, but he said it straight and uninflected, like he was delivering the news.

"Possible explosion," Kevin said.

"Can we agree on probable explosion?" Laura said. "I'm no expert, but I've watched my share of things blow up on TV, and that's exactly what that sounded like."

"OK, I can live with probable, but even then, it doesn't worry me."

"Even though we are trapped with a homicidal maniac?" Stuart said.

"Homicidal, likely, but the maniac part hasn't been established yet. But even then, yes, I'm not worried." Kevin leaned further back, tipping his chair onto its back legs. "It's not like the murderer, maniacal or not, has any reason to reveal himself . . ."

"Or herself," Laura interrupted.

"Or herself, by killing anyone else or really doing anything to attract attention to himself, or herself."

In retrospect Peter wished he had kept track of who had left the restaurant before the explosion. He had been looking out the window, not back into the room. He mentally enumerated the people he knew for sure had stayed. There was the one American who was not the Moosehead-loving Ted, the Canadian who had asked the question about safety, and his wife, or girlfriend, and Pyotr, and John, and who else? He was pretty sure Erin was around, and Nicole, and one or two of the housekeeping staff, and probably the other two young Canadians, although not for absolutely certain. But he wasn't sure about Cam, or Evan, or Ted, or Molly, or the other Belarusians, or the other staff. That was the problem with a dramatic event like an explosion, it tended to sharpen the recollection of the event itself at the expense of blurring what came before.

This was important because the more he thought about it, the more lightning causing an explosion resulting in a power failure didn't make sense. The only thing that could explode like that would be the diesel fuel supply, and those tanks were well protected against lightning.

John returned, looking pale, eyes wide, hair lank and wet, moustache drooping like a drowned caterpillar. Peter knew he was right. John sought Kevin out.

"The fuel tank blew up, Corporal Gudmundurson. The main generator sits on it, so it's gone too. We have another fuel tank we can fill jerrycans from to run the backup generator, but someone's disabled the backup. Smashed the control panel and on/off switch."

"Sabotage," Kevin said, sounding much quieter and softer than he normally did. "Who has access?"

"Everyone," John said, shaking his head slowly. He looked like he was about to cry. "The primary with its tank is beside the lodge, by the kitchen, and the secondary is by the utility shed, under a tarp. It's one of those ones on wheels."

"I'll go and have a look," Kevin said.

"Wait until the storm settles," John said. "It's pretty wild out there still."

Peter only half-listened to this exchange. His thoughts were looping around. *But why? Why cut the power? Who benefits? How do they benefit?*

CHAPTER
Twenty-Eight

The atmosphere in the restaurant became tense. There had been a frisson of adventure since the start of the storm that peaked after the power went out, but the practical reality of being without power was starting to weigh on people. A few drifted off to their rooms. Others sat silently in the semi-dark. The bar was still open, but the kitchen was going to have even more limited service without power. Once John got a grip on himself, he walked around from group to group, explaining that Evan would do something special for them as the propane barbecue still worked, but it would take some time. Molly, Erin, and Cam would be needed elsewhere for a little bit, but everyone was welcome to help themselves to snacks and drinks in the meantime.

Peter saw Molly step back into the room. She stood near the door and she looked upset again. Just then Evan came in from the kitchen, walked over to her, and put his hand on her shoulder. She shook it off. Cam was at the bar, lining up cans of beer, bottles of wine, and bags of chips on the bar. He saw this and took a step toward Evan and Molly. It looked like he was about to say something when Evan walked away from Molly, brushing past Cam without acknowledging him before disappearing into the kitchen. Ted was back, if he had ever been away. He and his buddy were at the bar immediately. The Canadians were all gone now, and Pyotr was the only Belarusian Peter could see, although another one might have been sitting behind the stuffed angry bear.

Peter was about to ask Laura what she thought of the strange interplay between Molly, Evan, and Cam when Pyotr came up to them, grinning. "Is like home! In Belarus sometimes power, sometimes not power. I was there when Chernobyl went boom." He made an exploding motion with his arms. "That was big explosion. This was small explosion." He pulled up a chair from the empty neighbouring table and sat down. "What do you think happen?"

Stuart and Laura made "beats me" facial expressions while Kevin regarded him with overt suspicion. Pyotr was oblivious to this as he had directed the question at Peter and was looking at him expectantly.

"I don't really know, but it seems like quite a coincidence that both generators are down after one lightning strike." He decided to leave out the details John had provided. Perhaps Pyotr was trying to find out how much they had guessed for reasons other than casual curiosity.

"You think explosion from lightning?" Pyotr asked.

"Maybe?" Peter shrugged.

"Maybe," Pyotr agreed. "But second generator, something else, not also lightning?"

"Probably not also lightning."

"Is interesting, yes?"

"Yes, it is interesting." Peter wondered where this conversation was headed, but Pyotr stood up, shook everyone's hand, and declared that he would go and look for John and ask him some questions.

After he left, Laura said, "I wonder if John will tell him everything about the possible sabotage?"

"I don't trust the guy," Kevin said.

"You've mentioned that a few times," Peter said, "but have yet to supply anything resembling a motive for a Belarusian mycophile —"

"Mushroom lover," Laura interrupted.

"Thank you," Kevin said.

". . . to shoot a Borealis pilot while he is on approach, thereby also killing a flashy entrepreneur and a local Indigenous politician."

"This also sounds strange to me," Stuart said. "The entire crime is strange. Why would a murderer, any murderer, whether the Belarusian or someone else, not simply shoot his target alone at a convenient time and place, rather than also kill two bystanders? Unless, of course, he is simply a homicidal maniac, as I suggested previously."

Peter opened his mouth to answer, but Kevin cut him off. "First, to answer Pete's question, I haven't supplied said motive because I don't have one. And I don't have one, because I'm not investigating the case. As I mentioned before, I bet Todd finds some kind of link. The key thing is that the Belarusians had the means and the opportunity. That goes for both crimes, in fact."

"So do all kinds of people," Peter said. "I bet those Americans are handy with a rifle, and there are quite a few different liver toxins. Google is very helpful for the prospective poisoner."

Laura spoke up. "Or the staff. Or those Canadians we don't know anything about."

"Fair, fair. I'm just sayin' I don't trust the guy. But to Stu's question, the perp would wipe out the whole plane to create confusion and doubt about the target, plus put a bunch of evidence deep under water. All of that slows down the investigation and gives an out-of-town scumbag time to amscray."

"Amscray? Are you a Jersey mobster from the '50s?" Peter said, chuckling.

"Myco-whatever? Are you an Oxford tight-ass from the '90s? And I mean 1890s?" Kevin said, visibly pleased with himself by his rapid-fire comeback. "And, I will add, that said amscraying is particularly valuable if you're from somewhere where I don't think we even have an extradition treaty." He pursed his lips and gave a sharp nod as if that settled the matter.

"I still think we have 21 suspects," Stuart said.

"I agree," Laura said.

"And that does not make me happy when I am in a dark place, and I do not know who to trust. Other than you three, of course," Stuart said. "I believe there were only 12 on Agatha Christie's Orient Express."

"Yes, 12. But I hope this doesn't end with all 21 suspects involved!" Laura said, giving a short, tight laugh while running her fingers through her hair.

"Is that how *Murder on the Orient Express* ends?" Kevin said, looking genuinely shocked.

It was hot, almost unbearably so. They were unable to open the windows all day because of the smoke, and now especially so because of the storm. The lodge didn't have air conditioning anyway, but the power outage had stopped the big ceiling fans in the restaurant, which had at least stirred the air before. Now the air steadily became denser, heavier, hotter, more humid. Much more humid. Peter tried to make a quip about states of matter being on a continuum rather than just three, or four if you counted plasma, discrete states, and how they were experiencing the normally gaseous state of air become something else on its way to the fully liquid state. Nobody responded. Laura might have smiled weakly, but in the light and with his eyes, it was hard to tell as she was bent over her knitting. Stuart had angled the newspaper up to be able to see the crossword better, mostly hiding his face. Only Kevin was looking up. His face looked like a cooked ham. He stared straight forward, eyes glazed, expression blank.

Then he snapped out of it, giving his head a slight shake. He reached over, picked up the water jug, poured some water on his hands, and splashed it on his face. "This sucks."

"It does," Peter agreed.

Kevin was quiet again, water dripping off his face. Peter could hear Pippin panting under the table and thought about getting him some water, but instead he lapsed into a daydream, his thoughts gliding over the concepts of matter. In his mind's eye he saw a vacuum with no atoms in it way off to the left, and the densest naturally occurring matter way off to the right. He had recently read that the densest element was osmium, a metallic substance that weighed one hundred grams per teaspoon. He didn't know what it looked like, so he just pictured something shiny and extremely hard and heavy. Between the two extremes he pictured the osmium atoms gradually pulling apart and vanishing, like a colour fade tool in Photoshop, eventually resolving to blank nothing. The atoms wanted to stay together, to be closely bound together, but applying energy forced them apart.

Want to stay together.

Energy forcing apart.

And then his thoughts suddenly lurched to the side, crabwise.

He pictured people.

He thought maybe he had a solution.

This process was always mysterious to him. His mind would meander somewhere that was pleasant but felt irrelevant, and then it would leap across a void to an unseen path that had been running in parallel all along. He wished he understood it so he could harness it properly, but at least it existed at all.

Peter snapped out of his reverie and looked around him.

Laura was still knitting. Stuart was still doing the crossword. Kevin was still looking parboiled and vacant. Someone had given Pippin a bowl of water.

The storm continued outside but was now abating quickly. The thunder sounded increasingly distant. The wind and rain only came in short bursts. The sky was still dark, but the air was possibly less smoky. More of the lake was visible, although the distance was still a blue-grey blur.

Peter wiped the sweat off his face, stood up, and walked to the window.

"There wasn't too much rain. Probably not enough to put out any fires, but at least there was enough to wash the particulate matter out of the air," he said.

"So, maybe we can crack a window open?" Kevin asked.

"I don't see why not. But maybe let's ask one of the staff." Peter looked around and spotted Cam coming in from the lobby.

"Sure, go for it," Cam said in response to the question. "We just need to be careful not to set off the smoke detectors. And please close it again if you guys leave the room."

"Will do. Any update on dinner?"

Cam glanced at his watch. "Yeah, it's getting late. How about half an hour? I know John promised barbecue, but everyone's pretty distracted and stressed, so we're just going to put out a cold spread. Sandwich-type stuff and things from the fridge that need to get eaten before they go bad. Sound OK?"

"Perfect, thanks. I wondered when John talked about barbecuing. Being a good host now is much less important than saving the lodge so he can be a good host for many years ahead."

"On that note, John, Jacob, and I are just going out to check on the fire."

"The lightning might have started some new ones, and with the pumps off . . ." Peter trailed off.

"Yup."

CHAPTER
Twenty-Nine

Dinner was even more haphazard and casual than Cam had said it would be. At one point Evan came out of the kitchen and announced that anyone who was hungry could come in and help themselves to whatever they could scrounge. Evan's chef's whites were dirt- and soot-stained. His face was a mask of weariness and stress. He had just been out with some other staff digging another firebreak to try to block a new blaze on the far side of the lodge from the one on the road, which was also still burning. Pyotr stood up and said that they were eager to help, and that other guests probably were too. Evan waved him off with a thanks, maybe later, but they had it under control now.

The light was especially poor in the kitchen because the windows were much smaller. Peter and Laura found what they guessed might be a quinoa salad in a big bowl under plastic wrap. They didn't want to ask Evan. He was slumped in the corner, chin on his chest. Whether he was actually sleeping or just resting was hard to tell in that light. Kevin and Stuart found cold cuts, cheese, pickles, and lettuce. Peter overheard Kevin telling Stuart that he was going to teach him how to make a proper Dagwood sandwich. Stuart's response was polite but skeptical.

"What kind of rabbit food is that?" Kevin asked as they sat down at what was now "their table," near the window, by the angry wolverine.

"Quinoa salad," Peter said, having confirmed it in the better light of the restaurant.

Kevin grunted and then gingerly set down the two wobbly-looking, six-inch-high sandwiches he had constructed. He glanced at the window.

"Storm's just about blowed itself out. I'll eat this quick and then go look at the messed-up generators." Kevin maneuvered his sandwich and gaped his mouth to take a bite. "A real Dagwood is thicker," he said, his mouth full, crumbs of bread falling out of it. Stuart looked horrified. "But I didn't want to be a pig."

Peter wished he didn't have to conserve battery power on his phone, because Stuart's facial expression was priceless as he gingerly picked up his monster sandwich as if it were a piece of unexploded ordnance.

It was a moment of levity that marked a general uptick in the mood. The storm had ended, and the smoke was definitely thinner. A short while later John stopped by to check on them. He sounded optimistic about the firebreaks holding until morning when they could hopefully start landing planes again. That was so long as the smoke didn't build up again. Which he didn't think it would. This was in marked contrast to Evan's more dour statements. Noting that John had been overly optimistic before, and seeing that Evan was exhausted, which tended to bring out pessimism in people, Peter assumed the truth lay somewhere between.

Kevin chewed quickly and swallowed hard, his Adam's apple in violent motion as if he had just sent a whole egg down his throat. "Sounds good. Give me a sec, John. I'm gonna head out right away and look at those generators."

John nodded, not taking his eyes off the smoky sky.

After Kevin disappeared, the other three tried to play crazy eights, but fatigue was taking hold. It had been a long day. A long, exceptionally hard day. Peter kept looking for an opening to explain his epiphany to them, but somehow the time never felt right to blurt out, "I'm pretty sure I know who the killer and dog poisoner is." With the storm gone and the lack of noise from fans or music due to the power failure, he also worried they might be overheard. And there was always someone else nearby, like Ted coming to look out the window, or Pyotr stopping by to ask what game they were playing, or Molly clearing away their plates. Also, Peter was so tired that he was concerned about his ability to explain himself clearly. This could be tricky for him at the best of times.

They set their cards down, each waiting for someone else to suggest another round, but nobody did.

Stuart said very quietly, "Look at that." He was pointing out the window.

The sun was setting behind the lodge, on the opposite side from the view. The smoke had filtered the horizontal light and rendered it red, painting the clouds in the east. Even the surface of the lake was red. Points and splashes of flickering orange dotted the far shore where the fires were active. Everything else was dark. Red and orange. Black and grey. The world's colour palate had been reduced to a vision of hell and anarchy. Yet it was beautiful to behold.

They watched this for a long time. Everyone else in the restaurant gathered by the window. They were all silent. Even Pyotr. Peter assumed everyone was thinking the same thing — please let the fire and smoke stay away until morning.

Kevin returned just as they were beginning to worry. Dusk was long and slow, so he wasn't in danger of running out of light right away, but none of them could understand what was taking so long. And they all wanted to go to bed. The restaurant had emptied out after the colour faded from the clouds.

"Sorry, guys, you didn't need to wait for me. John's still there trying to fix it, but I'm pretty useless with that stuff."

"Fix the backup generator? I thought the controls were smashed," Peter said.

"The generator's totally buggered. I'm talking about the radio. The UHF. Someone has taken a wrench or something to it too. John thinks maybe, just maybe, he can get it working again. Knows something about electronics."

"The radio? Are you serious?" Peter asked.

"No, I'm joking," Kevin said, sighing deeply. "Of course, I'm flipping serious."

"Sorry. It's just so . . ."

"Messed up? Yes, it is. Totally friggin' messed up."

"Where's the radio?" Peter asked.

"In John's office. But it wasn't locked. So, anyone could get in there. Happened sometime since mid-afternoon because that was the last time John went in to talk to the wildfire service people."

The restaurant was semi-dark now, so Peter couldn't make out anyone's faces. They were all quiet for a long moment.

"Let's try to get some sleep," Kevin finally said. "We'll secure the door as best we can."

The other three started to stand but Peter remained seated. He said, "I know who it is. At least I think I do."

They all sat down again.

CHAPTER
Thirty

"**T**he bald eye-patch guy?" Kevin asked.

"Yes, Cam, the bartender. Cameron Schmidt."

"And how do you know this?"

Peter noted that Kevin suddenly sounded crisp and alert. The beer, the sleep deprivation, and the stress of the day seemed to be handicaps he could push to the side and lock away in some compartment. At least temporarily. He supposed it was the same for him if a life-threatening emergency came into the clinic at the end of a crazy day.

"'Know' is overstating. 'Think' is more accurate. It's the theory that makes the most sense."

"I'm all ears." Kevin adjusted his seat and leaned forward.

In the gloom, Peter could see Laura and Stuart looking intently at him too. Pippin had gotten up when the others did, and now lay back down again under the table with a soft grunt.

"I believe it's a love triangle. Cam was jealous of Ned, who was in a relationship with Molly. Jealousy is one of the most common motivations for murder. And he had the means and opportunity. I also got information from Dwayne that Cam was in Stoney for weapons charges."

"I might quibble with how common jealousy murders are later," Kevin said. "But let's take that at face value and move on. So, in a jealous rage he killed three people in a weirdly elaborate sniper plot?"

"Like you said yourself, Kev, it was to try to cover it up. He probably hoped it would take even longer to recover the bodies up here. He knew that part of the lake was deep. It was premeditated. Not really a jealous rage, but the colder, more calculated kind."

"And how do you know Cam loves Molly? Because that seems to be the key element your theory hinges on. I agree that he had the means and the opportunity, but I need a little more convincing on the motive."

"And what about the dogs?" Laura said.

"The dog part is simple. He's jealous of John too. I've seen John hug Molly in what I assume was an innocent way, just friendly and supportive, but a jealous mind wouldn't see it that way. I also think we need to worry that he might go after Evan next. Evan pays a lot of attention to Molly."

"One weird theory at a time, dear. Back to the dogs. So, he'd hurt the dogs rather than John?"

"We've always believed the poisoning wasn't the act of someone who hated dogs, but of someone trying to get at John and didn't have the conscience to care about the dogs."

"But why wouldn't he just shoot him too?" Laura pursued.

"If he had shot John, there'd be a lower chance of being able to shoot Ned, who he hated far more, because the police would be crawling all over the lodge, questioning everyone. And if he tried to shoot John after shooting Ned, it would increase the chance of him getting caught. This was very clever. Hurt John in such a way that nobody, well, almost nobody, connects the crimes. And the timeline indicates the dog poisoning was first, which was clever too. Do the damage without drawing too much attention."

"Uh-huh. But back to Cam loves Molly," Kevin said.

"You saw Cam and Molly arguing, right?" Peter answered.

"Sure, but . . ." Kevin began to say, but was interrupted by a sudden growl from Pippin. The dog stood up and stared toward the dimly visible lobby door.

"What is it?" Peter asked.

Then there was a gunshot, followed by a scream. A man's scream. Something falling. Something heavy tumbling.

"What the . . . ?" Kevin jumped to his feet.

Footsteps.

Another scream, this time a woman.

Shouts.

Footsteps now approaching quickly.

All four of them were standing now. Kevin took some steps toward the lobby door.

Stuart had activated the flashlight on his phone.

Molly burst into the room, shouting, "Doctor! We need a doctor!"

Peter had spent his entire professional life worrying about a moment like this. Every time there was a request on an aircraft for a doctor, he'd look nervously about him, unsure what he would do if nobody stepped forward. Could a veterinarian be useful in a human emergency? Most airplane emergencies were heart attacks, and that was one of the few medical problems veterinary patients didn't share. They never clogged their arteries. But shot . . .

An image of Pippin from last year flashed across his mind. Blood-soaked. Carried into the clinic by Laura. Shot.

All this in a flash before Peter blurted out, "Has John been shot?" He should have told Kevin of his suspicions sooner. Now it was too late.

Stuart's flashlight lit Molly's face. Her expression was wild. The shadow of her head was enormous against the far wall.

"John? No! Cam! Cam's been shot!"

CHAPTER
Thirty-One

"**W**here is he?" Kevin asked.

"Onthestairs," Molly said, slamming all three words together. She spun around and pointed.

"Who did it?" Kevin asked.

"Don't know. It's dark. Shot came from the upstairs hall."

By our rooms, Peter thought.

"I was in the lobby, below the stairs," Molly went on, breathless, still speaking quickly. "Come quick, Dr. Bannerman! I think he's alive."

Peter was going to protest but didn't. He knew Molly would have known whether any of the other guests were doctors or nurses or paramedics or anything else more useful than a veterinarian in this situation. Ted, the American, was a dentist. A vet made much more sense.

There were shouts from upstairs and the sounds of doors opening and closing.

Kevin quickly said, "Laura and Stuart, get into the kitchen and bar the doors. I'm going with Pete."

"Grab a gun first from John's office?" Laura asked, pushing her chair aside forcefully.

"Local cops impounded them all. I'll be fine. Go!"

Peter and Kevin followed Molly across the restaurant, dodging taxidermy and tables.

Peter's mind was awhirl. Not Cam, then. But who? John? Jacob? Evan? Erin? Other staff? Or one of the Belarusians? Or an American? But none of that made sense. The faces all swirled together. His thoughts were a rapid-fire disjointed mishmash.

Then this: maybe Cam still. Maybe a love triangle still. Maybe he did kill Ned. Then Molly found out and shot Cam and is covering up?

Oh my god.

For the smallest fragment of a second, Peter considered shouting for Kevin to stop. But he didn't. What would he say?

And then they were in the lobby, where it was even darker. Molly reached behind the reception counter as she ran past. Peter's stomach lurched.

She pulled out a flashlight. It cast a pale-yellow circle of light on the bottom of the stairs.

Cam lay there, head down, eye patch askew. Blood, shiny, almost black in this light, oozed from a wound in his right shoulder.

He was breathing.

Peter ran up to him and knelt down. He checked Cam's pulse — rapid — and his colour — pale. He pulled off his blood-soaked T-shirt as quickly as he could while still being gentle enough not to disrupt the wound.

Where was the subclavian artery in humans? More medial and lower? This doesn't look arterial.

Peter balled up Cam's T-shirt and pressed it against the wound. Then he shouted at Molly, "Grab the first aid kit!"

"John's office!" She ran off.

Kevin was up the stairs, past Peter. Out of the corner of his eye he saw flashlight beams up there, criss-crossing in a confused jumble.

Good. Kevin will take charge up there. Calm everyone down. Look for clues in people's reactions.

Peter carefully lifted Cam's right shoulder to be able to look at the back. It was difficult to see in the poor light, but fortunately his eyes had improved so he was able to see something. There was a small hole halfway down Cam's back, the darkness of the hole contrasting with his pale skin. The exit wound. Some blood was pooled on the floor beneath it. It glistened in the small amount of available light.

Why is he unconscious and totally non-responsive? He didn't lose that much blood. Did shock cause loss of consciousness? Usually not this profound, at least not in animals.

Peter kept pressure on the entry wound with his right hand while exploring the back of Cam's head with his left hand. It came back sticky with blood.

He was knocked out by the fall. Concussion. Maybe subdural hemorrhage. Damn it.

Molly was back with the first aid kit and the flashlight. Peter rummaged around in the kit, not sure what he was hoping to find. Once the bleeding stopped, he could use the disinfectants and bandages to dress the wound.

Then he pulled out an EpiPen.

For anaphylaxis. Makes sense at the lodge. Cam could be in shock as well as concussed. Epi isn't the first choice in shock when you have other options, but better than nothing.

He plunged the EpiPen into Cam's thigh.

Then he took the flashlight from Molly and looked at his good eye. The light wasn't focused enough to allow for a proper examination, but at least he could see that the pupil constricted slightly.

"Good. They're not fixed and dilated," Peter said, realizing he hadn't told Molly anything yet.

"So, he'll live?" she asked, voice quavering.

"Too soon to say, but hopefully yes. I think the bullet missed the major arteries, so the big thing now is how hard he hit his head falling. No idea what the damage is, but it's knocked him out."

He checked the colour of Cam's gums. They were still pale, but not worse. Not white. So maybe the epinephrine helped.

Kevin appeared at the edge of the light, or at least his feet and legs did. The rest of him was shadow on shadow.

"How's he doing?"

"Alive," Peter replied. "But badly concussed, or maybe bleeding in the brain."

"John couldn't fix the radio. So, we've got to keep him alive until morning. I'm sure RCMP or MWS will come to check on us at first light because of the radio silence, so long as the fire doesn't flare up."

"John was upstairs?" Peter asked.

"No, I think he's on fire patrol. I told everyone to get into their rooms, bar their doors, and stay in there for now. I just don't know that everyone's accounted for. I didn't do a headcount, and it's even darker up there than it is here."

Peter nodded, although he doubted Kevin could see it. He wondered how to get Kevin alone to air his concern about Molly.

Cam made a noise, like a very low moan. Kevin and Molly heard it too and both bent forward to look. But Cam appeared to be otherwise unchanged. Peter checked his vitals again.

"Stable."

"Thank god," Molly said. She stifled a sob.

"OK, good," Kevin said. "Molly, what's the layout up there? I know you're not housekeeping, but do you know who's in which room?"

"Let me grab the book. John uses a ledger when guests arrive. Thinks it adds a homey touch." She said this as she ran over to the reception desk. "We have six rooms, three on either side of the hall. Four are occupied by guests for tonight and two by staff, one for male and one for female. Normally we're in the staff cabins, but John didn't think they were safe."

"Wow, you guys are packed tight. We've got four in our room, and we feel like sardines," Kevin said.

"Yeah, five of us girls, and six guys, but the plan was for shifts of two at a time to be up for fire protection." She paused. Peter heard the soft rustle of a book being leafed through. "OK, as you know, you guys are the first room on the right. Next to you are the two American guys, and next to them, the male staff. Across the hall from you are the Belarusians, then the two Canadian couples in the middle, and me and the girls at the end."

"Thank you. And there's an exit to the outside at the far end of the hall, right? I haven't been that way yet."

"Yes, there's a little sitting area there, a shared bathroom for the last two guest rooms, and then stairs down to the guest exit and the library. Plus, all the rooms have balconies. Yours are 'lake view' and the other side is 'forest view.'"

"Do you know who's on fire protection patrol now?" Kevin asked.

"I'm not sure, but John wrote up a roster. Hang on a sec. It's on his desk. I should have grabbed it before."

Peter took Cam's vital signs again.

Molly was back from the office quickly.

"Here it is. John and Evan between ten o'clock and midnight. I'm supposed to be on with Jacob at 4 a.m."

"OK, so those two won't be in their rooms, but everyone else would be?"

"I think so. I mean with the power out and the plan for an early start tomorrow, I'm not sure where else anyone would be."

All three of them were quiet. Peter could practically hear Kevin thinking in the dark, as if his neurons were making faint sparking noises. Peter checked to see if the bleeding from Cam's shoulder had been staunched. It was still oozing, so he continued to apply pressure.

"Molly?" Kevin finally said. "Who do you think did this?"

"I . . . I don't know. I really don't. Who would want to hurt Cam? He's so nice to everyone. Do you think this has something to do with the three people killed on the plane?"

Peter didn't believe her. She was hesitant with her first words but then spoke more confidently as she went on. That sounded like lying to him, although he knew he wasn't very good at reading people.

Kevin took a moment to reply. "Are you sure you don't even have a guess?"

"No, I can't. I don't know. I'm freaked out by everything that's happening."

"We all are." Kevin's tone was gentle. "But anything you can tell me that might be a clue could help. Anybody acting unusual today. Anything that caught your eye."

Molly sucked her breath in sharply. "Officer Gudmundurson, there's a gigantic forest fire, and a crazy storm, and a power failure, and a broken radio . . . The whole effing day has been 'unusual.'"

Peter was taken aback by the hard edge in her voice and looked up.

"I'm sorry, Officer. I didn't mean to sound like that. I'm just super stressed."

"No sweat. I get it." Kevin took a deep breath. "I guess I'm going to have to do a Hercule Poirot and call everyone into the restaurant for questioning. See who cracks. Whose story doesn't hold up."

"And who's not there," Peter added.

CHAPTER
Thirty-Two

P ippin.

In all the chaos, Peter had completely forgotten about Pippin. How could he forget him? He looked left and right in a sudden panic, but there he was. He could make out the distinctive shape of his dog, lying quietly on the floor of the lobby, just behind Molly.

Peter had an idea.

"I need water to start cleaning the wound. Can you get some from the kitchen, Molly?" he asked.

"The bathroom is closer."

"Actually, Laura and Stuart are in the kitchen, so I also wanted you to tell them it's safe to come here."

"Am I going to be safe going there?"

"The shooter is either hiding upstairs or went down the far stairs to the guest entrance. There's no way he can get to the restaurant without either passing us or going outside and then back in through the kitchen's back door, in which case we would have heard something from Laura and Stuart. So, from here to the kitchen through the restaurant is safe."

"OK." Molly sounded doubtful but got up and left as directed.

As soon as she was through the swinging restaurant doors Peter said, "I wanted her out of here so I can ask you about a plan I just thought of. I don't completely trust her."

"Oh? Tell me quick then."

"I can get Pippin to sniff for the gun. We just need to find the bullet to give him the scent. It went right through Cam."

"It should be in the far wall, or maybe the floor if the down angle was sharp," Kevin said.

"Yeah, the exit wound is quite a bit lower. It may even be in the floor right around here."

Kevin pulled out his phone, muttering, "Six percent battery."

He turned on the flashlight and began to pan around the floor at the foot of the stairs where Cam lay. As he did so he said, "Good thinking, Pete. Once I do a headcount, we'll know that it's safe, that the perp isn't roaming around here somewhere with the rifle. A smart gunman would have quickly stashed the rifle and then blended into the confused crowd up there after the shooting. We find the gun and we're much safer, and maybe one step closer to figuring out who pulled the trigger."

There was the sound of a door opening from upstairs, and footsteps.

Peter looked up. A shape loomed above them.

"Officer." It was Pyotr's voice. "What is plan? We are sitting goose up here."

"I'm going to gather everyone in the restaurant. We'll be safer together there. And then I can also see who is not there in case the gunman is still on the loose."

Smart, Peter thought. *Don't hint to anyone that we think the gunman discarded the rifle.*

Molly reappeared with Laura and Stuart, who were both holding kitchen knives.

"How is he?" Laura asked, bending down beside Peter.

"Alive, but unconscious and borderline shocky."

"OK, guys," Kevin said. "We're going to get everyone into the restaurant. Laura, you and Stuart stay with Cam. Pete will tell you what to do. Unless Pete thinks he can be moved?"

"No, not yet."

"Shouldn't I stay with him instead?" Molly asked.

Kevin shot Peter a quick glance, his face half-lit by a flashlight beam. "No," Kevin said. "I want you to go upstairs and round everyone up."

Peter showed Laura where to apply pressure to the wounds, and how to check Cam's colour. He asked her to also keep track of his pulse and respirations. Molly moved past them to go upstairs while Kevin spoke quietly to Stuart off to the side.

Peter turned on his phone's flashlight. The battery icon was flashing red. *Always charge as soon as you get the chance*, he thought, aggravated that he had allowed exhaustion and stress to interfere with that principle when they arrived at the lodge. He swept the light across the floor.

"What are you looking for?" Laura asked.

"The bullet."

"Why —" Laura was interrupted by a clamour of people moving and talking at the top of the stairs. Flashlight beams swept down on the four of them as they looked up. Peter was blinded. He squeezed his eyes shut. He was still sensitive to light.

There were gasps and a jumble of voices.

"Oh no!"

"Isn't that the bartender?"

"Is he alive?"

There was such a confusion of rapidly shifting bright light and black shadow that Peter had a hard time sorting out who was saying what.

Kevin reassured the crowd, "Yes, Cam's been shot, but Dr. Bannerman says he's stable and will be OK. Just move on into the restaurant, please, and I'll explain our plan. Keep together, please."

Molly was the last to pass by. She stopped and said, "OK, that's everyone except John and Evan."

"Great, thanks," Kevin said.

Peter considered which of the seventeen people — nine guests and eight remaining staff — who filed into the restaurant should be considered the top suspects. Could he rule any of them out?

And then the image of Marty Sullivan popped into his mind.

Maybe it wasn't safe to assume Pippin would only find a rifle rather than a rifle attached to a killer . . . He decided to keep this thought to himself. It was highly improbable and would only muddy the plan.

Molly stood there, looking at Cam.

"Please go in with the others, I'll be right there," Kevin said.

Molly's flashlight was trained on Cam. Peter couldn't see her face but heard her take a deep breath. There was a moment's silence and then she said "OK" quietly and left.

The room was dark again, other than the small circle of light from Peter's phone on the dark wood lobby floor.

"Here it is." A glint of brass was visible in a blackened hole in the wood.

"Why are you looking for the bullet?" Laura asked.

"I'm going to get Pippin to do some nosework so we can find the gun."

"That makes me nervous," Laura said.

"I get that, but isn't it better than waiting for the gunman to retrieve the gun, sneak up in the dark, and pick us off one by one?" Peter showed Pippin the bullet hole as he spoke, and quietly commanded, "Sniff."

"What if we miscounted? Or someone else from outside came in and shot Cam?" Laura asked.

"As much as I hate to admit it, Pete's right, sis," Kevin said. "The risks are much bigger if we don't find the gun. At some point I'm going to have to let someone go to the bathroom, or they'll make a diversion, or something, where they can grab the weapon again. We need to find it."

The door to the restaurant swung open. Two men stepped into the lobby. Peter could only see their silhouettes.

"Officer. Kirill and I help." It was Pyotr.

"Thank you, but it would be best if everyone stayed in the restaurant," Kevin said.

"We not afraid. We have training. We can hunt this man," Pyotr said, pulling a dagger out of a sheath on his belt. Stuart had turned his phone's flashlight on. The dagger caught the light and reflected it into Peter's eyes. It had a vicious serrated edge. It looked extremely sharp.

"Thank you, but right now, protecting the people in the restaurant is the best idea. And everyone is accounted for, so the man we hunt is in the restaurant anyway. I need to begin questioning, but if you can keep any eye out for anything suspicious, that would be very helpful, thank you so much." Peter smiled to himself at Kevin's effortless transition to his smooth, authoritative, professional persona. He wondered why he didn't insist on Pyotr surrendering his knife, but assumed Kevin knew what he was doing. In this regard anyway.

"OK, Officer. But say if need help. We have training." The knife went back into the sheath and the two men left the lobby.

Peter turned his attention back to Pippin. The dog was sitting up, alert, looking at him.

"He's got it," Peter said. "OK, Pippin, seek."

CHAPTER
Thirty-Three

"**I**'m coming too," Laura said.

"What? No," Peter said. He turned to Pippin. "Wait."

"You're going to be focused on Pippin. You know how you get tunnel vision in these situations. And speaking of vision, yours can't be a hundred percent yet. You need someone along to watch out for anything else."

"But . . ."

"No buts. Stuart can look after Cam, and Kevin is in charge of everyone in the restaurant."

"She has a point, Pete. It'll be much better with two of you," Kevin said. "I'll prop the restaurant door open, so I can keep an eye on Stu and make sure he's safe up here."

"I have a lot of battery still," Stuart said. "I can keep the light bright here. Then Kevin can also see the front door. We will all be fine. But you need someone with you. I think Laura is the perfect person. Small, quiet, very smart."

"Thank you, Stuart," Laura said. She stepped over to pet Pippin, who was waiting at the bottom of the stairs, looking up them, nostrils flaring.

"I suppose," Peter said, standing up.

His phone's flashlight gave out.

"Do you have a working flashlight, Laura?"

"Yes, I have about 20 percent battery, but we won't use it. Pippin can navigate completely by smell, so we'll just follow him closely and let our eyes adjust to the dark. That way we'll be less obvious if anyone is out there."

"See, Pete? Laura's got this," Kevin said. "Stu, you OK here? I'm going to head into the restaurant now and make sure the Belarusskis haven't tied everyone up."

"Yes, I am fine. I have a little bit of first aid training from when I was in the Boy Scouts."

"I didn't know you were a Boy Scout," Kevin said.

"There are many things you do not know about me," Stuart replied, flashing a tense smile before turning to take a pulse rate on Cam.

Pippin moved up the stairs quickly and then slowed down when he got to the upstairs hallway. It was pitch dark ahead, with the only light coming from Stuart, behind them at the bottom of the stairs. It felt like entering a coal mine.

He could feel Laura on his right and feel and hear Pippin on his left, now moving slowly and sniffing continuously. They passed one set of doors, then another, and then a third.

The rifle's not in any of the rooms, Peter thought, but that made sense as all the rooms had been occupied at the time of the shooting, so unless a whole group of guests was in cahoots with the killer, he wouldn't have run back into the room carrying the rifle. And then it occurred to him, that even without a rifle, someone dashing back into one of the rooms after the shooting would look odd to their roommates, unless they had the excuse that they had stepped out for a smoke — the Belarusians for sure were smokers — or to use the bathroom. This train of thought made him uneasy. Something didn't add up.

They came to the sitting area on the landing at the far end of the hall, and the bathroom the last two guest rooms shared, the ones that had been occupied by staff.

Pippin sniffed at the bathroom door and then moved quickly through the sitting area to the top of the back stairs.

Peter wondered how they were going to handle going down the stairs to the guest exit in the dark, but as Laura had predicted, his eyes were adjusting, and he could sense the railing as much as actually see it.

There was a sound from the bottom of the stairs. Indistinct. Soft.

Peter put his hand on Pippin to stop him from going down yet.

He could tell Laura was holding her breath. He strained to listen for anything else.

Nothing.

He leaned toward Laura and cupped his hands around her ear. He breathed, "What do you think?"

She did the same in reverse and whispered in his ear, "Don't know. Let's go down slow. Hope there are no squeaky steps."

Peter nodded, although he knew she wouldn't be able to see it. He took his hand off Pippin. The three of them, first Pippin, then Peter, then Laura, started to go down the stairs, one slow step at a time. Pippin either sensed the need to go slow or needed to anyway to follow the scent trail.

They arrived at the bottom. To the left was the door to the outside. To the right was a small guest library and lounge. Beyond the library, Peter knew there was a narrow hallway that led past what he thought were storage rooms, emerging into the lobby beside the reception desk. John's office was somewhere there too, behind reception. But he wasn't sure if it had a door into that hall too. There was also a bathroom for restaurant patrons to use near reception, but his memory was hazy on its exact location. Stress. Too much stress. Normally he had a near-photographic memory.

There was faint light from a window in the outside door. In the distance Peter could see flames. He had forgotten about the fires.

Pippin sniffed the door carefully and then turned toward the library.

Peter tried to recall the layout of that room. He was pretty sure the doors were on the middle on each side, so that if there was light, and both the doors were open, you could see through the library, down the hallway all the way to reception. He remembered the right side of the room had two big leather armchairs, reading lamps, and magazine racks. The left side had a table, several smaller chairs, and bookcases covering the walls. There was taxidermy in this room too. He thought he remembered an owl and a fox on the bookshelves and something larger against the wall behind the reading chairs. Was it a caribou? Yes, definitely a caribou. Not that it mattered.

The door was closed. It was a solid wooden door.

Peter turned the knob, hoping it wouldn't creak. It didn't. The door swung easily and noiselessly into the library.

Pippin brushed past him. Laura followed. The dim light from the window in the exit door didn't reach the library. It was blackest black. The far door must have been closed too as otherwise some of the light from Stuart's phone in the lobby would have been faintly visible in the distance.

Laura touched Peter's shoulder and gave it a light squeeze to signal him to stop. He heard Pippin stop as well. He listened.

There was the tick of a clock, and a murmur of heavily muffled voices, probably from the restaurant. He wondered briefly whether Kevin was grilling the guests, pacing back and forth like Hercule Poirot, twirling his beard braid.

He could also hear the wind outside. It had picked up again. That wasn't good.

He felt Laura stiffen. She squeezed his shoulder a little harder.

There was something else. The sound of someone breathing very quietly? Maybe?

He realized with a sudden tightening of his stomach that although the room was dark, the three of them were silhouetted against the faint light in the doorway.

"Come in," said a voice. Peter recognized it but couldn't place it.

"Zealandia," Laura said, half to herself.

CHAPTER
Thirty-Four

Zealandia? Peter thought.

Before he could try to make sense of that, the voice spoke again. "Please step inside and close the door behind you. I am disappointed that it is you, Dr. Bannerman. I was hoping for your brother-in-law, the cop. A cop, I can shoot. A vet, no. I love animals too much."

Now Peter knew.

They did as they were asked. Once Peter closed the door the room was plunged into complete darkness.

There was the sudden flare of a match from the right, first illuminating a man's hand and a ghastly-looking head of a caribou behind it and then moving to reveal the top of a white apron, and the lower half of a face with two stretched earlobes with large black plugs.

Evan Lundquist.

He lit a cigarette and shook the match out. The room was dark again other than an orange glow from the tip of the cigarette.

"Hang on a sec," he said.

A rustle and a click.

Then Peter and Laura were blinking in the light of a lantern on a small round wooden table beside Evan's chair. It was one of those battery-powered Coleman camping lanterns.

"Made sure it had fresh batteries before I took out the generators," Evan said.

Peter and Laura stood silently. Pippin sat down beside Peter. He could feel the dog's tension.

Evan regarded them for a moment and then said, "How's Schmidt? Dead, I hope."

More on instinct than by forethought Peter said, "Yes. Now you have another murder on your record."

"Doesn't matter. I'd get life anyway. One, three, six, twelve murders. Doesn't matter." He took a long drag from his cigarette and turned his head to blow the smoke toward the caribou. "Life if I don't die here tonight, that is, and if they catch me alive."

Peter was about to blurt how he possibly thought he could escape, but Laura spoke first.

"You love Molly, don't you?" She said this softly. Peter considered "love" the wrong word for the violent, evil obsession Evan had, but he understood why Laura used it.

Evan tilted his head slightly, frowned, and then smiled. "You know, you look a little like her." He took another puff. "But yes. Always have. Always will. And she loves me too."

"Did she tell you that?" Laura asked, voice still gentle.

"A long time ago, yes. And then . . . But it doesn't matter. We were just about to get together again when then that fucking Australian . . ."

"Ned Fromm?"

"Yes, Ned fucking Fromm. He waltzes into our lives and . . ." Evan screwed his eyes shut and set the rifle on his lap.

Is this my chance? Peter thought. He was on the cusp of jumping for the gun when Evan opened his eyes again and shook his head. "But now that fucker's dead as fucking dead can be." He laughed.

"And Cam?" Laura asked.

"He was in there right away, the prick. Pretended to be my friend."

"In there? As in comforting Molly?"

Evan snorted. "Comforting? Sure, you can call it that. But I know his game."

"And you think killing them will bring Molly back to you?"

Evan took several slow puffs and looked at the floor.

The mantel clock seemed to be ticking louder than before. The wind was definitely louder. Peter could hear his own pulse in his temples.

"Eventually, yes, I do. Murder, like love, is passion. It comes from the same place. I'm taking her into the woods with me. I know how to survive out there. I've learned a lot working here." He held his hand up. "I know what you're going to say. They'll come looking for us. They will. I know. That's the point. The world is going to shit. You guys know that. Don't lie to yourselves. Either we go down weak with this dying world, or we go down strong on our own. If they find us, it will be Romeo and Juliet. Passion, love, death. Together in eternity. She'll see the truth, the deep truth, before they come. She has to. My Juliet."

Peter bit his tongue. He so wanted to rebut this. This was so twisted, so insane, so disconnected from reality. But as Laura didn't say anything in response, he thought the better of it.

Evan stubbed his cigarette out on the floor, picked up the rifle and lantern, and stood up.

"OK, enough chit-chat. Where is everyone else?"

"In the restaurant . . ."

Evan interrupted him with a laugh. "That is awesome. Best news of the evening so far. Saves us from having to head out in the dark. We can wait till dawn now. This makes it much easier to stop you guys from following us. Dawn was Plan A anyway, but I couldn't pass up that beautiful opportunity to take Cam out. Fucking prick . . ." He took a deep breath. "Anyway. Everyone's there? Every last person?"

"Except Stuart who is by the front door with . . . the body. And I imagine John is still out watching the fire line. By the way, how did you leave him?"

"I just said I was going to check over at the far side of the lodge, because the wind was picking up. It was the perfect excuse. Anyway, let's go." He waved the tip of the rifle at them and pointed at the far door.

"That's a good dog," he said, smiling at Pippin as they turned toward the door.

"Yes, he is," Peter said.

"I love dogs."

"Then why did you try to kill John's dogs?"

Evan looked genuinely confused. "John's dogs? Atlas and them? I had nothing to do with that. How could you think that, Dr. Bannerman? Like I said, I love dogs. Go." He nudged Peter with the barrel of his rifle.

Passing into the hallway they could see Stuart's light ahead. Peter had no doubt Evan would put a bullet in Cam's head if he knew he was still alive.

"Peter!" Stuart said.

Peter held his finger to his lips, knowing Evan wouldn't be able to see the gesture from behind, especially with Laura in between. Cam looked the same as he had before. The movement of his chest with his slow breaths was only perceptible if you watched carefully.

"You," Evan said to Stuart when he saw him. "Into the restaurant. No need to watch the door anymore. Or the dead asshole."

Stuart's eyes widened and his mouth opened slightly, but Peter could tell he had comprehended the situation immediately.

Stuart, Peter, Laura, and Pippin walked into the restaurant. Someone had lit candles, presumably to save on flashlight battery power. They lent an eerie flickering glow to the various anxious faces gathered around a cluster of tables in the centre, under the antique dogsled.

Kevin turned around and was just beginning to say, "Hey guys, wha—" when he saw Evan and his rifle. He reached for a kitchen knife tucked in his belt.

Molly gasped.

There was a general murmur. And then a thick silence.

"Easy, Officer," Evan said. "Nice and slow. Drop the knife on the floor and hands up where I can see them."

Kevin eyed him. He didn't move. His hand remained on the hilt of the knife.

Evan took a step forward and in one startlingly quick and fluid motion swung the rifle by the barrel so that the butt connected with the side of Kevin's head. He crumpled to the floor like a ragdoll.

"Kevin!" Laura shouted.

"Shut up!" Evan said, pointing the rifle toward her.

Molly began to sob loudly.

"You too, Mol, shut up. Nothing to be sad about here. You're going to help me now."

She shook her head violently. "No, Evan, no."

"Yes. Help me, or someone else gets a bullet. I've got lots. As I was telling Dr. Bannerman, what's one more murder?"

Silence.

"I take that as a yes. OK, get the duct tape we keep behind the bar. Please and thank you. In the meantime, you three" — he inclined his head to Peter, Laura, and Stuart — "grab seats. And everyone arrange their chairs in a big semicircle around me. Just like in kindergarten. I'm the teacher." He laughed.

Nobody moved.

"Now!" he shouted and raised his rifle to aim at Jacob's head. He lifted it slightly and shot at a post behind him, hitting a stuffed grouse. The shot echoed in the large room, accentuating the moment of shocked silence that followed.

Then gasps and rapid shuffling and scraping of chairs into place. As demanded, they were in a large semicircle facing Evan, who sat down now as well, near the bar.

"Erin and Jacob, move the tables to the side so I can see everyone nice and clear. And put some of the candles on the bar here. For mood lighting." He laughed again. "And Mol, with that duct tape, I want you to tape up everyone's wrists together behind their chair backs. I hope nobody's dumb enough to try anything when I'm the only one with a gun, but you never know who might feel like being a martyr tonight."

"Evan, please," Molly said.

"Molly, please. Do as I said and nobody else has to die. Up to you." Evan shrugged. "I really don't mind blowing a few heads off, but I'm guessing you'd mind. And so would the owners of the heads."

It took about ten minutes, but then everyone had their hands taped up behind their backs. Peter noted that it wasn't especially tight. Pippin was under his chair, very quiet.

"For you, Mol, just keep your hands on your lap. I don't feel like setting the Mauser down to tape yours. And you have beautiful hands."

"Evan," Molly said quietly, between sobs, as she sat down. "How is this supposed to end?"

"You don't have to worry about that. It's all planned. Trust me. We'll head out just before daybreak. We'll take one of the boats. Disable the others. I have supplies stashed."

"What do you mean? Where are we going?" she said, alarm replacing sadness in her voice.

"Shh," Evan said. "Hush now. No more talking."

Time began to pass in an odd formless way. Evan said nothing further. He just hummed and whistled lightly. Everyone else was quiet. Kevin lay on the floor, breathing but unconscious. He moaned once or twice, causing Evan to chuckle, but he didn't move. Peter was grateful Evan hadn't followed up on his statement regarding not minding killing cops. Not yet anyway. He was probably too busy running through his crazy Romeo and Juliet fantasy in his mind. But if Kevin woke up and tried to move . . .

It felt like they had been sitting a very long time. Maybe it was after midnight already? He tried to calculate how quickly candles would burn down.

Then he remembered something about midnight.

CHAPTER
Thirty-Five

A short while later there was a sound from the lobby. Everyone turned to look.

John appeared at the door. "What the . . ."

Bang.

Evan shot him in the left leg.

"Motherfucker!" John hollered as he dropped to the ground.

The huskies next door in the conference room began to howl.

Pyotr leapt forward, hands still taped behind his back, but he cleared them over the back of the chair. He hurled himself at Evan. Head aiming for his stomach.

Evan whipped around and struck Pyotr on the head with the barrel of his rifle. The Belarusian fell to the floor.

Peter had hoped that when John returned from his shift at midnight, he would have noticed or sensed something and would have snuck in cautiously instead and overpowered Evan. No such luck.

"Sorry, John. Itchy trigger finger. And sorry, Pyotr, but that was stupid. Really stupid."

"Jesus H! Motherfucker!" John was writhing on the ground, clutching his thigh.

Pyotr groaned.

"Let me help them," Peter said.

"Sit tight, Doc. Doubt I hit an artery. And the other one is fine. Anyway, collateral damage. Happened before. Might happen again."

John took some ragged breaths and half sat up. "Don't know what the hell's . . . going on here." His words came out in gasps. "But wind's . . . really . . . picked up . . . May have to . . . evacuate soon."

Evan cocked his head. "How close is the fire?"

John winced and adjusted his position. "Not . . . sure now. Maybe . . . two hundred . . . metres from the . . . north side."

"Plenty of time. We're waiting."

John groaned and gripped his leg tightly.

"Evan, please," Peter said.

"He'll be fine. Drama queen."

Peter was to Evan's furthest right, nearest John and the door. From his angle he could see one of the big windows. He thought he caught sight of something moving out there. Probably just the wind in the trees.

Then he saw it again. He sensed that Laura saw it too because she shifted slightly in her seat.

Someone was in the gloom outside the lodge. They were moving toward the kitchen.

Someone with a large white beard.

Sullivan saw that Peter had noticed him. He held his finger to his lips. He raised the rifle in his hands and pointed toward the outside kitchen door.

"Evan, really, please. You can keep the gun pointed at my head. Just let me help these guys."

"I may not have gone to vet college, but I'm not stupid. I've read the news about you. I know you think you're an amateur detective. These two losers will be fine without your vet help. You're planning something. Come to think of it, it makes sense to put you more in the cop category than vet category. So, I'm going to keep the gun on you anyway, while you stay sitting."

"Then we have a good old-fashioned Mexican stand-off, Evan," came a booming voice from the kitchen door.

A tremor of shock ran through the group. There were several gasps and a quiet "Who the fuck is this now?" from Ted.

"Marty," Evan said slowly, drawing out each syllable, "is that you?"

"Of course it is."

Peter saw a flicker of fear on Evan's face.

"We do have a stand-off. I don't mind dying. But I presume Dr. Bannerman minds. Slowly move round to where I can see you. And lower your gun."

"My bullet will be zipping through your puny brain before you can pull the trigger, Lundquist. You've got until the count of three to lower *your* gun before I engage in some frontier justice. I'm sure Corporal Gudmundurson will understand."

Pyotr suddenly stood up. Evan's eyes flickered away from Peter toward the Belarusian. In that instant Molly flew at him. Before Evan could react, she had knocked the rifle to the floor.

Sullivan was on top of him in a blink of an eye later.

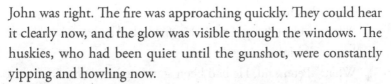

John was right. The fire was approaching quickly. They could hear it clearly now, and the glow was visible through the windows. The huskies, who had been quiet until the gunshot, were constantly yipping and howling now.

Kevin came to during the commotion. He was confused and could only watch as Evan was trussed up. Once this was done and John's wound had been bound, they all headed quickly down to the beach, taking Cam in a makeshift stretcher fashioned from blankets. Despite the goose egg on the side of his forehead, Pyotr insisted on helping to carry him. Kevin limped along with Laura's help. Sullivan's dog,

Dancer, was tied up outside the kitchen and joined them. Nicole led the seven huskies down using improvised leashes. Peter couldn't help but think that she looked like a Manhattan dog-walker lost in the wilderness. Pippin was excited to see all the dogs but stuck close to Peter.

The dogs, the stretcher, the wounded, the lame, the tied up . . . All the people and animals descending to the shore looked like a demented parade in the flickering light of the fire. Hieronymus Bosch.

From the lakeside they could see the scale of the renewed fire. The fires across the lake appeared to have settled. But behind them, a tremendous wall of flame towered over the lodge like a vindictive god.

John directed people to get the canoes and the motorboats ready in case they had to take to the water. The motorboats had hardly any fuel in them, but it was better than nothing. Peter noted that there wasn't nearly enough space on the canoes and motorboats for everyone, especially with the dogs and with Cam on a stretcher. And it was too deep here to wade far enough to make a difference.

Sullivan came up to Kevin when he was done arranging the boats. He handed his rifle to Kevin and extended both of his arms straight out toward him.

"You can arrest me now too, officer. Or just leave me behind if the fire reaches here."

"What are you talking about?" Kevin blinked and shook his head.

"I poisoned John's dogs."

"What?" Peter said. He had been standing beside Kevin. Kevin looked deeply confused.

"It was wrong of me. I thought I got the dose right to just make them sick. I don't know why some got so much more sick. I feel terrible. I just wanted the police to investigate and then take Comet's death seriously. I'm sure she was poisoned too."

"I don't understand," Kevin said, glancing at Peter.

Peter frowned and nodded. "Some dogs ate a lot more —"

He was interrupted by a tremendous noise. A whoosh like a rocket igniting. They all turned to look.

The lodge had caught fire. In seconds it was ablaze with such intensity that everyone stepped back toward the water. They squinted against the brightness, wincing at the heat.

John yelled something Peter couldn't make out.

"In the boats!" Peter heard him clearly now. He wondered how they were going to manage this *Titanic* lifeboat situation.

Then Kevin spoke up. "Strong swimmers, stick by me. We're going to the end of the dock. We'll take one canoe and take turns hanging onto the sides." His voice was weak and shaky, but still had a ring of authority to it.

This struck Peter as a crazy idea. But he didn't have a better one.

All three Belarusians stepped forward, as did two of the Canadians, both Filipina housekeepers, and Jacob.

Peter saw Cam's face. He was conscious. He looked utterly bewildered.

Pippin began barking. Peter looked at him. Pippin normally remained very calm in a crisis. The dog was half in the water, barking out at the lake.

Peter looked.

Then he saw it. First one, then two, then eight or more lights moving toward them.

"Hey! Guys! Look!" he shouted to the others.

Moments later he could hear outboard motors.

Several people pointed their flashlights out to the lake, their beams white bands dancing across the black and orange water.

Finally, Peter could make out a face in the lead boat.

It was Lawrence Littlebear.

"I guess it was a good thing you guys turned off your radio," Lawrence said, grinning, when he was close enough to be heard.

"Otherwise, we wouldn't have gotten all worried. Old Agnes Simpson, she said, take all the boats to the lodge. That fire over there is going to move fast, she said. I always listen to her."

He hauled Peter onto his boat and gave him a hug. Then he noticed Cam on the stretcher and Evan with his hands tied. He looked at Peter, raising his eyebrows.

Peter shrugged. "Long story, Lawrence. Really long story."

"Well, good thing I love long stories, cousin. And we got lots of time now."

CHAPTER
Thirty-Six

M uch of the southern end of Dragonfly Lake was still obscured by smoke, but Peter was able to make out the black smouldering remains of the lodge as the plane banked and began to climb. He shook his head with a lingering sense of disbelief. He felt guilty that his first thought was a mournful one regarding his lost tent and sleeping bag. There had been no way to go back. The plane banked again, and he could now see the ruined Friendly Bear Lodge as well. The amount of destruction was astonishing. Not just the two lodges, but so much forest. At least the DLFN community had been spared the worst of it.

And then the dead, and the injured. The murders weren't connected to the fire, but it all ran together in Peter's mind now as the plane climbed further and Dragonfly Lake began to disappear from view.

Three dead and one gravely injured.

All because of one man's distorted view of love, fatally poisoned by obsession and jealousy.

Kevin was beside him, gripping the armrests. He declined Peter's invitation to look out the window. Laura, across the aisle, was looking out her window, as was Stuart, leaning over Laura. Both were quiet.

After they reached cruising altitude and Kevin relaxed a tiny bit, Peter asked, "Are they going to charge Sullivan?"

"Todd's call, but I doubt it. Mitigating circumstances and all that." Kevin was still staring straight ahead. Laura and Stuart had both pulled out books.

"There was so much going on when we arrived at DLFN that I forgot to ask, but did you find out how Sullivan ended up at the lodge when he did?"

Kevin smiled a small tense smile. "Lucky break for us, eh? Turns out his cabin had burned down, so he dragged his other canoe back through the woods to Dragonfly, figuring he could hole up at the lodge until the fires ended. As he approached it, he could see Evan and his gun through the windows. Didn't know about the love triangle thing — good call on that by the way, Pete, even if you didn't get the players completely right — but apparently never trusted Evan and figured he probably wasn't performing a public service with his Mauser there in the restaurant." Kevin relaxed more as he spoke and chuckled at his own joke when he finished.

"And why he was out at Parsons? No chance he torched Friendly Bear, is there? Remember that empty jerrycan?"

"No, that wasn't arson after all. That Bev woman, the owner of Friendly Bear, was out to lunch. Apparently, she's out to lunch a lot. And Sullivan's canoe trip? Just like he said, it seems. Just showing his pup the trapline."

"That reminds me, any idea what happened with his other dog's death? Are the local Mounties going to investigate that now?"

"Doubt it. Guy's a bit of a loon. In talking to Todd, the leading theory is that he accidentally poisoned her himself with bad food. Maybe he realized that at some level and was overcompensating with his crusade. Or secretly wanting to get caught to punish himself. But it doesn't matter. Sullivan will drop it now. He knows he's on thin ice."

"Wild coincidence, these two crimes at the same time," Peter said. He looked out the window, hoping to see the lakes and forest, but it was cloudy. A good thing for the remaining fires, he supposed.

"It's that French fish thing you always talk about," Kevin said.

"French fish thing? Oh, you mean a Poisson clump?"

"Yeah, that thing. Where people think that just because two similar things happen together, they must be related. Even though they could be coincidences."

"You're right, it was a Poisson clump." Peter still wished he had been completely right, but at least he was partially right.

They were quiet for a few minutes while the flight attendant passed around small plastic cups of water.

"The other thing that's been bugging me is what happened around DLFN," Peter said after he took a few sips. "Why did Evan leave the first rifle, the murder weapon, there where it would be easy to find? Why not sink it in the lake? And why take that shot at us from by the community that morning I visited Lawrence?"

Kevin snorted. "Come on, Pete. This should be like two plus two for you."

"Wanted to make it look like someone from the community was the killer?"

"Bingo. Especially with Edna and that hydro guy being possible targets. Could have been plausible. But totally amateur. Todd and Emily and them saw through it right away."

"Speaking of rifles, Kev, do you know how Evan learned to shoot like that? I mean specifically the shot that killed Ned Fromm, the pilot," Peter said before finishing his water.

"In Zealandia, that little town in Saskatchewan where he and Molly grew up," Kevin said. "Evan goes back every fall to go duck and goose hunting with his dad. He's been hunting since he was a boy."

"Come to think of it, he mentioned hunting to us once. Remember, the venison he served you?"

"Right. And it was delicious. Back in Zealandia, that's how he started on the path to becoming a chef. He learned to smoke the goose breasts and make duck jerky when he was a teen and got inspired."

"Duck jerky —" Peter was interrupted when the aircraft hit a small patch of turbulence. Kevin gripped his water cup tightly. He looked like he wanted to say something else but waited until the air was smooth again.

"Yeah, duck jerky. Heavenly stuff. And that's where the whole drama with Molly started. Small dating pool in a town like that. He always believed they were fated to be together. They did date for a while around the time they came up to Dragonfly."

"But then Ned . . ." Peter said.

"But then Ned." Kevin agreed.

"And where does Cam fit in?"

"They haven't been able to interview him yet. Still in the ICU. But best as everyone can figure he might have had a little bit of a thing for Molly too. Emphasis on might. But regardless he was protective, and she definitely saw him as a big brother."

"Maybe a love quadrangle then?"

"Quadrangle? Regular people say square. But no, not really, more like one of those squishy squares where one side is really short."

"Trapezoid?"

"Sure, if it makes you happy."

"When you saw them argue, do you know what that was about?"

"Molly says Cam was warning her about Evan, but she didn't want to believe him. It looks like Cam was playing amateur detective. Kind of like you, but even more amateur, if that's possible."

"Hard to imagine," Peter said, chuckling.

"Isn't it? But anyway. He might have started with suspicions about John regarding the dogs, which would explain why he warned you not to fully trust him. And I'm just speculating here, but he might have originally wondered about John and his guns and the plane and whether he had something for Molly too. But it's only the suspicions about Evan we know about."

"He told Molly that he suspected Evan of murder and dog poisoning?"

"Not dog poisoning, and he didn't tell her outright about murder. He just told her that Evan was not to be trusted and to be careful around him because he might become violent. She couldn't believe that about him, so that's why they argued."

Peter shook his head. As much as he tried to study people, he still mostly did not understand them.

"But changing the subject, there's something I forgot to ask you," Kevin said. "What about the sick huskies, especially the lead one? Do you know how they're doing?"

"Yes, I spoke to Karla just before we took off. Atlas looks like he's going to be able to leave the hospital tomorrow. Incidentally, the lab report came back from St. B. and confirmed the PCP. If Sullivan hadn't confessed, it would have been handy info."

Kevin nodded. "Would have put a big hole in my Belarusski mushroom theory."

"And my xylitol theory. I didn't mention this to any of you, but I was beginning to wonder about John's sugar free diet and . . . Well, anyway, back to Atlas. He won't be able to race again, and he's going to need regular monitoring, so he should stay in the south. John wants to find someone to adopt him."

Stuart looked up from his book and turned to face Kevin. "You should adopt him."

"I agree," Laura said. "That's two votes for Atlas living with Kevin. Pippin would love a friend."

"Make it three votes," Peter said, grinning at his brother-in-law.

The plane's engines thrummed while Kevin stared at the back of the seat in front of him.

He sighed, and shaking his head slowly said, "Make it four."

Peter looked at his brother-in-law. Kevin was smiling.

Here's a sneak preview of Philipp Schott's next
Dr. Bannerman Vet Mystery:

Three Bengal Kittens

PROLOGUE

They were hungry. Very hungry. Normally the food man filled their bowls two times a day. The first time was after he got out of his bed and made his hot black liquid. They would mew at him and wind around his legs. But he insisted on having his hot black liquid first. Then one morning he did not get out of his bed. They mewed at him and danced on his chest. But he still did not get out of bed. This happened before when the food man had been looking at his noisy light box all through the night. But later, in the middle of the day, he always got out of his bed and filled their bowls. This time he had not been looking at the noisy light box and now it was the middle of the day, and he still did not get out of his bed. So, they stopped mewing and began screaming. They were small, but they could scream loudly. Still the food man did not get out of his bed. And then it was night. It was time for their second feeding. Now they screamed in his face. But he did not move.

It was a terrible night. They were so very hungry and now they were scared too. What if the food man never got out of his bed again? Who would fill their bowls?

The next morning there was a knocking sound at the door. And a ringing sound. Then more knocking sounds, much louder. Then the door opened, and a new man came in. The new man made loud noises. The new man went to where the food man was lying in bed. Then the new man made even louder noises. They ran up to this man and rubbed on his legs and mewed. Hopefully this was a new food man.

CHAPTER

One

"**H**e called again," Theresa said. She flashed Peter a smile after she said this, but it was a wry smile, and her tone was sympathetic. "Do you want me to write the message down?"

"Same as before?" Peter asked.

"Pretty much."

"No, that's fine then, Theresa. Thanks. That makes, what? Six times in the last two hours?"

"Only five." Theresa chuckled. She swivelled back and forth on her chair behind the reception counter, absentmindedly petting Cantaloupe. The big orange cat was basking in a bright sunbeam beside Theresa's coffee mug. He had only been named "official clinic cat" for New Selfoss Veterinary Services two weeks before, but he already had assumed regal command of the space.

"I'm sorry he's bothering you," Peter said, sighing, running his hand through his unruly hair. "I'll call him back right away and tell him to stop."

"It's no bother at all. He seems to be in a good mood today. And anyway, it's a slow morning."

It was true. Susan Gislason had cancelled because Dieter, her dachshund, had suddenly started eating again after a mysterious three-day-long hunger strike. And the cat spay had turned into a neuter when Peter discovered Princess was actually a prince. Neuters were much quicker surgeries.

"When am I supposed be at Chernov's to look at that bull?"

"Not until one o'clock, and you've only got Michelle Nyquist before then, so you've got plenty of time if Sam's chatty."

"Not if Michelle's chatty too," Peter said.

They both laughed.

•

Peter stared at the messages on his desk, as if looking at them just the right way might somehow change their content. He stretched his long arms and rolled his head around on his neck a few times. It was a gorgeous late September day out there. His very favourite type of day. Not too warm, not too cold. Aspen and birch glowing. Smell of earth. Crunch of leaves. But he was in here. Waiting for Michelle Nyquist. And avoiding calling his brother back.

Sam Bannerman had moved back to Manitoba that summer. His existence as an artist in Toronto, which had always been tenuous, had become unsustainable as rents continued to climb and sales of his paintings continued to dwindle. Sam had confessed to Peter that he hadn't sold a single canvas in two years and was living off a combination of welfare and stretched credit cards, having long since spent the last of the inheritance they had both received from their parents. The only solution was to move back to Manitoba, where it was cheaper to live. New Selfoss had a tight rental market and Sam had nothing but scorn for his old hometown and for small-town life in general, so, with Peter and Laura's financial help, he moved to Winnipeg. To a small bachelor suite in the North End, on Burrows Avenue. "This is going to be OK after all," Peter told Laura.

Then the calls started.

Problems with the landlord. Problems with social assistance. Problems with his doctor. Strange noises. Strange smells. Strange thoughts.

Peter picked up the first message. Theresa had numbered them, obviously anticipating multiple calls:

1.   *Sam called*
2.   *Sam called again — says it's urgent but was polite*
3.   *Sam called again — says it's about cats*
4.   *Sam asked again nicely but sounds worried*

Something urgent to do with cats. Peter considered that his brother had probably picked up a stray. His North End neighbourhood was full of them. Sam had owned a ferret in Toronto. But after Nosferretu died, in a rare moment of rationality, Sam decided that his apartment wasn't a great place for pets, so he didn't replace him. His new place on Burrows was no better, what with the canvases, painting supplies, and garage sale "treasures" stacked floor to ceiling in every available space. He couldn't possibly keep a cat there. So, what on Earth was . . .

Peter stopped himself.

He was allowing his mind to stumble down a pointless path of speculation. He hated it when he did that. It was a waste of brain power and a waste of time. As always, data was needed to quell the speculation.

He'd have to call Sam.

"Hi, what's up?" Peter asked, forcing a cheerful tone to try to conceal the annoyance he felt at having to have this conversation. Today's annoyance was just a thin layer stacked on top of decades of layer after layer. By now it was a tower. A tower of annoyance.

"I'm sorry, man. I'm really, really sorry to bug you. You know I hate bugging people because I hate it when people bug me. You know? So,

I get it. I totally get it. You know that I get it, right?" Sam sucked in a long, ragged breath.

"Yes, I know," Peter said. He suppressed a groan and glanced at his watch. It was going to be one of *those* conversations.

"Cool. That's cool. So, I called — and again, I'm sorry for calling like a gajillion times because I know you're super busy and all what with vet stuff and whatever — but anyway I called because there's these cats next door. Don't know the guy's name or anything. Seen him a couple times in the hall. Old and sketchy looking, you know? So, I didn't like say 'hey neighbour' and stuff. But I keep hearing his cats. Like right through the walls. They're like paper. The walls I mean. Even over my TV I hear them. But last couple days they're like extra loud. Extra extra loud. Like screaming and stuff. So, I thought about talking to the dude, but like I said he was sketchy looking, and I don't want to get into some kind of feud or something. A pissed-off neighbour can make your life hell. Total hell, right? Don't need that. I got enough problems, right? So, I tried to call the landlord, but they're not answering. And then —"

Sam was cut off by a knocking sound.

"Do you need to get that?"

"Nah, probably Mormons or Jehovahs or something. No security system here. I wrote an email to management about that, and they were like —"

Sam was interrupted again, this time by much louder knocking, followed by a loud voice: "Winnipeg Police! Please open up!"